Pride of the Fleet

Ixan Legacy Book 2

Scott Bartlett

Mirth Publishing
St. John's

PRIDE OF THE FLEET

Library and Archives Canada Cataloguing in Publication

Bartlett, Scott

Pride of the Fleet / Scott Bartlett ; illustrations by Tom Edwards.

ISBN 978-1-988380-12-4

To those who stand on principle.

CHAPTER 1

Kick Down the Door

Amber lights pulsed as Seaman Jake Price ran down corridor after corridor, trying to concentrate on finding his way through Tartarus Station despite the alarm's constant assault on his ears.

He'd been able to make it out of the Outer Wing easily enough. The Union bureaucrats had kept him there so long that he knew that part of the station by heart. But the moment he'd reached the hatch that let into the rest of the station, he was lost.

Something must have gone pretty wrong. The desk jockeys would never have left that hatch unguarded unless all mayhem was breaking loose.

That was certainly what the blaring klaxon suggested. It had woken him from a deep sleep, and absurdly, his first thought was that he'd slept through breakfast.

Never would have happened in the Steele System. His daily routine was slowly losing the clockwork rigor left over from life in the Darkstream military. The bureaucrats were keeping Jake and the other Steele System refugees in a state of limbo—cut off from the rest of the galaxy, alone, wholly unsure of what would become of them.

It had been affecting all of Oneiri Team; the elite team of mech pilots he'd found himself commanding during what they now called the Mech Wars. *A fitting name, considering the most notable combatants.* The Progenitors hadn't been able to keep his pilots down, but lately, it seemed the bureaucrats were succeeding where the aliens had failed. Ash, Beth, Marco, Maura...Lisa and Andy...they all grew increasingly listless, sleeping longer and speaking less. Showing less and less interest in what might be happening in the galaxy around them, and in what might become of them.

And yet, when the screaming alarm and blaring lights had spurred Jake from his bunk, he found the Outer Wing empty, as well as the other Oneiri members' bunks. Apparently, they'd chosen today to be on time for breakfast.

The station only had two cafeterias, centrally located so that meals would disrupt the station's routines as little as possible. For every meal, guards had escorted Oneiri and the other refugees through a labyrinth of corridors, until they came to a sea of metal tables and chairs, where they ate the sort of freeze-dried gruel that served as food in space.

Now, Jake racked his brain to remember the route, which he'd paid only passing attention to before. Every intersection looked familiar, which made sense, since they all looked basically the same. *Was it a left here, or a right?*

Not for the first time, his inability to use his implant to contact his teammates made him curse. Away from Steele's system net, the things were next to useless, and integrating them with the station's narrow net had not been at the top of the bureaucrats' to-do list.

At last, he reached the cafeteria to find it milling with thousands of people—well beyond its official capacity. Clearly, it was being used as some sort of staging area. *Or as a corral for panicking station workers. That seems more likely.*

Keeping track of the time was one of the few things his implant was still good for: it took fourteen minutes of searching to track down Oneiri Team. He found them in the usual arrangement. Marco Gonzalez sat with a hand on his chin, staring into space, no doubt turning something over in his mind. Ash Sweeney and Beth Arkanian leaned back against a cafeteria table, joined at the leg. Andy Miller and Lisa Sato sat apart from the others, having some sort of lovers' quarrel, from the looks of it. And Maura Odell sat alone, wearing a faint grimace, as though wondering how she'd ended up here.

Seeing Andy and Lisa together brought Jake a sharp pang, even though they were arguing. It had taken him a while to figure out what those pangs meant, which had helped him to realize just how out-of-touch with his feelings he truly was.

Is not knowing your own feelings a male thing, a soldier thing, or a human thing? He found it hard to tell.

"Oneiri, *attention!*" he barked.

For a moment, they all just looked at him, blinking. It was the first time since they arrived back in the Milky Way that he'd given them an order of any kind. Then Marco, of all people, jumped to his feet first, planting his right foot firmly on the ground and holding his arms at his sides like iron rods.

The rest of Oneiri followed suit—first Maura, then Ash and Beth. Andy and Lisa stood last, twin frowns flashing across their faces before vanishing as quickly as they'd appeared.

That was like Andy, but it wasn't like Lisa. Ever since they'd picked her up, adrift in space, after she'd escaped from the Progenitor ship...ever since then, she'd been different.

"What is this, exactly?" Jake asked, sweeping his hand in the air to take them all in. "What are you all doing?"

"Waiting to see whether we're about to get blown up or not," Andy said. One of his legs ended at the knee—a souvenir from the conflict in Steele. Since arriving on Tartarus, he'd been fitted with a prosthetic that seemed to serve him as well as the leg had. *The bureaucrats did that for us, at least.*

"Andy, you didn't undergo the training that the rest of Oneiri did. You only served with us during the final fight, back in the Steele System. If you'd been with us from the beginning, you'd know that Oneiri doesn't sit around and wait to get blown up. Oneiri *acts*, and when opportunity knocks, we don't just answer—we kick the door down. *This* is opportunity," Jake said, glancing past them at the chaotic cafeteria. "And for the rest of you, there's absolutely no excuse for failing to capitalize on it."

"What would you have us do, Jake?" Marco asked. "We're just as cut off as we were before."

"You're cut off by your own sloth," Jake snapped, and Marco recoiled slightly at the hardened tone. "It's pitiful, how quickly you've let the desk jockeys make you weak. The same goes for me—I'm big enough to admit that. We haven't kept up our PT. Take us away from our mechs, and we're apparently fine with letting ourselves slowly fall to pieces. Even Gabriel Roach would have known better than that."

That remark brought some winces. But not from Beth. "Marco's question was good. What are we supposed to do?"

"What do soldiers do when faced with a situation full of unknowns? We gather intel. This is the first time we haven't been under the watch of armed guards. Do you think everyone in this cafeteria is just as in the dark as we are? The bureaucrats deliberately kept us isolated and ignorant, and my money would be on *everyone* knowing more about the current situation than we do. My guess is, these people are here because they're civilians. But that doesn't mean there aren't sensor operators, administrators, shuttle pilots fresh from a run—people with knowledge about what the hell is going on. People who have never heard the phrase 'operational security.' I want you to spread out through this cafeteria, pretend to be whoever you need to be, and get me answers to the following questions: what the hell is going on? And where are our mechs?" He glanced around at them one last time. "Please tell me I don't have to order you not to phrase the second question like that."

"No, sir!" Maura Odell said.

"Good," Jake said. "Now go, and report back in ten minutes with answers!"

Twenty minutes later, they were all jogging away from the cafeteria and toward one of Tartarus' three flight decks—which, according to a mid-level systems administrator, had been shut down and sealed off seven months ago for no real reason. That timing happened to coincide with the Steele refugees' arrival in the Milky Way.

As for what was going on: according to a lidar tech who'd required some persuading, multiple ships had suddenly appeared in the Hellebore System, ships with profiles that matched those fought by Captain Vin Husher during what the lidar tech had called the opening battles of the Third Galactic War. Whether that was an exaggeration or not, it certainly told Jake a lot more about the current climate in the galaxy. Before, they'd only heard that Husher was putting a sour taste in the Interstellar Union's mouth, but the specifics had been hazy.

Now, Jake felt pretty sure he knew why: the Union wanted to avoid war at all costs, but Husher knew it was inevitable. He was engaging with reality, while they were engaging only with their own ideology. It *all* made sense, now.

"Lisa Sato!"

Jake noticed Lisa jump at the deep, rumbling voice, which was followed by heavy footfalls that vibrated through the deck.

Turning, Jake saw Rug pounding up the corridor after them. The enormous quadruped cut an intimidating figure, to be sure—flanks heaving as she galloped toward them, she resembled a cross between a panther and a bear, and she was larger than both. He could almost understand Rug's approach startling Lisa...except that she'd known the Quatro for longer than he had.

Strange.

Lisa walked forward, extending her arms toward the alien, almost hesitantly. "R-Rug, it's good to see you! Where were you?" At last, she wrapped her arms around the Quatro's broad neck.

"I saw you leaving the cafeteria, but it took some time to make my way through all the humans without trampling them."

"I'm sure they appreciated that," Jake said. He'd forgotten about Rug in his desperation to find his mech, but now he wondered whether her own quadruped mech might not be with Oneiri's. The Quatro's machine seemed to share its origin with Jake's—there was good reason to believe they'd both been built by the Progenitors, especially since mechs of similar make had driven several humans and Quatro pilots mad. Gabriel Roach had become one of those crazed pilots. He'd allowed himself to permanently fuse with the alien mech he piloted, and soon after that, he'd murdered one of his own teammates. "Rug, the system is under attack, and we're pretty sure we know where our mechs are. Does that interest you?"

"It does, Jake Price," Rug said, dipping her massive head. "One way or another, I suspect we are about to step onto the galactic stage. Meanwhile, the Quatro Assembly of Elders negotiates still with your Interstellar Union. I already know what one of their requirements will be. They will demand to be given custody of my brethren and I, who fled from the Elders many years ago. I will not allow that to happen."

"The Union is no government of mine," Jake said. "But I take your point. Either way, our short-term goal is the same. Let's get those mechs."

Unlike the Outer Wing hatch, the hatch leading into the flight deck *was* guarded. Neither Jake nor the other Oneiri members were armed, and they approached with hands up, keeping Rug in reserve in case things came to blows. The great alien hunched out of view from the guards, ready to charge, in case things went south.

It turned out that wasn't necessary. The guards saw the sense in allowing seven trained mech pilots to join the fight for the system, and when Rug padded past to follow Oneiri onto the flight deck, Jake saw the guards look at each other and shrug.

Jake spotted his alien mech straight away, towering over the MIMAS mechs that stood in formation around it.

The hulking, shapeshifting monstrosity reacted to him as he approached, its front folding down to reveal a cocoon waiting to envelop him. As for the MIMAS mechs, they all responded to the short-range commands sent from their pilots' implants, hatches popping out to lower to the deck behind, becoming ramps.

As he climbed into his mech, Jake wondered whether the Union bureaucrats had been able to gain access to it, or whether they'd tried.

"Can I bum a sedative?" Jake called to Marco, and his teammate tossed over a fat, red pill after digging it out of a compartment inside the hollow of his MIMAS.

Jake slapped the pill into his mouth, descending into the mech dream within seconds.

Both MIMAS and alien mechs were controlled using a technology called lucid, which Darkstream had developed after fleeing the Milky Way. Lucid gave structure to your dreams, using them as a platform to run simulations, which were incredibly immersive in the way a dream was for the dreamer. Installed in mechs, lucid merely simulated a very specific dream: a dream identical to reality, except that in it, the dreamer became the mech.

Inside the dream, Jake rose to his full height, massive shoulders rolling back and metal hide rippling in the halogens. He wore the mech's power like a glove.

We missed you, the alien mech whispered to him. *We are ready to kill.*

Ignoring it, Jake turned to the others. "Let's do this."

CHAPTER 2

Dishonorable Discharge

"Captain Vin Husher, do you know why you've been brought before this special commission?" The Winger, who resembled a blue jay, leaned forward as she spoke, perhaps attempting to pin Husher to his seat with her beady eyes.

"I have a pretty good idea," Husher said.

"Oh? Why don't you outline your *idea* for us, then?"

"Well, I'm sure you've received multiple being rights complaints from citizens of Cybele, and maybe even a few from members of my crew. That's one reason. Then, there's the fact that by attacking Teth in the Concord System, I dashed your attempts to strike a peace deal with him." Husher locked eyes with President Chiba as he delivered this last reason. The president of the Interstellar Union, a Kaithian, sat next to Kaboh, who shared his species. Kaboh was Husher's former Nav officer—he'd resigned just a week ago, after a month of waiting around in Feverfew to see how the IU would decide to handle Husher.

The president didn't sit on the commission running this hearing, and neither did Kaboh. Several Union politicians did, though. The commission was made up both of Union politicians and Integrated Galactic Fleet members in equal part. They sat at a long, curved table that half-ringed the room. A platform kept the table well above the rest of the chamber, and the spectators sat in chairs below. Everyone faced Husher, who sat alone, scrutinized by all.

"Those sound like potential grounds for a dishonorable discharge to me, Captain," the Winger said. Her name was Ryn, and she chaired the commission. "Would you agree?"

"No."

"Why not?"

"Because my version of 'respecting being rights' differs dramatically from those of my accusers. Their version involves dividing society up and pitting the parts against each other, so that short-term, ineffectual 'solutions' might be forced down everyone's throats. I agree that we have a problem when it comes to interspecies relations, but because my methods for dealing with the problem differ, I'm branded a pariah."

"I think you may be sidestepping the issue," Ryn said. "When you consider some of your—"

"I'm not finished," Husher said. "My accusers claim to follow 'liberal values,' but they're utter hypocrites. One value they piss all over is the idea that it's possible to rehabilitate anybody—that everyone, even criminals, are capable of reform. Allow me to illustrate the way they've completely abandoned that principle: let's for a moment entertain the false assumption that I'm wrong to suggest alternate methods, and that they're right. Even if I acknowledged that, I wouldn't be given the opportunity to change my ways and follow a new course. No, now that I've been branded 'toxic,' I'm to be stripped not only of my position but also every platform for speech available to me. Even if I 'reformed,' my accusers would still try to silence and marginalize me. Why? Because this isn't actually about protecting marginalized groups. It's about targeting groups they perceive as more powerful than they are. And since I belong to such a group, they will never stop targeting me. If my accusers actually cared about underprivileged beings, then they would try to give 'offenders' an incentive to reform. They'd embrace those who 'changed their ways.' But it isn't about that. This isn't a 'just cause'—it isn't any cause at all. It's a power game, and one that's being played at the highest levels. I refuse to play it with you. Do what you will to me—I won't play your game."

Ryn nodded, barely reacting to Husher's words. "And how do you justify your unsanctioned assault on Concord?"

"Just twenty years ago, Teth and his father strove to wipe out all sentient life in the galaxy. They nearly succeeded, and if it hadn't been for Captain Keyes's sacrifice, they would have. The idea that Teth would adhere to even a temporary ceasefire is absurd. He was always going to strike to kill—now, at least, we'll be on wartime footing when he does."

"It is true that you've forced the Interstellar Union's hand," Ryn said, her eyes never leaving his. "Because of your aggression, we are indeed committed to a war that will doubtless prove costly and bloody. But not everyone on the commission agrees that this war was necessary. You are a talented captain, but you need not think you've won yourself job security. Both your rank and your position as captain of the *Vesta* are under review."

"The Progenitors will hit us with wave after wave of highly advanced warships," Husher said. "If you don't deploy every experienced captain you've got, you're fools."

"Then you'd best hope your rash actions don't prove as destructive as I believe they will," Ryn said. "Do you have anything else to add, Captain?"

"What about subspace tech? The Fleet needs to start implementing it."

"That is also under review," the Winger said. "This commission will adjourn."

CHAPTER 3

Distress Call

Husher left the government building and stepped out onto Zakros, where a cool wind blew rhomboid leaves across asphalt. The system's sun shone above, a pale circle offering some warmth, but not much.

Before hailing a taxi to take him to his next destination, he glanced back at the building, which his Oculenses painted with bright colors meant to represent the four Union species. Here on a civilian colony world, he didn't have access to the captain's privilege of switching off the Oculens overlay. He wondered what the building truly looked like underneath, but it wasn't worth removing the lenses.

He eased himself into the taxi, which got underway the instant he fastened his seatbelt—it already knew his destination from when he'd used his com to order it. Leaning back, he permitted himself the leisure of wondering how things were on the *Vesta*. His Oculenses told him that the supercarrier's orbit would soon take it directly overhead.

She'll be with me during the trial ahead. In a sense. The funny little thought brought a smile to his lips.

Causing the Interstellar Union an interstellar headache had not been the only effect of his attack on Concord. It had also helped the tens of thousands of people living in Cybele, the city located in the bowels of his ship, to contend with the reality of living on a warship: in particular, the fact that eventually, warships went to war.

The struggle with Teth had resulted in twenty-nine civilian deaths, with well over a hundred more injured. Even for those unhurt, it must have been a terrifying ordeal. Probably, it should never have come to pass that civilians had been allowed to live in a place where they would inevitably experience the horrors of war firsthand.

But the capital starships themselves had always been a bargain with the devil, and those that chose to continue living in shipboard cities like Cybele would almost certainly encounter war again.

Hell, so will many who live in planetside cities. Even so, Cybele's population level was plummeting in the wake of Husher's attack on Concord, with people selling their cubic residences at rock-bottom prices. It was a trend reflected across all eight capital starships, though nowhere was it so pronounced as aboard the *Vesta.*

That trend would continue, Husher knew. What he hadn't expected was that it would be accompanied by a different trend: an influx, significantly smaller, of new residents.

What kind of civilians flock to a city certain to find itself beset by war and death? He would soon find out...provided he was allowed to stay in command of his ship.

The taxi ride lasted fewer than ten minutes. He paid, and once the computer registered the transfer, it unlocked the doors for him to exit.

He stepped out onto a busy sidewalk, the coffee shop that was his destination rearing above him. *Neutral ground.* He stepped inside.

The coffee shop's interior mimicked the style popular among the galaxy's youth: closed clamshells distributed throughout, accessible via a small opening, across which both a curtain and a privacy shield could be drawn. These enclosures were ideal for conversations one would rather not have in public, but as far as Husher knew, they rarely got used for that. Mostly, patrons sat inside and immersed themselves in digital worlds using their Oculenses, occasionally ordering real-world beverages to justify their presence. If a given customer failed to order drinks with a certain frequency, it was customary to charge them a base fee for use of the space.

Husher knew what clamshell he was meant to insert himself into—it had been agreed upon in advance. As was his habit, he ordered a cup of black coffee through the narrow window at the back, which brought the customary odd look from the employee. Usually patrons ordered from their clamshells, using Oculenses. Many shops featured a conveyor system that delivered the drinks, eliminating the need for actual human contact altogether.

Coffee in hand, regretting that it wasn't alcohol, Husher slipped inside the agreed-upon clamshell to find his daughter, Iris—or rather, Maeve Aldaine, now—and his ex-wife, Sera Caine.

"Hello, Vin," Sera said, her voice icy.

"Hi, Sera. Maeve." His daughter had chosen to continue using the name her mother had given her before she was old enough to remember she'd ever had another. He wanted to respect the decision. Either way, Maeve didn't return his greeting.

Mother and daughter sat separated by three feet or so, and Husher took up a position across the broad, ovoid table. Reaching behind him, he shut the privacy shield.

"Why did you ask us to come here?" Sera said.

"Why did you come?" Husher answered.

"I have no idea."

"Maybe you came for the same reason I invited you: so we can all reach some sort of shared understanding about what the hell happened to our family. So that, just maybe, we can help our daughter make sense of what we've done to her."

Maeve's expression remained impassive, other than a momentary tightening of her lips, almost undetectable in the clamshell's dim lighting.

"What *we've* done to her?" Sera said. "You're the one who flew her into a battle, even after you knew she was your daughter."

"And you're the one who lied to both of us," Husher said quietly. "You let me think my daughter had died, and you let our daughter believe she had no father."

"She doesn't have a father," Sera said, glancing at Maeve, maybe hoping for some support. Maeve didn't react, not even to meet her mother's eyes.

Husher let that play out, and when Sera turned back to him, she seemed somewhat crestfallen. "The Gok blew up our *home,*

Vin," she went on. "They might have done it again. I did what I had to do to protect her.

"That didn't work out very well, did it? She ended up in the middle of a war all the same."

"That wasn't my doing," his ex-wife snapped, her glare piercing. He'd first met Sera while they both served aboard the *Providence*, under Captain Keyes. She'd been marine commander, and she still seemed to have some of the hardness command required.

"What *was* your doing, Sera?" Husher said, still managing to keep his voice level. Ever since defeating Teth over Klaxon, he found it much easier to regulate his mood. "Is there anything you're willing to take responsibility for? Yes, I flew the *Vesta* into battle with full knowledge that my daughter was aboard. But it's not my fault she chose to go to school aboard a military vessel in the first place. Why do you think she did that?"

"What are you implying?" Sera asked, eyes narrowing. "Are you saying she wanted to get away from me?"

"No. I'm trying to tell you something I realized recently. It's impossible for parents to shelter their children from danger. We can keep them at home and coddle them, keep them wrapped up safe in our arms, but it doesn't matter. Eventually they become adults and enter the dangerous world all the same, except they're less prepared to face the danger because of our coddling. Maybe Maeve chose Cybele University because she deeply craved some risk and danger in her life. Because she knew, on some level, that she'd been starved of it, and that she needed to confront it if she was to going make it in the world."

"So you're blaming me," Sera said.

"I'm actually not. Listen, Sera. I get what you did. I get the desire to protect your daughter, because I feel that too. But there comes a point when being a good parent means letting go, no matter how much it hurts. We can give Maeve our love as best we can, and we can try to help her. But we can't protect her anymore. Not really."

"The hell we can't," Sera said, rising to her feet and turning to Maeve. "Come on, sweetheart. I have a couch you can crash on until you find your own place. If you like, I can even do up the spare room, and you can stay as long as you want."

Maeve was sitting between Sera and the exit, so that Sera couldn't leave until she got up. Instead, she met her mother's gaze.

"I'm not staying. I'm going back to Cybele to finish my studies."

Eyes widening, Sera began to tremble slightly. "You can't," she said, her voice coming out more high-pitched than she'd likely meant it to. "There are plenty of good schools here, sweetheart. You can't go back on that ship."

"I can," Maeve said slowly. "And I will." With that, she slid open the privacy shield and left the clamshell.

Sera's eyes were fiery as they found Husher's once more. "Rot in hell," she said, and chased after her daughter.

Raising the coffee cup to his lips, Husher sipped through the tiny opening. *Still warm.* He drained the contents, then ordered a taxi.

He didn't see this as a victory—in fact, he'd hoped the conversation wouldn't become as combative as it had. Besides, Maeve hadn't spoken to him once the entire time.

A priority alert reached him moments after he got in the cab, causing him to immediately change his destination from his hotel to the nearest spaceport:

"HELLEBORE SYSTEM UNDER HEAVY ASSAULT. ALL NEARBY IGF VESSELS ARE TO ANSWER THE DISTRESS CALL WITH ALL POSSIBLE SPEED."

CHAPTER 4

Munitions

Commander Fesky met Husher at the shuttle's airlock with a crisp salute. He returned it, along with a warm smile.

"How's my old girl holding up?"

The Winger clacked her beak. "I am not old, and I'm *certainly* not your girl."

"I meant the ship," Husher said, though he was pretty sure Fesky knew that already. She had that twinkle in her onyx eye that said she was messing with him.

"As good as you left her, and maybe even a little better," Fesky said as she spun on her heel to head deeper into the *Vesta*. Husher fell in step with her. "Our stock of munitions has been replenished and expanded to wartime levels, and I've had Engineering working overtime to repair the damage we took during our recent engagements, particularly the main capacitor bank."

He nodded, and now his voice grew somber. "Have you had a chance to look at any of the data coming in from Hellebore?"

"Mostly, I've been coordinating with the Feverfew coms relay and cross-referencing with Fleet databases, to figure out who's supposed to be where—what ships we can count on being close enough to back us up in Hellebore. But I did have a glance at the data from the Hellebore sensor web."

"And?"

The question brought a gust-like exhalation from his XO. "We're going to have quite a fight on our hands. There are four of the diamond-shaped destroyers Teth commanded, and five of the big vessels we termed carriers. At the last update, the destroyers were wreaking pure havoc on the system's defenses, and all seven ships were belching Ravagers at everything that moved."

Husher cursed under his breath. "So we're picking a fight with an eight-hundred-pound gorilla."

"Nine of them," Fesky said with a nod. "On top of that, we have no idea how these new aliens will react. The data shows dozens of their ships, just sitting there."

"Hmm." Officially, neither of them was supposed to know about the alien fleet that had been sitting in Hellebore for weeks. But word tended to get around, and now the system's sensor data had confirmed it. "Well, we didn't join the Fleet to sit around on our hands. What are we looking at in terms of backup, assuming the new aliens don't intervene on either side?"

"There's one other capital starship whose patrol has it and its battle group close enough to arrive in Hellebore within a meaningful timeframe. They'll arrive soon after us. Other than that, one destroyer, two missile cruisers, a corvette, and three frigates were already in-system."

"None of them nearly a match for our enemies." *And us without a battle group.* "We'd better hope the other capital starship is making haste. Which one is it?"

"The *Mylas*. Sir...I'm not sure we can win this."

"Have we ever been sure, even of surviving any given day?"

Fesky shrugged. "I guess not."

"We have our orders. Our job is to figure out how best to execute them."

Still, as they joined the *Vesta*'s other first watch officers in the Tactical Planning Room, Husher's palms began to feel clammy, and a coldness was spreading through his chest.

But as they went over the coming engagement, and as second watch took the supercarrier toward the Feverfew-Hellebore darkgate with all the acceleration she could muster, his fear gradually lessened.

His Oculenses showed him a shared view of the latest known configuration of the battlespace in Hellebore, displayed over a tabletop. And as he worked through the possibilities and tactics of the upcoming battle with his officers, Husher even began to take heart.

Yes, the odds against them were daunting. But when hadn't they been? He'd always known it was a tossup for whether the galaxy would endure the coming invasion. But staring at the miniature representations of enemy ships, he suddenly felt certain that Teth was aboard one of them.

That wasn't all: by attacking Hellebore with such force, Teth was doing exactly what Husher needed him to do. Exactly what the *galaxy* needed him to do.

Despite Husher's assault on Concord, the Union was still dragging its heels when it came to accepting the reality of the war.

But after this, they wouldn't be able to help but confront that reality head-on.

Teth was playing right into his hands. It was entirely unlike him to do that, but maybe the defeat in Concord had rattled him. *I guess having to flee in an escape pod would rattle anyone.*

At last, they finished running possible scenarios and coming up with the optimal gambit in each one. It wasn't every engagement they got to break down in advance like this, so that was another reason to be grateful. "All right, everyone. Good work. Time to head to the CIC."

His officers filed out of the Tactical Planning Room in orderly fashion. Chief Benno Tremaine was last to leave, other than Husher and Fesky, and Husher was about to follow him when his XO motioned him to one side.

He walked over, eyebrows raised. "Yes, Fesky?"

Feathers stiffening, Fesky said, "I wasn't going to tell you this until after the battle, but I'm thinking there's no good time to tell you, and it's better for you to know sooner than later."

"What is it?"

"With the influx of people to Cybele, we're getting a lot of interesting...characters."

Husher frowned. "I'm guessing interesting doesn't mean good, here."

"Maybe it's nothing. But background checks indicate a lot of them belong to some fairly extreme political groups. Groups known for taking their ideas into the streets."

"Do I know any of the groups?"

"I'm sure you've heard of the Sapient Brotherhood."

"I have," Husher said, suppressing a sigh. The Brotherhood believed humanity should never have joined a union comprised of nonhuman beings. Mostly they railed against the Kaithe, but ultimately they resented all alien influence on human affairs—although, they did have a soft spot for the Ixa, mainly because of their dedication to keeping their own species 'pure.'

The Sapient Brotherhood is also the group my critics accuse me of sympathizing with. It was a ridiculous notion—he believed in the Interstellar Union. At least, he believed in the principles it was built on. And he believed in the Integrated Galactic Fleet.

But that didn't matter. Society was hyper-polarized now, and anyone occupying a moderate position would be labeled with an extreme one by those who disagreed. *Which only polarizes society more.*

"Thanks for letting me know, Fesky," he said, heading for the exit into the corridor. "There's not much we can do about it, but it's good to know what we're dealing with."

CHAPTER 5

Hellebore

Husher had never seen his CIC's tactical display so cluttered—and he'd rarely been so shocked at the contrast between the intel he'd received and reality.

They'd transitioned into Hellebore minutes ago, and according to the hundreds of glowing ships represented in miniature on the display, the system was teeming.

Did they filter ships out of their sensor data before broadcasting the distress call? It wasn't a sentiment he wanted to speak out loud, but then again, there was no hiding the fact from his CIC crew.

Tartarus Station was located here—home to the Department of Interplanetary Immigration and Travel, one of the Union's biggest bureaucracies. *What have they been up to?*

Ensign Scot Winterton, Husher's primary sensor operator, could always be counted on to report reality as his sensors showed it, whether that reality conflicted with his superiors' version or not. "The unidentified alien fleet is far bigger than intel suggested, Captain," Winterton said. "Visual analysis puts the number at one thousand three hundred and forty-two, though there's a high probability that over a third are nonmilitary vessels."

Still... Husher blinked to clear his head, trying to process what his sensor operator had told them. Even if only two-thirds were warships, that fleet came close to rivaling the entire Integrated Galactic Fleet in size. "What's their posture?"

"They're still showing no sign of involving themselves in the engagement. But that's not all, sir. There's also a battle group of eleven UHF-era warships holding orbit over Imbros, with dozens of civilian ships trailing behind. Some of the nonmilitary vessels look newer, though their profiles don't match anything I've seen before. There's also a ship with them, almost certainly a warship, which resembles those of the enormous alien fleet."

Husher puzzled over that for a few moments—then, the answer fell into place in his mind. "Darkstream," he said, his voice coming out as a low growl. He had no idea why the alien ship was holding formation with them, but who else would have so many UHF ships from the same era? "Eleven was the number of ships they stole from us before they fled the galaxy." *But what are they doing here, orbiting Imbros like it's the most natural thing in the world?*

As the *Vesta* approached missile range with the Progenitor battle group, Husher turned his attention to the actual engagement. No surprises there, at least. There were nine enemy ships being engaged by five Fleet ships, with debris clouds to account for the missing two. Except—

"What's being represented by the tactical display, there?" Husher said, gesturing at the CIC's main display. He'd already paired his Oculenses with Winterton's, so he knew the sensor operator was looking at the same thing as him. "Those seven blips, almost too small to make out."

Frowning in concentration, Winterton tapped at his console. "Those...those appear to be seven bipedal robots, sir." Winterton looked up, and for the first time Husher could remember, the man looked a little helpless. "They're aiding our ships in fighting the enemy."

If Winterton can't properly account for what he's seeing, then I probably shouldn't try. "Very well," Husher said, nodding and then clearing his throat. "Let's move to back them up, then. Helm, engines all ahead. Nav, I want you to collaborate with Tremaine on an approach vector and deceleration profile that allows us to maximize kinetic impactors, which I want sprayed at the enemy ships at optimal intervals."

"Aye, sir," said Chief Noni. She was a Tumbran, and his new primary Nav officer, following Kaboh's resignation.

Ensign Fry spoke up. "Sir, I'm getting a transmission request from one of the enemy destroyers."

"Accept, and put it on the display with open access to all." Husher knew who it was, even before Teth's hideous face appeared, with its bare bones protruding through cracked, whitened scales. *So I was right.*

"Captain Husher," the Ixan hissed. "Right on time."

Husher's mouth quirked. Teth had a sharp tongue, and letting his crew in on whatever bile the Ixan had to spew was risky, from a morale perspective. But to take the transmission in his office, or even to take it privately—so that only he could hear Teth's words—would have reeked of weakness, and no captain could afford to let his crew think him weak.

Maybe I can beat him at his own game. "Teth. I see you've acquired a new ship. It looks a lot like the last one I blew out from under you."

For once, the Ixan had no response, and though his expression didn't change, Husher knew he'd struck a nerve. According to Teth himself, that ship had held the last of the Ixa. Now, other than Ochrim, Teth was the last of his kind.

"I want to thank you for coming to Hellebore today," Husher continued. "The Union's been reluctant to go to war, and this attack is exactly what was needed to convince them."

Teth's forked tongue made a brief appearance between pointed teeth. "What, this skirmish?" he said. "This is psyops more than anything else. I barely have to fight this war, Captain Husher. I have complete confidence that *you* are going to win it for me."

Husher shook his head. "What are you talking about?"

But Teth had already vanished from the display.

"Not one of his best speeches," Husher said, which brought a round of chuckles, although he heard a nervous edge in the laughter. *Moving on.* "Tactical and Nav, how are those firing timings coming along?"

"We're ready to lock them in, sir," Tremaine said. "We have the first salvo timed just before deceleration, to take full advantage of our current acceleration."

Chief Noni nodded. "We've also introduced a slight curve into our trajectory, to ensure no impactors hit our allies."

"Good work."

"Sir, the UHF ships near the planet appear to be coming online," Winterton said. "Shuttles have been coming and going from them ever since we entered the system, and now heat signatures suggest engines being started up—yes, a corvette just broke formation with the others."

"Is she headed toward the engagement?"

"Negative. She's heading...uh, nowhere. There are no meaningful destinations along her trajectory. It's possible they plan to circle around the engagement and make for the darkgate."

They're fleeing. "Coms, send them a transmission to the effect that we could use their help, over here. I don't like the idea of teaming up with Darkstream, but I like the idea of losing to the Progenitors even less."

The moment he finished speaking, Winterton said, "One of the Progenitor carriers just disappeared, sir."

"Acknowledged. I want active scans of our immediate vicinity. Tactical, ready Banshee salvos to fire along every axis, and Fry, let Commander Ayam know he may be scrambling Pythons sooner than expected."

Seconds later, his preparations proved unnecessary, when the carrier reappeared—not beside the *Vesta*, but right behind the old UHF-model ship attempting to flee. The carrier vomited forth a cloud of its savage robots, and though the corvette did its best to shoot them down, there were far too many.

Sailing past the corvette's point defense turrets, the metal attackers lighted on her hull, burrowing inside her in dozens of places. The carrier vanished, then, reappearing back near the engagement, its dark work done.

Long, tense minutes ticked by as Husher and his officers watched a zoomed-in view of the corvette. Then, she ruptured, expelling gouts of flame to be instantly snuffed out by the void.

CHAPTER 6

The IGS Mylas

"Firing opening salvo of kinetic impactors," Tremaine said.

Husher nodded, watching the tactical display. Before the first impactors arrived, Tremaine loosed another volley.

Almost simultaneously, an IGF frigate and the sole corvette exploded under enemy particle beams. The smaller ships were much more vulnerable to the weapons—any significant superheating and their hulls would rupture.

"Coms, send a recommendation to the other IGF captains that they keep up lateral movement in relation to the enemy, to avoid presenting them with a still target."

"Aye, sir."

Winterton leaned toward his console, scrutinizing whatever he saw there closely. "First impactor salvo arriving now, sir." He frowned. "The ship we had the best bead on has vanished to avoid getting hit. Other impactors are raining down on the hulls of one destroyer and two of the carriers. Hmm. We've succeeded in destroying a primary turret battery on the destroyer."

Tremaine sent five more salvos at the enemy ships before the *Vesta* closed with them, and Winterton kept Husher updated on the success of each one. None did more than superficial damage, but that was about what he'd expected. At this range, with the enemy's ability to simply vanish from the line of fire, kinetic impactors could only be counted on to soften up targets.

That's better than nothing. We've put holes in their point defense systems for our Pythons to exploit.

"Have Commander Ayam scramble the entire Air Group, Coms. With this many Progenitor ships, we'll need most of our fighters on missile defense duty, but tell Ayam to assign four squadrons to apply some pressure. Either the system's defenders will throw them off enough to give us an opening or vice versa."

"Sir, the *Mylas* has just transitioned into Hellebore with all four of her battle group ships in tow," his sensor operator said.

Husher nodded. "Welcome news, but we won't be able to count on their help for over an hour. In the meantime, we need to do some damage."

With just the *Vesta* and six of the system's defender ships remaining, they were still outgunned by the nine Progenitor ships, and the strange alien fleet still showed no sign of moving to help either side. Still, Husher believed in his Air Group, and he believed in the *Vesta.* The sheer might brought to bear by one capital starship simply couldn't be discounted, and if they could hold on until the second one arrived...

This is far from over.

He briefly considered reaching out to the hundreds of alien ships in distant heliocentric orbits, but quickly decided against it.

Even he could see that doing so would be stepping well outside his bounds as a Fleet captain. Negotiating with a foreign power, especially one of that size, would be tricky business under the best of circumstances. But sitting down to the negotiating table with a foreign power that had just saved you from military disaster...it wasn't what Husher would call an enviable position.

"The enemy battle group has started taking us seriously, sir," Winterton said. "They're directing most of their robot-missiles at us, now."

"As expected. Tremaine, stand by to fire Banshees at any missiles that make it past our Pythons. Whenever you can, try to neutralize them near the maximum range of our point defense turrets, to avoid any wasteful overlap."

"Aye, sir."

"That's not all. Sneak some Gorgons into the mix—say, one for every ten Banshees fired. I want the Gorgons programmed to make their way at a leisurely pace toward the nearest ships: split them evenly three ways between the nearby destroyer and the carriers lingering off her stern."

"I will, Captain."

"Forward the Gorgon's telemetry to our Air Group, but tell them not to make it too obvious that they're making way for stealth missiles."

Husher took several long breaths as he monitored the tactical display to see how his gambit would play out. The Darkstream ships in orbit over Imbros were still peeling away, one by one, on trajectories that took them essentially nowhere, but which left room to loop around the *Mylas*'battle group and slip through the darkgate.

The Progenitors didn't appear to want that. The first Darkstream ship in line was a missile cruiser, and when it neared the debris cloud that had once been the corvette, the same Progenitor carrier disappeared, showing up right behind the cruiser and overwhelming it with an even bigger cloud of the robotic killers.

Another IGF frigate went down—and then something surprising happened. One of the enemy destroyers ruptured in a brilliant flash that reminded Husher of watching Teth's destroyer go down over Klaxon's moon.

"What caused that?" he asked.

"It would seem the seven bipedal robots managed to neutralize the enemy ship, sir," Winterton said. "With minimal aid from IGF vessels."

"Show me a visual closeup of those things."

Winterton did. The CIC's main display zoomed in to show the seven robots flying through space in formation, toward the nearest carrier. One of them was much bigger than the other six, and while the others had a human aesthetic, with their sleek contours and recognizable weaponry, the big one seemed totally alien.

The carrier they were headed toward answered the robots' approach with a torrent of metal devils, and Husher watched as the alien robot *shifted*, its arms becoming spinning blades that shredded any missile-bots they came into contact with. Several missiles made it past the hulking biped, prompting an explosion of shrapnel to burst from its back, which took down multiple targets at once with precision accuracy.

"I see," Husher said.

Winterton spoke up again. "Sir, three of the six Gorgons fired were detected, but the other three detonated—one on the port aft side of Teth's destroyer, and the other two on the closest carrier. Those two struck together, blowing a sizable hole in the enemy's hull."

"Acknowledged. Tremaine, fire our primary laser at that hole, now."

"Yes, sir."

Husher watched on the tactical display as Tremaine dumped energy into the damaged ship—until, after several tense moments, it exploded, flinging shrapnel and flame in all directions and forcing some of the *Vesta*'s Pythons to peel away on evasion courses.

Cheering erupted inside the CIC—a rare sound in this war, so far. Husher let it play out for a few seconds until saying, "All right, people, we're not done yet. Tremaine, it's time to start—"

"Sir," Winterton said, so low he was almost whispering, but it was enough to make Husher break off.

"Yes?"

"All six enemy ships just vanished."

Slowly, Husher shook his head. "Have they retreated?" The engagement was far from over, and until the second capital starship arrived, he would have said the Progenitors still had the advantage.

"They—sir, the six ships just appeared behind the *Mylas* and her battle group. The IGF ships are coming about, but the enemy's already firing."

Husher toggled to a close-in visual display of the engagement, the knuckles of his other hand white from his death-grip on the command seat's armrest. The point defense systems of the IGF ships were working overtime, and their captains had already ordered that secondary lasers be used to supplement.

It wasn't clear that would be enough. "Nav, set a course for the *Mylas*, and Coms, send a request that the Hellebore system defense group follow us."

He knew the order was pointless—the *Mylas* and her battle group were much too far for the *Vesta* to reach them in time to make a difference. But he had to do something. The Progenitor ships were filling the battlespace with their robots, and the defending ships had already expended a significant portion of their arsenal keeping them at bay.

Next, particle beams lanced out from the enemy warships, heedless of the robots they caught in their beams. The robots melted, and so did the IGF hulls. A frigate went down first, followed by a corvette. Next, the destroyer and missile cruiser were neutralized in almost simultaneous explosions.

Total silence took hold in Husher's CIC, as they all held their breath, waiting to see whether the silent death being dealt would claim the *Mylas*.

Though he knew better, Husher felt a quiet confidence spread through him. *There's no way they're taking down a capital starship. The* Mylas *will hold on till we reach her, and then we'll show them exactly what they're dealing with.*

When the supercarrier ruptured in a blinding flash, at first Husher didn't know how to process it. Neither, it seemed, did his CIC crew—they all maintained their postures, mostly leaning forward and gripping their armrests.

"A capital starship," Noni said, breathless. "They just destroyed a capital starship."

No one else spoke, not even Husher, though he knew he had to say something, to try and salvage morale from the abyss it was tumbling into.

But there was nothing to say.

CHAPTER 7

Snapped in Two

At last, Husher did the only thing he could do, the only thing he knew how to do:

He acted.

"Tremaine, coordinate with Nav to come up with a formation that places the other IGF ships far enough away to disperse enemy fire but close enough that we can help each other out with missile defense. Send that formation to Coms for forwarding as an urgent recommendation to the other captains." He couldn't actually give them orders, but he'd be very surprised if any of them defied him in this. "Add in a reminder to stand ready to use lateral thrusters for particle beam evasion at a moment's notice." He swallowed. "They should also be prepared to fall back as needed, to buy time to deal with enemy ordnance—but do so judiciously. The Progenitor ships could just as easily appear behind us."

The *Mylas'* entire Air Group had been taken out in one fell swoop. At least that wouldn't happen to Commander Ayam's fliers, since they were already deployed. That should grant Husher the needed versatility to respond to enemy maneuvers quickly, even if the Progenitors appeared just off his stern.

Husher watched the tactical display, hating the silence that continued to reign over his CIC as the Progenitor ships crept closer across the battlespace. The silence was no different than any other time he wasn't in the middle of giving orders or coordinating with his officers—except, it was vastly different, wasn't it? A capital starship had fallen. Even Husher, who'd given voice to the probability of this happening once the Ixa's creators returned, was having difficulty processing the reality of it.

The capital starships formed the backbone of the Integrated Galactic Fleet, and it felt like that backbone had just been snapped in two.

"Sir," Winterton said. "The alien fleet is in motion."

Husher called up an expanded tactical display, one that showed the entire system. There, at Hellebore's periphery, he watched dozens of alien ships breaking formation at a time, to become a great wave bending away from their previous heliocentric orbit—toward the *Vesta* and the ships around her.

Idly, he toggled to a visual display, zooming in on one of the ships as far as the sensor could go. At this vast remove, the image was blurry. All Husher could see was a tapered ovoid, thinner at the fore than at the aft, and royal purple in color.

"What should we do, sir?" Noni asked.

"Absolutely nothing. The *Vesta* may have the legs to make her way around the Progenitor ships to escape through the darkgate, but the other IGF ships don't. And we're far too deep inside the system for any of us to go to warp. We're not going to leave the other IGF crews to die." *Besides, public morale is going to be bad enough after losing a capital starship.*

"Should we prepare to engage the approaching fleet?"

"Negative. We don't have a prayer against so many ships. We're going to stick with our current line of action, and we're not going to try to influence something we have no control over."

He took a moment to wonder why the alien fleet had finally decided to get involved. Had the Union requested it, or were they doing so of their own volition? Either way, contacting them would be pointless. Requesting their help or begging would only degrade whatever leverage the Union had with the new species.

Then there was the possibility that the recent arrivals were actually allies of the Progenitors. Husher didn't like to dwell on that one, since it would mean certain death if it proved out. But he had to admit it was possible.

At first, he was sure the Progenitors were going to reach them before the alien fleet did. But then he noticed how fast the purple vessels were traveling. It was difficult to tell whether their starships' engines were more advanced that those fielded by the IGF, or whether they were just grossly overtaxing them. Whatever the case, the new ships were closing the distance rapidly.

When the eight nearest ships of the unidentified fleet drew just within the *Vesta*'s maximum missile range, they loosed a volley of missiles—twenty each, totaling one hundred and sixty. They screamed toward the *Vesta* and her companions.

"Sir," Tremaine said, his head twitching toward Husher. "Should I—"

"Do nothing." With her Air Group, the *Vesta* was likely capable of holding off such a barrage by herself. But the same principle applied: if the newcomers were targeting the IGF ships, they would be sandwiched between them and the Progenitors, and nothing they could do would stay death for long.

The next row of alien ships loosed a comparable volley, and so did the next.

The Progenitors continued to approach. The *Vesta* and the other IGF ships stayed where they were, doing nothing, Pythons milling around them.

At last, the first missiles sailed past, automated guidance systems keeping them well clear of Pythons and warships alike.

When the Progenitors registered that fact, they fired a volley of robots, many of which were obliterated the instant they encountered the guided missile barrage. Several missiles slipped past the bots, however, and the nearest carrier exploded.

Husher's heart leapt. The six remaining Progenitor ships abruptly reversed course, struggling to deal with the onslaught. More missiles landed on the hull of one of the destroyers, Teth's destroyer, taking out a turret battery here, blowing open a gaping hole there—

Then all six enemy ships vanished from the system. The remaining guided missiles looped around, rocketing back toward the ships that had fired them. *A salvage function.* He hadn't seen that before, but it seemed like a great idea, so long as stringent precautions were taken to prevent armed missiles from exploding on their return.

The CIC remained silent as they all waited to see whether the Progenitors would reappear. But Husher didn't think they would.

"Send our new friends a blanket transmission request," Husher said. "I'd like to speak to whoever's in charge. Include our warm thanks in the broadcasted request."

"Sir, the suspected Darkstream ships have reached the darkgate, nonmilitary vessels included," Winterton said. "The single ship resembling the ones that just helped us also appears to be leaving with them."

"Well, they paid a heavy price for their escape," Husher said. "Let them have what they bought."

Chasing them down would take a while. Besides, other IGF ships would likely apprehend them before they got farther than Feverfew.

CHAPTER 8

Predator

The *Predator,* successor to the *Apex,* flickered through the dimensions along a predetermined route, ending up back in what Teth thought of as the Prime Reality.

Unlike the last time his destroyer had fled from the *Vesta*—when he'd ended up far from any destination of strategic importance—this time, he knew exactly where he was. The *Predator* now sat roughly equidistant between the Hellebore system and its neighbor, well outside the distance inside which it could be detected within a meaningful timespan, let alone harmed. On the sensor board, he watched as his five companion ships reentered the universe all around him, flickering in and sitting there, awaiting his next command.

Everything that had happened today, including the loss of two carriers and one destroyer, had been according to his design. He'd sewn the seeds of the Union's destruction, and the main agent of that destruction would be none other than Vin Husher. Teth knew Husher like he knew himself. He knew the sort of person the battle in the Baxa System—which the Union now called the Concord System—had turned Husher into.

The man wasn't capable of the kind of rapid change needed to avert the catastrophe waiting for him and for everyone he sought to protect. No, he would forge ahead, confident in the lessons he'd so recently learned, and those lessons would take him apart piece by piece.

Slowly, Teth rose to his feet, staring vacantly into space. Today had been a total success. So why did he feel so hollow?

"Immaculate One," his strategy auxiliary said.

Teth turned toward the Ixan. "Yes, Breka?"

"Perhaps we should initiate repairs to the *Predator*'s damaged hull. There is much to do."

Slowly, Teth nodded. "Do so." Then he walked around his command seat, which resembled a hulking throne, and drew the massive broadsword strapped to the back, holding it before his face and studying its perfection. At one time, the sword—a gift from his father—had filled him with pride and purpose. Now? Nothing.

He paced around his warship's bridge, the blade's hilt dangling from his grasp. Each auxiliary he passed shrank away from the weapon. All except Breka.

Only Breka would have the courage to speak the words that needed to be spoken to his Command Leader. Teth's strategy auxiliary was the perfect Ixan—of the purest bloodlines. Confident, competent. Dominant.

Breka didn't remember how Teth had sacrificed him in order to inspire the rest of the crew. He'd decapitated Breka with the sword he now held, in full view of everyone aboard, despite the

Ixan's supreme worthiness. It had been a demonstration of the exacting sacrifices that victory demanded.

But Breka had no memory of it, just as the rest of the crew failed to remember how Teth had spent their lives in the battle over Klaxon.

That was because Breka was a clone. A replica. Just like the rest of the crew, and just like the sword Teth now held.

Breka looked like Breka. He *smelled* like Breka, and he said everything Breka would have. His unwavering gaze was just like Breka's, along with his iron will. But sometime during his death and rebirth, Breka's spirit had been wrenched from him, and what remained was just an empty shell. An automaton, which acted like Breka without knowing it was imitating anyone.

But it wasn't truly Breka, and the sword Teth gripped was not the one his father had given him. The Breka clones aboard the other two destroyers, who remained totally unaware of each other's existence, weren't Breka either.

Teth had escaped the confrontation with Husher in the Baxa System, barely, but what if he hadn't? The Progenitors would simply have cloned him, too, and given the clone the task of coordinating the war's opening campaigns. Functionally, it wouldn't have mattered—not to the Progenitors, certainly. But Teth could smell the clones' falsehood. He had no idea how, but they reeked of it.

Unable to take it any longer, he marched off the bridge before the impulse to murder everyone on it overtook him.

Storming through the barren corridors, he brooded. He hadn't bothered to replace the black, white, and scarlet banners he'd ordered hung around the *Apex.* He no longer saw the point. He'd spent Breka's life under the conviction that he'd been building something—power. An empire in which everyone and everything bent to his will. But in encountering the clones' fakery, he'd also met with the lie of his own beliefs.

His father was gone, and there was no hope of turning his brother to his side—Ochrim's intentions had always been ultimately self-sacrificing, and now that he knew Baxa's and Teth's never had been, he was lost forever.

Even the Ixa were gone, replaced by a species of shams. Teth was left alone, all alone. But with his isolation came a blessing that gleamed darkly, in the form of bald truth:

Life was suffering.

Strip away the pretense and false promises, and that was all that remained. He should know; he'd inflicted plenty of the suffering himself. And now, suffering was all he knew, which was the eventual fate of every living being, until they died.

But only until they die. The universe was malevolent, a cruel jokester, but Teth had not been wrong to be an agent of suffering. *No.* He had stumbled on the fundamental morality of the universe, and by embracing it, he would join the ranks of the most moral actors who ever lived.

Life was suffering. The only true antidote was death. And so, Teth vowed to become the most efficient agent of death he could possibly be.

The just and unjust alike. The guilty and the detached. They would all die, and if they knew what Teth was truly doing for them, they would thank him. They would call him Saviour.

They still might, he reflected as he about-turned and made his way back to the CIC, to set the next phase of his plan into motion.

CHAPTER 9

Divided and Deployed

It took President Chiba less than a day to travel to Tartarus Station, and Husher was surprised by his speed, even though the politician had only been coming from the next system over, via darkgate. Husher was used to sluggishness from the Interstellar Union, and for the galactic president to travel anywhere involved a lot of moving parts, least of all his massive security detail.

The fact that Chiba had moved so quickly meant the Union was finally taking the Progenitors seriously. *Good.*

To speed things even more, the president had sent a message ahead by com drone indicating that he wanted the upcoming meeting with the alien newcomers to occur aboard Tartarus Station.

The same message requested Husher's presence at the meeting. That was how he found himself walking with Fesky from one of the station's three flight decks toward a central conference chamber, accompanied by their own security detail, which consisted solely of Major Peter Gamble.

Gamble had wanted to bring more marines along. The man had pushed for an entire platoon.

"We're in Union space, Major," Husher had said.

"Yeah, just like we were in Wintercress. And Saffron. Didn't help us much there. Besides, who knows what these new aliens might pull?"

"The Quatro withdrew their fleet to the edge of the system again. They've only sent one shuttle to Tartarus."

"Yeah, but I hear these guys are huge."

In the end, Husher had taken Gamble's concerns under advisement, but ultimately he'd decided they were unwarranted. If the president of the galaxy was willing to meet aboard a space station—a much more vulnerable venue than a planetside building, or even better, a fortified underground facility—then Husher was fine with just his marine commander as escort. They needed to convey a certain level of trust to the Quatro. He would have gone without any escort at all, but he knew Gamble would have turned himself inside-out over that. The man *fretted*.

There wasn't much room aboard Tartarus, which was the case inside most space-based constructs. Not capital starships, of course, but that was one of the many reasons the capital starships represented such a leap past anything else in the galaxy. Achieving that leap had required staggering resources, along with some of the finest engineers to be found among the four Union species.

Space constraints meant that even the meeting chamber the president had chosen to meet with the Quatro was somewhat cramped. After leaving Gamble in the corridor, Husher and Fesky entered to find the quadrupedal aliens were every bit as large as rumor held. There were five of them, all in repose on the carpeted floor, and together they took up almost half the room. One of the two curved tables had been shoved back against the bulkhead to make space for the aliens, since Tartarus had no furniture designed for Quatro.

Husher and his XO were almost last to arrive, leaving only the president missing. Flanking them at the human table were Union functionaries Husher couldn't put names to, but opposite them, on the other end of the table's curve, sat a boy who was staring at Husher, next to a girl who was doing the same.

What are they doing here? He doubted either one of them was even twenty. *I haven't met very many diplomacy prodigies.*

As he returned their scrutiny, he picked up on subtle cues that gave him a slightly clearer picture of their identity: defined jaw lines, short-cropped hair, unwavering gazes. *They're military.*

But that didn't give an answer to what were they doing here. They were too young to hold high rank.

It was a mystery, but he wasn't about to ask. He returned their gazes with one eyebrow hiked up until they looked elsewhere, first the boy, then the girl.

The president entered, along with a single armed guard who took up position against the bulkhead behind him. *I don't think that guard is going to accomplish much if these beasts decide to attack.* Chiba's head-tail swayed as he took his seat in the table's center, and he folded his small, blue-white hands before him as he studied the Quatro with the eternal calm of a Kaithian.

The central Quatro rose to its full height, pointed ears brushing the ceiling. Thick, scarlet lines radiated back from its snout through otherwise purple fur, and it regarded the president with enormous orange eyes. Its face looked menacing, but Husher wasn't sure it was capable of adopting a configuration that didn't look menacing, in the same way that the predatory cats who'd stalked prehistoric humans across the savanna had struggled with looking friendly.

President Chiba spoke first. "We thank you for your help in dealing with the invading battle group."

The alien dipped its giant head in response. "This enemy, who you may know as 'Progenitor,' is why we have come," it said in a deep, resonant purr—or rather, the device hanging around its neck did. *A translator. Remarkable.* "They drove us from our home, and we were fortunate to escape with the numbers we did. As for our aid in fighting them, your people did not request it of us. We volunteered it. Nothing is owed for this. Our aims clearly align, and Quatro also benefit from the destruction of Progenitor ships."

Husher raised his eyebrows, surprised to hear the Quatro giving up the leverage they'd gained in helping with the defense of Hellebore. Verbally, anyway—the leverage remained, no matter what they said. *But still.*

"That's very gracious of you to say," Chiba answered, which suggested to Husher that the president's thoughts mirrored his own. "To avoid offense, I should seek some clarification—I'm given to understand that you are Eldest of the Assembly of Elders, and that you are male. Is that right?"

"Yes."

"And the Assembly is a governing body of some kind?"

"That is correct. And what position do you hold among this...assortment of species?" The Quatro glanced along the curved table, though the gesture stretched the word to its limits—even a glance seemed momentous when performed by the great being. His gaze took in those seated, which included humans, Kaithe, Wingers, and Tumbra.

"I am President Chiba of the Interstellar Union."

"Then it would seem our conversation has potential. I thank you for honoring our presence with yours, though I must acknowledge that we have been waiting in this system for some time, conducting seemingly circular negotiations with low-level dignitaries. And yet, once we expelled the Progenitors from your space, you rushed to meet us. Is military might the only thing you respect?"

"No," Chiba said. "Quite the opposite, actually."

That's for damn sure, Husher mused.

Chiba continued: "What is your name, Eldest?"

The alien regarded the president in silence for a moment. "Name?" he said, as though turning the word over in his mouth to see how it tasted.

"You don't have names? Designators for individuals?"

"I am Eldest among the Assembly of Elders. Other than that, I am equal among my drift, though unlike others, my drift includes all Quatro."

"We, too, prize equality," Chiba said. "That's an interesting notion, that names might be tied up in keeping us unequal." The president paused, as though momentarily lost in thought.

Oh, God. Husher cleared his throat.

Chiba glanced at him, then met the Quatro's gaze once more. "The reason I delayed in meeting with you has to do with galactic security. When the president goes anywhere, it's a news story, and we were reluctant to draw unnecessary attention to what was happening in Hellebore until we knew who we were dealing with. We've had two unexpected arrivals, recently—a group of humans who fled this galaxy twenty years ago, who we managed to transport to this system undetected by the media, and you, who arrived in this same system not long after. If there is such a thing as fate, it would seem it's at work in Hellebore. But I digress. The returning humans I mentioned were also accompanied by Quatro; a much smaller group, mostly aboard a single ship that resembles yours, though it's clearly based on older technology. I understand you have an interest in those Quatro."

"Yes," the Eldest said—a little too quickly, in Husher's estimation. "They must be folded back into the drift."

The boy and girl sitting across from Husher tensed at the Quatro's words. *Interesting.*

"I see," Chiba said. "As I'm sure you detected during the battle, the Quatro ship in question has already fled the system. But I fear this discussion is becoming as aimless as you suggested the other negotiations were. I think it's time we communicate our respective desired outcomes for today's meeting. If I may jump ahead a little, it seems likely that we both need each other's help in fighting an enemy that's quickly proving a threat to not just the galaxy, but perhaps even the universe. Am I correct in that assumption, Eldest?"

"You are," the Quatro said, but Husher barely heard him. At Chiba's words, adrenaline had washed through his entire body, and it made him want to leap to his feet, pumping his fists in the air and yelling like a maniac.

A threat to the universe. *I think we might finally be getting through to them.* This felt like an even bigger victory than the one he'd achieved over Klaxon.

"Excellent," Chiba said. "Now that we've established that, the only thing that remains is to determine the conditions under which we both will be able to collaborate."

For a meeting involving the Union, this one had proceeded at what Husher would have called breakneck speed, so far. Of course, that didn't last. After deciding they wanted to work together, the president and the Eldest took a while to arrive at what seemed to Husher like very simple terms. *This is why I'll never be a diplomat.* Beside him, Fesky began to shift in her seat.

The Quatro warships would be divided and deployed according to direction given by the IGF, mostly to protect and defend the various Union systems. In return, the Quatro would be granted three suitable Milky Way systems in which to make their new home, with the promise of more once the alien's apparently rapid reproduction rates filled those up.

Other than that, diplomatic relations would be kept open, with provisions made to address the evolving needs of both the Union and the Assembly.

"It's also vital that you refrain from opening any more wormholes," Chiba said. "Ever. I know the reasons why have already been outlined to you, but I'd be remiss if I didn't underscore them. Compromising the underlying structure of our universe is obviously something that would impact us both."

One thing kept cropping up throughout the discussion, and Husher credited it with most of the blame for the meeting taking so long: the Eldest wanted those escaped Quatro back.

"I'm afraid that isn't something I can guarantee," Chiba said. "Amid the confusion surrounding the attack on this system, both the Darkstream ships and the Quatro ship were allowed to slip through Feverfew and onto much less populated systems."

"We *must* have them back," the Eldest said. "As soon as it can be done."

"May I ask why you want them back so badly?"

"They are wayward and proud—far too proud. Their pride is such that they place themselves before their drift, and they hold to toxic ideas that we consider antithetical to the operation of a healthy society. They *must* be folded back into the drift."

"Toxic," Chiba said, nodding. "I see. They're criminals, then?"

"Worse."

"Well, I will notify our warship captains that they are to do everything in their power to apprehend them, should they encounter them. How does the Assembly typically deal with criminals?"

"You already have the answer, though you do not know it."

The Kaithian tilted his head to one side. "Hmm? How do you mean?"

With that, the two Quatro on both ends of the group stood, bowing their heads low toward their leader. Neither bore the red face markings of the Eldest, or the yellow lines that adorned the other two Quatro's heads.

"These two are guilty of crimes against their drift," the Eldest said. "And yet here you see them, walking free. Indeed, I have brought them to what may well prove to be the most significant event in our species' history."

"They are reformed," Chiba said.

"Yes. But you should hear them recount their experiences themselves."

The rightmost Quatro fixed Chiba with an unwavering gaze, eyes wide with conviction. "Before the Progenitors destroyed our home, which spanned a galaxy just as yours does—before that on-slaught, we lived in paradise. The Assembly provided everything we could possibly need. No one wanted. Everyone enjoyed plenty, and all were equal. That is still our way. All are equal, with only the drift elevated above all."

"And the Eldest is the only one whose drift is made up of every Quatro," Husher interrupted.

Heads swung toward him all along the curved table, and the Eldest regarded him as though he was considering making a meal of him. Chiba was glaring, too. Fesky clacked her beak softly.

"Yes," the Quatro criminal answered, haltingly. "As I said, all are equal...even the Eldest..." It turned until it was looking just past the Eldest, who dipped his head. The reformed criminal re-turned to staring wide-eyed at Chiba. "I was selfish, once. I sought more than others, and I competed with my drift to get it. I placed my drift beneath myself, and I harmed it to satisfy my whims. But I was not put to death. We are permitted to believe whatever we want. I was simply taught the supremacy of the drift."

The Quatro lowered itself to the floor, then, and so did the other criminal, who hadn't spoken.

"So you see," the Eldest said. "We treat our criminals very well. We fold them back into the drift."

"Okay," Chiba said. "I expect we may be finished for today, unless anyone has anything to—"

"What about subspace tech?" Husher said. He didn't like bringing up the new tech around freshly minted allies, but then, he wasn't telling them how it worked just by naming it, and he didn't know when he would get the opportunity to apply this kind of pressure again.

"What about it, Captain Husher?" Chiba growled.

"We've already agreed that the Progenitors are an existential threat. So it's rational to move ahead with anything that might improve our combat effectiveness. Subspace tech will do that, especially since I'm fairly certain our enemies are already using it."

The Kaithian clearly hated to give him what he wanted, but it would be the height of irrationality to disagree with him now, and the Kaithe were nothing if not supremely rational.

"Very well, Captain," Chiba said, his words still clipped. "I will work with you to make this a reality. Will that be all?"

"No. Before I left Zakros, I was told my rank and position as captain of the *Vesta* are under review. Is that still the case?"

The Kaithian opened his mouth to reply, revealing twin rows of tiny, pointed teeth. Then he closed it again. Clearly, he was surprised Husher would bring that up at this meeting. Husher was a little surprised too, if he was being honest.

Chiba shook his head, as though to clear it. "If the special commission finds you guilty of the charges brought against you, I will grant you a presidential pardon, conditional upon your unqualified obedience throughout the remainder of this war. It's an unusual way of doing things, but I tend to agree with you that we need to leverage every asset at our disposal, and you are such an asset."

"Thank you, Mr. President," Husher said, trying not to grin too broadly.

"Where do we fit into all this?" said the boy sitting across from Husher, his tone one of barely restrained anger. "We were also driven from our home by the Progenitors, and we also have tech that can help win this war. Why haven't we been acknowledged at all during this meeting?"

"Who are you?" Husher asked, squinting.

"I'm Seaman Jake Price. I lead the team of mechs that took down a destroyer while you were busy letting a supercarrier get destroyed."

Husher stared at the boy, mentally checking to make sure his mouth wasn't hanging open. *Jake Price. The one Teth is so keen to get his claws on.* "Not what I'd call a fair representation of the recent engagement," Husher said, grateful his voice was so steady. "But even so—we have a lot to talk about, son."

CHAPTER 10

Prison Planet

To Captain Bob Bronson, lingering inside a cell on Imbros for what already seemed like an eternity felt too much like the weeks he'd spent in the *Providence*'s brig. Keyes had kept him there, alone and ignored, at a time when Bronson should have been captain. The UHF admiralty had granted him command of the supercarrier, but it didn't matter. Keyes had staged his little rebellion, for which he was rewarded lavishly in the end. Of course, that had involved overthrowing the entire Human Commonwealth, but even so...Keyes had deserved nothing good.

Ah, well. He got his in the end.

Unlike Keyes, Bronson was still alive. Still here. True, he was in prison, and a guard had done him the courtesy of informing him that his destroyer was gone—taken out of the system, probably by other Darkstream employees. Or ex-employees, now. *Whatever.*

During the confusion of the skirmish with the Progenitors, most of the Steele System civilians and Darkstream personnel had apparently managed to find their way into orbit and onto the parked ships. The Quatro, too, most of whom hadn't gone down to Imbros in the first place, choosing instead to live aboard their own warship.

As far as Bronson knew, no one had made an attempt to spring him from his cell.

Ungrateful bastards.

A door opened somewhere, and he heard the slow crescendo of approaching footsteps. A woman he recognized as the warden appeared at the shatterproof glass that fronted the cell. The *Providence* cells had had bars, but here it was only spotless glass, which made him feel naked with someone standing there gawking at him.

Quinn. Eve Quinn. He'd only spotted her twice, but he recognized her. Uniform neatly ironed and tucked, not a hair follicle in disarray. A slight smile that said she knew exactly how much power she had over him.

"Bronson," she said, her voice coming through an octagon of pinholes just above her mouth. "*Captain* Bronson—isn't that what your pretend military promoted you to?"

He didn't humor her with a response.

"I have a couple news items for you. There's bad news, and there's—ah, should I call it good news? Which would you like first?"

He held his peace, envisioning the revenge he'd take on her if his designs ever panned out.

"We can do this all day, Bronson. I can tell you the news, but I want you to ask for it politely."

"Could you tell me the news?" he said at once.

Quinn's smile widened. "All right. The Darkstream board members have all been sentenced to life in prison for their crimes, without parole."

Despite himself, Bronson's eyes widened. The Progenitors had promised him that Darkstream would rise to power once again in this galaxy. But that was difficult to accomplish from a prison cell.

That was the least of his worries, now. Much more worrisome was what, exactly, the Interstellar Union considered Darkstream's crimes to be. *If they know about our collusion with the Progenitors…*

"What crimes?" he managed to rasp.

"Well, some of the members were left over from the board that fled the Milky Way through a wormhole, after they were caught poisoning our democratic process. As for the newer members…countless witnesses testified to how, during your time in the Steele System, Darkstream exploited people for ever-increasing profits. There's documentation showing the company instigated a war with the Quatro living in the Steele System, and more proving that citizens living in Darkstream habitats were allowed to become slaves, because of a deal the board struck with a local drug lord. This ringing any bells?"

"You've kept awfully informed for a prison warden."

Quinn nodded, looking genuinely pleased. "I do like to personally keep my prisoners updated on their individual situations."

"I can tell. What's my situation?"

"Well, that's the other part. The news of questionable quality, if you will. See, you're essentially free to go."

"Essentially?"

Quinn nodded again. "You have identified the most important word in that sentence, yes. In a moment, I'm going to release you from this cell, but you'll be under what we're going to call planet arrest. You can go anywhere you like on Imbros, even out into the wild, if you care to. Be a tree man, if that's to your liking. But the moment you leave the planet's gravity well, we'll know, and we'll intercept whatever bucket you've managed to slither into well before it leaves the system."

Feeling cautiously optimistic, Bronson said, "How will you know if I leave Imbros?"

"I was actually hoping you'd ask that. What we have in this system, as I'm sure you've heard, is the Department of Interplanetary Immigration and Travel. Lot of mumbo jumbo, to my ears, but it does mean we get a lot of tech geeks. Love their devices, do the desk jockeys of the Department, especially when it comes to devices that enable tracking and surveillance. Can you see where I'm going with this, Captain Bob Bronson?"

As Quinn spoke, a cold sweat had broken out all over Bronson's body, and he fell silent once more.

"I think you might, but I'll spell it out for you all the same. You see, we've taken a real interest in the computers that a lot of you Steele System folks had implanted in your head." Quinn poked a finger against the side of her skull and spun it. "And it turns out they're real easy to hack into! Almost like they were designed that way. Isn't that funny? Anyway. We decided not to go poking around inside the heads of regular civilians too much, not at this early stage, anyway. But we sure were interested in how those implants worked, and who better to unabashedly spy on than a jailed corporate suckhole who's probably guilty six ways from Sunday? Prisoners are at the forefront of tracking and surveillance, whether they know it or not. And once we hacked into your implant, we saw what you saw. Heard what you heard. Yeah, we knew every time you muttered in your sleep, farted, or took a piss."

Quinn sniffed. "Lucky for you, the implant logs you no doubt kept on everyone weren't stored on the devices, else we'd probably be able to nail you to the wall. As it stands, we've got to thinking that it might be useful to have you around." With that, Quinn produced a device from her pocket and clicked it. The glass slid a meter to the right, opening just enough to let him pass through. "So go ahead, Bronson. Go out and stretch your legs. When we need you, we'll know where to find you. And if you're a good boy, maybe we'll even toss you a few more bones."

Hardly able to believe it, Bronson rose to his feet. *I'm finally leaving this cursed place.* At that moment, with his admittedly conditional freedom spreading out before him, anything seemed possible.

He stepped past the glass.

"Remember," Quinn said, dropping her playful tone like a bad act. "I'll be the one watching you, so try not to act like too much of a slob, all right?"

He smiled at her, then turned toward the end of the corridor, where a guard was holding the door for him.

The same guard escorted him past two more rows of cells, an office, and then another row, inmates jeering and spitting at him the entire time. Bronson felt the urge to curse at them, not in anger but joy. He restrained himself. *I'm being a good boy.*

For now.

His personal effects—some of them, anyway—were returned to him at the front desk, and he was shown to a restroom where he could change out of the prison uniform.

Outside, the sun was just breaking through scant cloud cover, and he cherished the warmth on his upturned face. That was a pleasure he'd barely encountered during his twenty years in exile. Back in Steele, Eresos had been the only place where you could go outside without a pressure suit, and he'd rarely consorted with the human cattle who'd lived there. The artificial sun they'd had on Valhalla Station just hadn't been the same.

Now what? It occurred to him that he had no money, at least none they'd accept on Imbros. Hundreds of thousands of credits were tied to his implant, but that didn't mean anything in the Milky Way.

Surely they plan to keep me fed? Glancing back at the prison entrance, he briefly contemplated going back inside and raising the matter.

No way. He'd sooner die than step foot in that place again. *They've been very clever, with this 'planet arrest' nonsense.* Now they didn't even have to bother with housing him, with Imbros itself as his prison. Maybe he *would* have to enter the wilderness, just to forage something to eat.

The idea seemed preposterous on the face of it. A starship captain, forced to scrounge in the bushes like an animal. It made him want to laugh, though his mirth was quickly cut short by his rumbling stomach.

He started walking, and after a few blocks he came to what was clearly a soup kitchen. Judging by the position of the sun, it had to be around lunch time, and the line that stretched out of the door and down the sidewalk was an even better indication. Cheeks heating, he made his way to the back of that line and hunched his shoulders, to make himself as unrecognizable as possible.

With that bit of embarrassment over, and his stomach mostly full, he continued walking until he found a public park. He took the first bench he came across, which faced the road, where he watched driverless cars zip past each other until his vision blurred.

A humanoid shape appeared before him, and he focused again, before crying out and drawing his legs onto the bench with him. "Wh-whuh? What are you doing here?"

Standing before him was a Progenitor, or at least one of the telepresence robots they'd always used to communicate with him. He'd had one secreted inside his office on the *Javelin* for most of his twenty years in the Steele System.

"Compose yourself," the robot said as sunbeams glanced off its gold and silver plates, half-blinding Bronson.

Slowly, he lowered his legs back to the ground, feeling even more ashamed than he had waiting in line for soup. But as his initial fright subsided, rage began to replace it.

"How dare you show yourself here?" he said, though his voice still shook.

"Clarify."

"You betrayed us. We had a deal, damn it. You promised that Darkstream would rise to power after returning here, but the board members were all just sentenced to life in jail!"

"Is the board Darkstream?"

Bronson hesitated, the strangely philosophical question throwing him off. "I mean, basically!" he said at last. "Who else is Darkstream? The shareholders? Most of them are dead."

"In the Steele System, you provisioned us with a trove of data, which you harvested by discreetly monitoring every human living there. And yet, the breadth of your ignorance continues to impress."

"*Bastard.*" Bronson rose to his feet, fists clenched, and strode toward the robot. A mother pushing a stroller nearby shot him a concerned look, then hurried on. Suddenly, it occurred to him how odd it was that no one had reacted to the strange robot's presence, He stopped, squinting at it. "You're not actually here, are you?"

"Correct. I've co-opted your implant in order to communicate with you."

"Great job. The Union is monitoring my implant. You just blew your cover."

The robot cocked its oblong head to one side. "Again, your perceptions reliably mislead you. We have of course masked our interference from the woman responsible for surveilling you. Doing so posed us no challenge at all."

Bronson frowned. He didn't remember the Progenitor that lived in the *Javelin*'s closet ever speaking with such arrogance and sarcasm. *Am I talking to someone else, now?* "You must have a presence nearby for us to be talking in real-time."

"Yes. We have a shuttle concealed on Imbros' moon for the purpose of contacting you."

So there's an actual Progenitor, sitting in this star system as we speak? That's gutsy. "What do you want?"

"You accuse us of failing to lift Darkstream to power. I am here to tell you that Darkstream's dominance of this galaxy is all but assured."

"How?"

"Sit."

Bronson returned to the bench and sat down.

The Progenitor nodded, the front tip of its strange head bobbing toward the ground. "You must commit everything I say to memory, and follow my instructions to the letter. Listen well, Bronson. Engineering a galactic government's self-destruction is a delicate business."

CHAPTER 11

Getting Paid Again

For now, Oneiri Team was still bunking in Tartarus Station's Outer Wing, despite that the Union no longer had them under lock and key. The mech pilots had officially joined galactic society—for as long as it existed, anyway.

Jake was making the rounds, informing everyone of their next moves. This station was ultimately a civilian installation, meaning everyone had separate sleeping chambers—a luxury for low-ranking military personnel, no matter how cramped they were. He'd left Andy for last, since Lisa normally bunked with him, and calling on them always involved an element of awkwardness. It did for Jake, anyway. He wondered how they both fit in that narrow bunk, for one thing.

But his knock brought only Andy to the hatch, and the bunk was clearly visible from the entrance. It contained no Lisa.

"Price," Andy said. Joining Oneiri Team, which Jake had found himself in command of during the chaos back in Steele, hadn't done much for Andy's attitude toward him. He was pretty sure the guy only stayed on the team to keep an eye on Lisa, and he frequently made reference to the fact that he wasn't even military to begin with. Everyone on Oneiri referred to Andy as a seaman, since the Darkstream military had used naval ranks across the board, but officially Jake was a seaman, too.

"Where's Lisa?" Jake asked.

"Who wants to know?"

"I asked the question, didn't I?" Jake shot back, an edge creeping into his voice.

"She went on a snack run."

"Right. Well, I came to tell you—"

"About the big important meeting you found yourself at? President of the Union and all that? Hey, let me be the first to congratulate you, Fearless Leader. You're well on your way to becoming a top-level desk jockey."

Nodding slowly, Jake said, "You got that out of your system, then?"

"I guess we'll find out."

"Cut the wisecracks until I get out what I came to tell you, Miller. Captain Vin Husher was at the meeting too, and after he found out who I was, he started pushing hard for me to come with him aboard the *Vesta*. And when he found out I piloted a mech—"

"Wait. He gave a shit about who you were, independently of you piloting a giant alien mech?"

"Yeah," Jake said. "Trust me, I'm just as surprised as you are. Apparently the Progenitors know my name. An Ixan from the Second Galactic War, Teth, is one of their lapdogs, and getting access to me was one of his conditions during the negotiations the Union thought were a good idea."

Andy's eyes were narrowed, and he was shaking his head in disbelief. "*Teth* is still around?"

"You know who he is?"

"I've read up on the second war with the Ixa, yeah."

"You're just full of surprises, Andy. Anyway, I gotta admit, Husher impressed me during the meeting. He was throwing his weight around a lot, and getting results, too. I kind of get the impression he's had to deal with a lot of bull up to this point, and he's fed up with it. Can't say I blame him. He started asking me about Oneiri, right there in front of the president and all those bureaucrats, not to mention the Quatro leader. And within a few minutes, he'd arranged for us to be folded into the marine battalion aboard his supercarrier."

"All right."

Jake blinked. "We get to join a military outfit, Andy. We're getting paid again—that'll be nice, won't it? And we get to help fight this war."

"Did you remember to tell our new captain that the type of mech you pilot has a history of driving people insane?"

A pounding began in Jake's ears, and he fought to settle himself. "I have that under control, Miller. Husher doesn't need to worry himself with something that isn't an issue. The most important thing now is beating the Progenitors."

"Right. Listen, I think we both know that if Lisa wasn't so gung-ho about all this, I'd have left with her long ago."

Jake shook his head, eyes narrowed. "And gone where? Do you not get that the galaxy's in danger of getting wiped out?"

"Yeah, but that'd take a few years at least, to wipe it *all* out. You know? And I'd say there's a good chance they'll leave little shit-speck backwater colonies alone. If we cozied up there, we'd probably be fine." Andy grew a wistful smile, which made Jake want to punch him.

Their assignment to the *Vesta* wasn't the only thing Jake had come to talk over with Andy, and the conversation so far had convinced him even more that the next topic was a lost cause. Still, he didn't like to abandon something he'd resolved to do, so he gritted his teeth and had at it.

"Andy, have you noticed anything weird with Lisa, since we picked her up on the edge of the Steele System? Have you noticed her acting differently at all?"

Andy's smile turned venomous, then, which was all the confirmation Jake needed that this line of discussion was completely pointless. "Ah, I see what this is about," Andy said, chuckling. "Yep. See, Lisa has been acting differently, Price. You know how? She's finally acknowledged her feelings for me. I know you two were childhood buddies and all, but for Lisa, that's as far as it went. For you, though—you always wanted a little more, didn't you? Real sorry, buddy, honestly. Sorry things didn't swing your way. But is this really the way you're going to take out your frustrations? By asking me whether Lisa's acting *weird?* Kind of pathetic, don't you think?"

Andy's smile remained plastered on his face, and his eyes never left Jake's. For Jake's part, it was everything he could do to restrain himself, so that Andy didn't end up on the floor.

"Thank you for going over my concerns with me, Miller. Pack your things. We ship out tomorrow. And tell Lisa to do the same."

With that, Jake about-turned crisply and headed for his own chamber.

CHAPTER 12

Extremely Poor Taste

Husher knew Ochrim spent most of his time in the lab these days, so he didn't bother ringing the doorbell, using his com instead as he walked up the lane toward the Ixan's house. "Ochrim, you decent?"

"Decent? Oh. Yes."

"Wanna let me in, then?"

"You'll find the door unlocked."

"Thanks."

He let himself in, walked toward the rear of the cubic residence, and paused at the kitchen entrance, eyeing the fridge. It was usually well-stocked with beer, and he debated grabbing one, but thought better of it. He proceeded to the back room instead, where the floor panel had been left propped open to reveal the ladder stretching down into the ship. Now that subspace tech was known to more than just he and Ochrim, there wasn't as much need for secrecy.

"How do you like your new lab?" Husher asked as he stepped off the bottom rung. He'd ordered work started on expanding it before they'd left the Concord System, and in Hellebore he'd been able to outsource the rest of the job to a planetary contracting company.

"Much more spacious," the Ixan said. "And better company, too." He nodded at an enormous, transparent tank that took up an entire wall. Inside it swam Ek and her six offspring. One of Ochrim's main projects was to develop a method for Ek to once again walk freely, whether on land or a starship's deck—without her body degrading from the harmful affects of zero-g, this time. He hoped to do the same for her children.

Every other species injected themselves with Ocharium nanites, which then embedded within the body's cells. The Ocharium attracted the fermion matrix in every starship's deck, creating a perfect simulation of one g. But Fin cells rejected the Ocharium for some reason, and the years Ek had spent spacefaring had taken a nearly lethal toll on her.

The tank featured an extension that projected toward the lab's ceiling, which allowed the Fins to come up and speak with anyone in the lab. Having noticed Husher's arrival, Ek did so now. "Greetings, Captain Husher."

"Hello, Ek. How are you making out?"

"The tank is less spacious than the oceans of Klaxon. But we are grateful to have left that place, even so." Ek's six children regarded Husher solemnly through the shatterproof glass as their mother spoke.

"I should think you are," he murmured. Before the *Vesta*'s arrival, Ek and her family had been hunted for months by the Ixa, forced to cower in deep underwater caves and crevices to evade capture. Come to think of it, that was probably why the younger

Fins seemed so wary around Ochrim, especially at first. They'd warmed up to him considerably since their arrival here, which was a testament to Husher's idea that the best thing for interspecies relations was for the various species to simply spend more time around each other, rather than the oppressive, ineffectual policies so many in the Union tried to force on everyone.

"Ek, I recently attended a meeting between the IU president and the leader of a new arrival to the galaxy—a species who call themselves the Quatro. Their government is called the Assembly of Elders, headed by the 'Eldest.' I was surprised by how well the two parties got along. What do you make of that?"

"It is difficult for me to draw any solid conclusions based on a secondhand account, no matter how much detail you provide in that account. It is much better if I can observe behavior directly. Was the meeting recorded?"

"If it was, I don't have access to the vid."

"I see. Then, I can only offer the most superficial inferences, I am afraid. When two parties develop an instant rapport, it is often because each sees themselves reflected in the other. Sadly, I cannot offer more than that, Captain."

"I understand. Thank you, Ek."

"Will that be all? I can leave you and Ochrim to your conversing."

"That's all for now."

With that, Ek swam down the tank's extension to join her children in the main section.

The Fins' tank contained water from Klaxon's oceans, which had the right chemical composition for them to remain healthy—

it was very similar to that of their homeworld, Spire, to which the Gok had laid waste during the Second Galactic War. Husher had ordered two hundred thousand gallons of reserve water brought aboard as well, so that the tank could regularly be replenished with purified water. At the Fins' request, he'd had the floor laid with algae-lined rocks, to mimic the Klaxon ocean floor as closely as possible. Ek was obviously determined not to distract from the war effort, and so it had taken some urging from Husher to tell him that she'd also enjoy some aquatic plants, as well as some furniture modified to accommodate Fins. He made that happen, too.

He'd tried to do everything he could to make the Fins as comfortable as possible, but in the end, they were still living in a glorified aquarium. That was fine for a guppy, but for sentient beings it had to be torture.

Subspace tech had to take precedence over all else, however, and Ochrim could only fit in work on a solution for the Fins around his work on improving the new tech—chiefly, trying to reduce its enormous energy demands so that bigger ships could enter subspace. Right now, they only had the ability to send a starfighter, which was a far cry from the immense carriers the Progenitors managed to make vanish on a whim.

He knew the Ixan wasn't getting much sleep, since he was just as concerned about the Fins' welfare as Husher. Hopefully, a breakthrough would come soon. Husher wanted full-time access to Ek's keen perception. Feeding her data secondhand like this paled in comparison to what he'd seen her do during the Second Galactic War.

Ochrim was leaning against a steel table, looking resigned. Probably, he sensed that his labor was far from over. Husher felt a pang of real regret—he was sure there were even more whitened scales around the scientist's eyes than the last time they'd spoken.

He never would have expected to feel sympathy for the being responsible for hundreds of thousands of human deaths. *The universe is a bizarre place.* But since coming aboard the *Vesta*, Ochrim had proven himself to Husher, several times over. After Husher was stripped of command through political maneuvering by the Cybele city council and his old Nav officer, Ochrim had helped him, even though Husher had lost all his authority and influence. Indeed, the Ixan had helped him win that authority back.

Through his actions alone, Ochrim had convinced Husher that everything he did was intended either to minimize pain or serve the greater good. As twisted as it seemed, the Ixan had even been convinced that killing hundreds of thousands of people would lead to the future with the least pain. That act had been the most radical expression of the Ixan's ironclad philosophy, and while Husher would never condone it, he at least understood it, now.

Those deaths also demonstrated the limits of such a philosophy: even Ochrim, who'd believed he had access to perfect knowledge via his AI father, had committed an unspeakable atrocity that didn't even end up minimizing pain like he'd thought it would.

"At the same meeting I mentioned, the President gave the go-ahead to start implementing subspace tech throughout the fleet," Husher said. "We're first: the *Vesta* is on her way back to

Feverfew right now, to have a squadron of Pythons outfitted with spherical wormhole generators. I assume you know what that means."

"You'll need me at the shipyards tomorrow." The Ixan let a sigh escape his lips. "I wasn't even aware we were underway."

"Seriously?" Husher let a sardonic smile take shape. "Sounds like someone's falling behind on their narrownet reading."

The joke was in extremely poor taste, given how hard he knew Ochrim was working. But as he waved goodbye to Ek and started the climb back up the ladder, he still took pleasure in the Ixan's bland reaction.

The way Husher saw it, every supercarrier captain was entitled to the occasional tasteless joke.

CHAPTER 13

Technically Insubordinate

Back in the Feverfew System, Husher quickly found himself once again in front of the special commission jointly convened by the IU and the IGF. Today, he would learn whether he was guilty of any punishable crimes, in light of his actions during the opening battles with the Progenitors.

The commission's chair, Ryn, looked even more severe than she had during the initial hearing. Her feathers stood at attention as she leaned over the elevated table, pinning Husher to his lonely seat with her stare. "There's no use prolonging these proceedings," she said. "None of us like how things have gone. When captains skirt both regulation and law and get rewarded for it, it leaves a sour taste in the mouth of everyone who sits on this special commission. Nevertheless, Captain Husher, you have been found guilty of insubordination and also of multiple being rights violations. Given that President Chiba has seen fit to pardon you, this is a symbolic measure at best, but nevertheless, we prefer sending a message over no action at all. How do you plead?"

"I'm prepared to plead guilty to insubordination. It's true that I acted against the IU's wishes to conduct negotiations with the

Progenitors, even though I did so because that line of action would only have hastened our destruction. My actions prevented Teth from gaining a foothold in the Concord System, and clearly the IU agrees with me on some level, since they now have a battle group stationed there to prevent him from attempting it again." Those ships had arrived before Husher himself had left the system—during the weeks they'd waited in Concord while Ochrim developed a way to bring Ek aboard the *Vesta*. "But I was technically insubordinate, yes. As for the being rights violations, given they were leveled solely on the grounds of my failure to adhere to broken policies, I plead not guilty."

"Very well. Your pleas have been registered. I'll also remind you that this commission's findings will be made public, and are almost certain to be publicized all across the Union."

"I need no reminder," Husher said. "I've been given leave to fight the enemy seeking to wipe us from the galaxy. Public opinion is irrelevant to that mission."

Ryn clacked her beak. "I think you'll discover that assumption is thoroughly incorrect, Captain. You have been granted a pardon for now, but pardons can be revoked, especially when sufficient political pressure is brought to bear. Our society is in the process of ridding itself of men like you. You may think you've won your status back, but I can promise you, this reprieve will be temporary."

There were many things Husher wanted to say to that, but none that would do him any favors in the public eye. He stayed quiet and settled for returning the Winger's gaze.

But Ryn wasn't finished. "Although it isn't directly relevant to these proceedings, I would like to state for the record, and for your benefit, Captain, that your three marines who violated Human Nonattendance Day are all being dishonorably discharged from the Integrated Galactic Fleet."

"An obscene overreaction," Husher said, immediately wishing he hadn't.

The Winger's eyes widened—in satisfaction, as far as Husher could tell. "Care to clarify that statement?"

He was committed, now, though he doubted the public would like what he was about to say, and many Fleet officers would probably cringe when they heard it, too. "Enlisted soldiers have always gotten into scraps—in bars, mostly. It's essentially a fleet tradition. Proportionate disciplinary measures are always taken, of course, and these three marines have already spent plenty of time in the *Vesta*'s brig. But to dishonorably discharge them because of the political component sets a dangerous precedent."

"Your view will be registered," Ryn said. "I can assure you of that. But it's irrelevant to our decision. The marines will be discharged. As for you, Captain, consider yourself on notice. While you were in Hellebore, an extensive analysis of your ship's narrow net was conducted, which uncovered dozens of instances where extreme viewpoints were expressed, most notably in support of groups known for their hatred of nonhumans. This is the type of person your policies embolden, Captain. And indeed, as has been pointed out to you before, many of them name you as a figure of admiration."

Husher opened his mouth to answer, but clearly Ryn wanted to end on that note. "This commission is now indefinitely adjourned," she said. The Winger gave Husher a final, meaningful look, then stood and left the chamber, followed by the others on the commission.

CHAPTER 14

All It Took Was a War

"Making a squadron of Pythons subspace-capable has not been the only modification made during the last few weeks," Husher told the others as he led them past the squadron in question, which sat on a hangar bay inside one of the Feverfew Shipyards, orbiting the system's gas giant.

"As some of you are already aware," he continued, "what we know as the *Vesta*'s Supplies Module was originally meant to be capable of detaching from the supercarrier entirely and flying under its own power. You can probably guess the reason—it was meant to serve as a lifeboat for the civilians in Cybele, in case we were ever about to engage in combat. Kind of like we've been doing over the past several months. The designers scrapped the lifeboat concept, since they were afraid it would detract from the idea that capital starships are indestructible—why bother including a lifeboat in an invincible ship? But after Hellebore, we know capital starships are very destructible, and with starship city populations dropping even faster than they were before, the IGF is scrambling. These cities still serve as a major source of funding for our military, and for better or worse, command considers keeping people in them a priority."

Fesky trailed close enough behind Husher that he heard it when she clacked her beak. "All it took was a war to expose cities on warships as a ridiculous idea," she muttered.

Walking to her left, Tremaine chuckled. "When you're this invested in a bad idea, your only option is to double down."

"They're tripling down," Husher said. "But we have to deal with reality as it presents itself, not as we'd like it to be. Most of the supplies inside the Supplies Module have been moved elsewhere, and the connectors have been fitted with couplings that will allow it to detach and reattach at will. The Supplies Module is now the Lifeboat."

"Where'd we put the supplies?" Commander Ayam asked, sounding half-distracted, as he usually did whenever he wasn't inside a Python.

"Some of them are sitting inside my lab," Ochrim put in dryly.

Husher nodded. "We've put them where we can, for now. We do have a couple unused hangar bays, which we're in the process of stuffing full, and we also have a lot of vacant residences that have been filled up as well. Obviously, Command hopes that's a temporary measure. We've even relocated some to the brig, so I'd appreciate it if you'd all refrain from breaking any serious regulations."

No one laughed at his joke. *Ah, well. At least I know when they do laugh at one, it's because they actually think it's funny.* "Anyway," he continued. "The biggest change—other than the upgraded Pythons, which I think is a bigger change than anyone realizes—is the assignment of a new battle group to the *Vesta*. Two destroyers: *Resolution* and *Knight*. And two missile cruisers, *Hero* and *Impulsive*." Husher was having trouble keeping the excitement out of his voice. "The destroyers are real bruisers, arguably the best in the Fleet, and the cruisers are packed to the brim with Banshees, Gorgons, and Hydras. The Union may hate us, but they sure have given us some big guns."

"When do we set sail?" Tremaine asked, which made Husher grin. *The man must be picking up my nautical terms.*

But as he came to a stop, turning, the smile fell away. "That's the next thing I brought you here to tell you. It's also why I've run through these new additions so quickly. Seventeen star systems' sensor webs have been getting the same sort of anomalous readings that Wintercress did during the lead-up to Teth's first attack. Except, we now know they're not anomalous. The Progenitors are scouting our systems, flitting in and out, and Command thinks it's preliminary to a multi-system assault. Our best theory for why they do this was one Fesky hit on: they're mapping out points along the ecliptic plane where they can pop in and out, so they can make use of them when it comes time to engage."

"But that doesn't cohere with our understanding of subspace," Tremaine said, who'd been filled in on the modified Pythons' capabilities. "It offers true stealth, and it shrinks distances to a third, but we can only reenter realspace at the corresponding point in subspace."

Ochrim cleared his throat. "We believe the Progenitor mode of travel utilizes other dimensions. In fact, it isn't certain they ever enter subspace at all."

"I see," the Tactical officer said.

"Ultimately, it doesn't matter," Husher said. "That's all conjecture, and what's relevant to us is what we already know: the sensor web blips tend to precede attacks. We're being deployed to the Yclept System, and because our government's freaking out right now, they're leaning heavily on the Quatro fleet to help defend other systems. They consider a capital starship and her battle group enough to defend a single system, but there are only seven of us left, which leaves ten systems to be protected by a mix of Fleet and Quatro ships."

"I'm not fond of how quickly we've jumped into bed with this Assembly of Elders," Fesky said. "Did you notice how strangely that Quatro was behaving as it sang the praises of its government? I know they're a brand new species to us and we don't know how to read them yet, but everything about that Quatro screamed abject terror to me."

Husher nodded. "The alliance is hasty and ill-considered. But that's just how our government operates, these days. Besides, we're going to need all the help we can get to defeat the Progenitors."

"And what about the Gok?" Fesky said. "Do we know what they're planning, or has the Union bothered to check, other than to apologize for Concord and invite them over for tea?"

"Apparently the Gok government is 'distancing' themselves from the actions taken by 'rogue warships.'"

"And the Union swallowed that without question, I assume?"

"It's looking that way."

"Of course," Fesky squawked. "It's good to hear the Union is still finding creative new ways to remain vulnerable."

CHAPTER 15

Not a Psychologist

Major Peter Gamble leaned against a low garden wall and waited as bullets whipped through the night above his head and explosions sounded in the distance. Twisting around, he popped over the wall and returned fire at the steadily advancing Ixan commandos. There were only two of them, but if they reached the marine squad, they'd make short work of them.

We need to make a move. Five minutes ago would have been ideal, but now is much better than later.

Unfortunately, Gamble wasn't in command today.

"Jenkins?" he whispered into his lapel transceiver. "Orders?"

Newly minted Lance Corporal Jenkins stammered back. "Uh...uh...I dunno, Major. I got nothing."

Are you kidding me? "'Nothing' gets you killed in war, son. We need something, and we need it now."

"Um...maybe..."

Boy's all froze up. Cursing, Gamble took over. "Wilson and Moore, you're closest to the alley on our left. Knowing this city, there's a good chance it connects with one farther up. When I give the go-ahead, run for it while the rest of us cover you. Then move around for the flank, but check your angle first—I'm not in the mood for friendly fire today. My hope is the Ixa will spin around to engage you, then the rest of us can hit them hard from behind. Maybe toss a grenade or two. Everyone copy?"

A chorus of "Yes, Major," came back at him. *They know how to do that, at least.*

"Good. Wilson and Moore, move!"

They did, and Gamble popped over the garden wall again, sweeping his assault rifle across the enemy position. The gun clicked, and he ducked back down to swap in a fresh magazine.

The covering fire did the trick. His marines would be moving up the alley now, and soon they'd be in position.

Jenkins chose that moment to find his courage, rising to his feet—in full view of the advancing Ixa.

"Corporal, what you are you doing?" Gamble hissed. "Get down!"

"I got this, Major! This'll be an even *bigger* distraction."

With that, Jenkins ran out from cover and promptly got shot in the face.

"For crying out loud," Gamble said. "You're dead, Jenkins. *End sim.*"

The Oculens overlay depicting the city of Larissa disappeared, revealing the *Vesta* cargo bay where he'd been drilling the marine squad he considered the weakest in his entire battalion—Teal Squad. Captain Husher had kept this hold clear of boxes and things, knowing Gamble used it for running combat sims. He appreciated that, especially knowing just how many supplies the captain had had to relocate.

The 'heroic' lance corporal was avoiding eye contact, looking abashed and confused at the same time. Probably, the poor kid didn't even know what he'd done wrong. But that wouldn't stop Gamble from tearing a strip off him. "Jenkins, this isn't a video game. It's a combat sim, and it's considered a reflection of how we can expect you to behave in actual combat. As such, we take it very seriously. Squad tactics is not about rushing into enemy fire and going down in a blaze of glory. That might look good in the vids, but in real life it puts your squad mates in real danger. What if you were to get wounded by the enemy but not killed? What if the enemy took you hostage and started threatening your life to use as leverage against us? Don't you think that might complicate things a bit?"

Looking from marine to marine, Gamble continued: "Leadership isn't about trying to be a hero, because ninety-nine times out of a hundred, acting like a hero is a stupid idea and it'll probably get people killed. Leadership is about making sure your squad remains a tight, cohesive unit that executes the best tactic for a given situation. Now, after Corporal Martinez's death in Cybele, this squad is in need of a leader. But I can tell you right now, none of you are anywhere close to squad leader material. We're in a war, marines, and to be frank, war is not the time to be as sloppy as you are now. By next week, I need to start seeing marked improvement, and in two weeks' time I need you to be twice the soldiers you are now. Am I getting through, here?"

"Yes, Major," came the ragged reply, all of them with downcast eyes and red cheeks.

They want to do well. I can see that, and it's a start at least.

"Dismissed, marines. Talk to me if and when you want to schedule in some extra training time."

Teal Squad filed out of the cargo bay, and Gamble watched them go. As the last marine left, his com buzzed, and he took it out to find a message from Admiral Connor Iver informing him that Corporal Toby Yung, Private First Class Dion Mews, and Private Jordan Zimmerman were being dishonorably discharged from the IGF on the grounds of being rights violations perpetrated against the citizens of Cybele while off-duty.

Lips tightening, Gamble left the cargo bay to head for the marine quarters—for the bunkroom where he knew Yung, Mews, and Zimmerman slept. *Maybe I'll find them before they're gone.* Losing three competent marines, one of them very competent, was the last thing he needed right now. It was the last thing the war effort needed. There was nothing he could do to change the IGF's decision, but at minimum he could try to offer a few parting words of comfort and guidance. He'd never been good at that sort of thing, but he could try.

When he arrived at the bunkroom, he found it empty except for Yung, who was in the middle of stuffing things into a duffel bag.

The former marine glanced up when Gamble entered with a sharp rap on the open hatch. "Morning, Major."

"Morning, uh, Yung." Gamble was a bit taken aback at the man's tone, and he'd almost called him corporal when he remembered that the dishonorable discharge had included him getting bumped down to lance corporal, and he didn't want to remind him. "I'm sorry about what happened. If it's any consolation—"

"Don't mention it, Major. It's not worth stressing about."

Gamble blinked. "Huh? You're not upset."

"Not really," Yung answered, shaking his head. "Honestly, this feels like a fresh start more than anything else. You may not know this, but the captain gave me a stern talking to right before we went to help defend the Saffron System. He told me that I haven't worked to realize my full potential. And you know what? I think he's right. That's not all—I think this will let me start working on fixing it."

"Outside the military? What will you do?"

Yung's smile broadened. "Oh, I think there's plenty I can do, right here on the *Vesta*. I'm not leaving, Major. Mews and Zimmerman are, but not me. I'm gonna become a citizen of Cybele. I know they'll take me. They aren't turning down anyone, since the bottom started falling out of their population levels. That city is ripe for change. Lots of it. And I think I might just be the guy for the job."

Yung's smile widened, to the point where it was beginning to give Gamble a vaguely uneasy feeling. He had no idea what the ex-marine was talking about, and he had neither the skills nor the time to delve into it. He wasn't a psychologist, and he needed to move ahead with his day. Next up was figuring out how this new mech team was going to fit into his marine battalion.

"All right then, Corporal," Gamble said, before wincing. He hadn't meant to use Yung's rank. *Ah, well. Calling him Corporal still isn't technically wrong. Plus, he doesn't seem all that upset anyway.* "If you'll excuse me, I'd better get going."

Nodding, Yung said, "Things to do. I get it, Major. I'm sure I'll be seeing you around, before long."

Gamble gave the man one last look, which probably showed the confusion and concern Yung's behavior was causing him. But there just wasn't time to unpack it. He had to focus on his job. The one he was good at.

CHAPTER 16

Blood Moon

Gamble's command style would have turned a lot of commanders off. It involved maintaining a fairly warm, jokey relationship with his marines—for the most part. But when circumstance called for it, his demeanor could range from stern to harsh bordering on savage. His marines tended to fear and respect him intermittently, which usually resulted in getting exactly what he needed from them.

Because of his overall closeness with his men and women, he tended to be let in on their rumor mill in a way that most leaders weren't. As such, he knew that the mech pilots spent a lot of time coming in and out of Hanger Bay Zeta, which made sense. That was, after all, where their machines were being stored.

In keeping with what he'd heard, when he arrived in the hangar bay, he found Seaman Jake Price there. But that was where reality stopped conforming to his expectations.

"Seaman Price, isn't it?" Gamble said as he ambled up to Price, squinting slightly.

Price nodded, sticking out his hand. "It is. Yourself?"

"Major Peter Gamble, the *Vesta*'s marine battalion commander. I'm here to figure out how your Oneiri Team is going to fit in around here—both the mech you pilot and the MIMAS mechs." He grasped Price's hand firmly, and they shook.

"Ah," said Price, who suddenly looked like he didn't know what he should be doing. "Well, it's an honor to meet you, Major. I've been hearing about what you and your people did on Klaxon's moon. Seems like it's become an instant legend."

"My marines held it together admirably, but if I'm being honest, we would have been done for if it wasn't for the *Vesta*'s guns backing us up. I'm getting off-topic, though." He nodded toward the giant metal crate behind Price, which was one of eight scattered throughout the hangar bay in a haphazard fashion Gamble wasn't a big fan of. "Do you always keep your mechs in boxes, Seaman?"

"That's where the Tartarus Station desk jockeys put them," Price said, his voice a little hoarse but otherwise composed. "Probably wanted to keep them out of sight from prying eyes. The Union was keeping everything in Hellebore pretty hush-hush till you guys arrived."

"Right," Gamble said, shoving his hands in his uniform's pants pockets. "But you had the mechs out since you were on Tartarus. You fought the Progenitors with them, and after that the cat's been out of the bag, so to speak. So why'd they end up back inside the boxes?"

Price looked like a prey animal caught between a pair of high beams. "Uh...easier transport?" he said, his voice growing hoarser.

"Footage of the battle showed your mechs flying through space of their own accord. Seems it would have been easier just to have them rocket over."

"Right," Price said, rallying visibly, "but the secured crates prevent people from tampering with them, or worse, trying to climb inside them. I'm sorry, Major, but every Oneiri pilot except Marco was born outside this galaxy, and he was just a few months old when Darkstream left the Milky Way. We don't know your crew, and it's going to be some time before we're fully trusting. I think you know that'll be the case whether I say it or not, so I hope you don't mind me saying it."

"I don't mind, and I do understand your meaning. There's just one thing I'm struggling with. I remember seven active mechs from the battle in Hellebore, and I see eight crates here."

Price had obviously found his footing, and he had his reply already loaded in the chamber. "The eighth is a mech we've freely given to the IGF, for study and replication."

"I see." Gamble happened to know the eighth mech had already been transported to an IGF R&D lab on one of Feverfew's shipyards. But that was something known to only a few, and Price clearly didn't anticipate Gamble being one of them. *Not sure how long you think you can keep this up, boy. But you're clearly stalling for something.*

"All right then, Seaman," Gamble said. "I hope you don't mind my questions. The road of trust runs both ways, which I'm sure you've already figured out, even at your young age."

"I have, Major."

"Good." Hands still in his pockets, Gamble approached the metal crate, and he didn't miss the way the corner of Price's right eye twitched. "Let's talk about what Oneiri's role will be, going forward. I'm content to leave you in command of Oneiri, given I don't know the first thing about the machines you pilot. I'd like to rectify that ignorance, so that I can deploy you effectively, but you will remain squad leader."

"Thank you, Major."

"Of course. As for what operations you'll participate in, they won't be stealth ops, I can tell you that much." Gamble quirked one side of his mouth upward, indicating he was joking, and Price gave a stilted chuckle. "No, given the size and firepower of your mechs, I expect shock and awe to be the major tactic. Though I can tell you, I'm not sure how shocked the Ixa will actually be. With their augmentations, they're about as tall as your mechs, and they make scarily short work of a human in a para-aramid reinforced jumpsuit." Gamble sniffed. "Either way, though, Oneiri Team's going to draw attention wherever we send them. For ops requiring more delicacy, more precision, I likely won't deploy you at all. But for anything else, I'll put you wherever I'd like the fighting to happen. I have a feeling you're going to have a great big target painted on you wherever you go."

Nodding, Price said, "That lines up with my experience."

"I thought as much. Bottom line, I hope your team likes action, because you're going to be seeing a lot of it."

"Major, we like action."

Gamble grinned. "Good. Now why don't you open up this crate for me." He brought his hand back to slap it, hard, and he could have sworn he heard something give a small start inside.

Price had that caught-in-the-headlights look on him again. "O-open it, Major?"

"That's right. I said I wanted to get familiar with the tech, didn't I? There's no time like right now."

"Sure, but we already talked about trust. I don't feel like now is the time to—"

"With respect, Seaman, I don't give a damn what you feel. I understand it might take some time for you to start feeling comfy-cozy right-at-home aboard this supercarrier. But that's irrelevant to the order I just gave you. What's *relevant*, right now and for as long as you're under my command, is that you follow my orders promptly and without question. Is that very well understood, Seaman?"

The color having drained from his face, Price moved to a keypad on the side of the crate. "You'll want to move out of the way, Major," he said, his voice admirably steady. "The front opens onto the floor."

Gamble did, clearing out and watching from a safe distance with his hands folded behind his back.

The front of the crate cracked open at the top, then hissed to the ground to reveal a four-legged mechanical monstrosity, peering out at him from the shadowy recesses of the crate with eyes like a blood moon. It stepped forward, and it took all the steel in Gamble's spine not to take a step back.

I thought that crate's dimensions seemed a little off. Gamble withdrew his com from its holster and raised it to his mouth, rapidly pressing the sequence of buttons that would connect him directly to Captain Husher, a feature meant only for situations Gamble deemed legitimately urgent.

"Captain...we may have a problem."

CHAPTER 17

Too Far

Husher entered Hangar Bay Zeta at the head of a platoon of marines, who quickly ranged ahead and took up position in a tight semi-circle centered on the strange mech, weapons trained on it.

Thankfully, Gamble appeared unharmed, and he quickly backed out of his soldiers' line of fire, leaving Seaman Price alone with the quadruped.

Two of the marines broke formation to approach Price and yank him away from the crate, dragging him toward another one nearby and slamming him face-first against its side. Husher approached them, circling around to give the other marines a wide berth.

"Is this how you treat all your new allies?" Price grunted as Husher drew near.

"Is this how you treat yours?" Husher shot back. "You smuggled military hardware aboard my ship, clearly piloted by a member of a species I know next to nothing about. You must have known you couldn't keep it a secret forever. When were you planning to let me in on it?"

Price tried to twist around to get a better look at Husher, but one of the marines restraining him slammed him against the crate again, and the seaman spoke with the side of his face jammed against the metal. "I was going to tell you once we were far enough away from the Assembly of Elders that there was no chance of you handing Rug over to them."

"Rug? Is that this Quatro's name? I thought they didn't have names."

"Rug does," Price said, his speech somewhat strained by the pressure being applied by the two marines. "She took a name to better communicate with us, and so did a lot of the other Quatro we met in the Steele System. They're not with the Elders. They fled their home to escape them."

"Why?"

"The Assembly of Elders is corrupt. They claim they treat everyone the same, that they've always provided every Quatro with everything they needed, but in reality the Elders lived in luxury while widespread shortages were common. They say they support freedom of thought—that Quatro can believe whatever they like. But that only applies to the part of reality they allow their subjects to see."

"And you know this how?" Husher titled his head to one side. "Because this Quatro told you?"

"I'd trust Rug with my life. She's saved it enough, and she's saved plenty of other humans too."

"Right." Husher sniffed. "Maybe we can make this conversation a little more amicable. I'm going to need your friend to get out of her mech."

The Quatro stepped forward, eliciting a flurry of shuffling backward and shouting from the marines. Husher held up a hand to settle them. "She's only gaining enough clearance from the crate, I think," he yelled over the tumult.

He was right. The back of the mech opened, and the great alien stepped out before making her way around the side of the machine. In some ways, the strange mech resembled the one Price piloted. Outside of it, Rug studied Husher with calm, onyx eyes.

He took a moment to appreciate the Quatro's majesty. "Why didn't you go with your brethren, in the vessel that fled Hellebore?"

The alien's voice rumbled through the translator she wore around her neck. "I refused to leave Jake Price, Lisa Sato and the other Oneiri pilots. They are dear to me. Once I helped my people escape the Hellebore System, I returned to Tartarus Station."

"To be smuggled aboard the *Vesta*."

"Yes," the Quatro said, without a hint of remorse.

"How do I know you've told Price the truth about the Elders? Do you have any proof?"

"I do not," Rug said. Her voice was deeper than even a Gok's, but richer, more resonant. "But it should not seem so unlikely a proposition to you, Captain Vin Husher. I am sure the Eldest spoke to you about the Quatro way: placing drift above all else. This is an admirable principle, but like so many admirable principles, it has been taken too far, by individuals whose true motive is power."

"And?" Husher said. "How is that meant to convince me you're telling the truth?"

Price twisted against the marines. "Because the Interstellar Union is heading in the same direction!" he yelled.

One of the marines shoved him back against the crate, but Husher waved toward them. "Let him off that thing." The soldiers complied, but they each kept a firm grip on Price's upper arms. Husher turned back to Rug. "You agree with Price, I take it?"

"It is a possibility. Your Interstellar Union has not reached the stage of corruption and rot now occupied by the Assembly of Elders. But there are worrying similarities between your government's current state and that of the Elders during the years that preceded their tyranny. It is possible that their alliance will accelerate your government's transition."

"A lot of things are possible," Husher said, though the coldness in his stomach was at odds with his level tone. "Right now, the Progenitors are the most immediate threat. How can we be expected to beat them if we don't rely on every ally we have?"

"This is why the Union is in the state it's in," Price said, and the anger in his voice surprised Husher. "It's people like you in positions of power, making the choice that's most convenient for you in the short-term. I never believed the stories the Steele System old-timers used to tell about the Milky Way, and they might not have been true when Darkstream left. But they're sure true now. I can't believe how far you've fallen."

Husher returned the boy's glare with narrowed eyes. "Bringing up your Darkstream connection is not a good way to ingratiate yourself with me."

"I'm not trying to ingratiate myself with anyone."

Jaw set, Husher looked at Rug. "Your presence aboard my ship is a threat to the new alliance, and I'm not promising I won't turn you over to the Elders at the earliest opportunity. I have half a mind to throw you in the brig until such an opportunity presents itself, though I'm not sure you'd fit in any of the cells." Husher sniffed sharply. "We probably have a battle waiting for us in Yclept, and ultimately, I can't afford to waste any assets available to me. Rug, for now you'll operate as a member of Oneiri Team. I expect full compliance from all Oneiri—compliance not just with orders given by myself and Major Gamble, but also with our expectations. It's up to you to figure out what those expectations are. They should be obvious, and I don't have the time to break them down for you."

Husher glanced at Gamble and saw the light of approval in the major's eyes. Returning his gaze to Rug, he said, "If you want to justify the risk you pose by being here, you'd better toe the damn line." He turned back to Price. "Is there anything else you'd care to tell me about your team?"

After a few seconds of stony silence, Price finally spoke. "Right before we left the Steele System, Seaman Lisa Sato was taken by the Progenitors and held aboard one of their ships for a time. We picked her up on our way out, but ever since, she's been acting differently. Not like herself. Some disagree with me about that, but that's the way I see it." Price cleared his throat. "I should mention that I have personal feelings for Sato, and it's possible my judgment is compromised."

Personal feelings? Wonderful. "Can I expect problems to stem from these 'personal feelings' you hold for someone in your direct chain of command?"

"No, sir. She's with Miller, now. I accept that."

"Good. In the meantime, keep an eye on Sato's behavior, as I'm sure you're already doing. Other than that, I'm not sure what to do with what you just told me. She seems to be acting normal to me, though I don't really know her."

"Yes, sir."

Husher nodded, then glanced around at the assembled marines. "Dismissed."

CHAPTER 18

Fester and Grow

The Eldest had returned with Chiba to Abdera in the Caprice System—the seat of Union power ever since the end of the Second Galactic War. The planetary capital was chosen for its centrality: Caprice was equally accessible by every Union species, more or less.

"Our partnership pleases me greatly," Chiba said, turning his head toward the enormous quadruped that plodded beside him. They walked along a cobbled path that wound through one of the sprawling walled gardens spread throughout the presidential estate. The walls weren't visible from this part of the path, and Chiba's security detail were doing their best to be unobtrusive, as they knew their president preferred. He could almost believe he and the Eldest were walking through nature on Home, the Kaithian homeworld.

"Our partnership," Chiba went on, "and the fact we've established such trust so quickly, forged from our common need—it's the perfect expression of the principles upon which the Interstellar Union was built."

The Quatro dipped his head. "For our part, we are grateful that you have accepted us so readily into your home, President Chiba. We were truly at your mercy."

"I don't conceive of it that way. We are both beset by the Progenitors, who created the Ixa. And we have a shared duty to oppose species like the Ixa in every way possible. The Ixa's values are antithetical to ours. Their obsession with purity and sameness is distasteful. Repulsive. It can't be borne. I never thought I'd hear myself say it, but you've convinced me, Eldest. If they won't see the error of their ways, they must be stamped out."

"Then we should thank the stars that our alliance has bestowed a chance of doing so," the Quatro said. "But I hope it isn't necessary for me to point out that the problems you just named are not limited to the Ixa."

Chiba paused, taken aback for a moment at what was obviously criticism of the Interstellar Union. Then, Chiba sighed. *The Eldest is right.* "What you say is true. The galaxy's problems are extensive, and they begin with the advantages enjoyed by humans, leading to a wealth disparity that must be redressed, to make things fair for everyone. But the situation is much worse than that. There are radical elements within our own society that, perversely, have grown stronger as the Ixan threat intensifies."

"Indeed. And it is not difficult to see that the captain whose behavior was so offensive during the Tartarus meeting is a booster for such elements."

"There are signs of that," Chiba said, a little reluctantly. "I haven't decided whether Husher is as rabid as some loathsome individuals hope, but even if he is, we can't afford to put him down yet. We need him."

The Quatro leader didn't answer at first, and they walked in silence for a while. At last, he said, "I understand that we have different conceptions of how to imbue our societies with strength. However, even though Quatro civilization has endured many millennia, we only achieved true stability in the last several decades—after we finally learned that hateful elements, if not dealt with the moment they appear, will fester and grow, seizing power the moment times are hard. Hard times are here, President Chiba. If you do not act swiftly, your society too will fall into darkness."

"We need Husher," Chiba repeated. "But we won't need him forever. In the meantime, our conversations have helped me to recognize the danger to our society represented by groups like the Sapient Brotherhood. We do not need such beings, and they can be dealt with right away."

The Eldest dipped his head. "It is a relief to hear you say so."

"And I thank you for your insight," Chiba said, lifting his hand toward the alien in respect. "Before we part, I also wanted to arrange a meeting between the Assembly of Elders and the Galactic Congress, to discuss your integration into the Interstellar Union..."

CHAPTER 19

Mechs Complicate Things

"We're too late," Ensign Winterton said eleven minutes after they transitioned through the Larkspur-Yclept darkgate—long enough for lidar and radar sensors to update with data about the area surrounding Juktas, Yclept's only significant colony. The tropical world had once been overrun with insurgents, before being ravaged by the Ixa at the end of the Second Galactic War. But things had long since settled down for Juktas, and it was now considered one of the IU's major colonies. "The planet's already under attack."

Damn it. "Nav, set a course for the planet that makes the best use of the system's gravity well for maximum speed, with engines all ahead full."

"Aye," Chief Noni said, bending to her work. Luckily, Juktas' orbit currently had it on this side of the star, meaning the *Vesta* and her battle group could ride Yclept's gravity well the entire way there.

Husher's gaze snapped back to his sensor operator. "What are we looking at, Winterton?"

"Two Progenitor ships, sir: a destroyer and a carrier. The destroyer apparently appeared below the colony's orbital defense platforms, but the Juktas fighter defense group must have engaged it right away, since it hasn't succeeded in destroying any of the platforms from below."

Husher nodded. Ever since Teth's ship had first popped into existence below Tyros' orbital platforms in Wintercress, the importance of starfighters for system defense had risen sharply. "What about the carrier?"

"It's pounding the defense platform closest to the destroyer from above."

"They probably hoped the destroyer would make short work of the platform," Chief Tremaine cut in. "Otherwise, it would make no sense for the carrier to engage the platform's arsenal so close-in. They're going to get their rear ends handed to them."

"And yet they aren't," Winterton said, shooting an annoyed glance at Tremaine—a rare display of emotion for the sensor operator. "I wasn't finished. The carrier is in the process of deploying Ravagers en masse to the platform's surface, as well as the autonomous mechs we're calling Amblers. Dozens of robots have already made it to the platform's surface and are being engaged by defenders stationed there."

An urge to massage his forehead made Husher's hand twitch, but he willed it to remain on the command seat's armrest. "Ravager" was the Oneiri pilots' name for the little robots that Husher had been contending with since Teth had first appeared, and everyone seemed content to adopt the term. *It certainly fits.* As for the Amblers, Price had shown him footage of the things in action, but this was the first time he'd actually encountered them. Ten meters tall, the Amblers were two-legged war machines that bristled with artillery. Taking one down was no easy task, and if enough of them made it past the defense platform's guns, the soldiers there would quickly fall.

"Noni, a small addition to our course. During our final approach, I want us to level out over the planet, so that there's no risk of our ordnance hitting either the platform or the colony below. Fry, relay that to the other battle group captains, and order them to fan out in a dispersed battle spread formation, to make that carrier's job as tough as possible."

"Yes, Captain."

Given enough time, Husher knew his supercarrier alone would have proven more than a match for the Progenitor carrier. With the new addition of two destroyers and two cruisers, however, the enemy didn't stand a chance.

And yet, the enemy mechs complicate things. Neutralizing the Progenitor ships before they managed to blow a whole in Juktas' defenses wasn't just about winning this engagement. It was about keeping the colony secure against the next attack, and the next. The two ships in Husher's sights were almost certainly doomed— if they stuck around to fight, anyway. But if they succeeded in destroying a defense platform, the colony would probably be doomed too.

With that in mind, he opened up a two-way channel with Major Gamble. "Major, come in."

"Gamble here. I read you, Captain."

"Juktas is under attack by two Progenitor ships, and one of them is a carrier dropping Ravagers and Amblers onto one of the defense platforms. I want most of your battalion patrolling the *Vesta*'s outer corridors and guarding her vital systems, in case any Ravagers get in, but I need you to take two platoons to the surface of that platform and aid in its defense. Take Oneiri Team with you."

"Does that include the Quatro mech?"

"Yes."

"Are you sure that's a good idea, sir?"

Husher paused. "It's not like you to question my orders, Major."

"I rarely do, Captain. But I hope that'll give it more weight that I'm questioning them now. If word of us harboring that Quatro gets back to their Assembly of Elders, I can't see it ending well, for the alliance or for us. I doubt either the Assembly or the Union even knows a mech built for Quatro exists."

"The Quatro need the alliance just as much as we do, Major. As for the Quatro mech, I won't hold it back out of fear. For all we know, it could make the difference in saving that platform. I hear your concerns, but I'm not going to limit our force potential just to stay on the Elders' good side."

A brief silence followed from Gamble. Then: "I understand, sir. I respectfully disagree, but as always, I'll follow your orders to the letter."

"Your disagreement has been noted. Thank you, Major. Prepare to deploy your forces."

"Yes, sir."

Husher ended the transmission, his attention turning to his CIC officers as he wondered idly how much of the conversation they'd gleaned. It didn't matter, ultimately—by now, everyone was used to the latitude the IGF gave subordinates when it came to questioning their superiors and offering "constructive" criticism.

Even so, Husher wasn't used to Gamble questioning him, and it did give him pause. *Am I being hasty in deploying the Quatro mech?*

He swept the idea aside. *A starship captain can't let doubts undermine his own confidence in himself.* Besides, he had to hold to the same principle he'd held to even before the war began.

Victory at all costs.

CHAPTER 20

Whirlwinds of Steel

"The station defenders and the robots are fighting over the eastern side of the platform," Gamble said over a wide channel that included both platoons as well as Oneiri. Since the platform maintained a geostationary orbit over the planet, it was simplest to use cardinal directions in planning their assault. "That makes sense, since it's the side closest to their carrier—they're trying to consolidate their efforts to take out as many guns there as possible. Once the platform's weak point has been expanded enough, they'll obliterate it. The platform's destruction is important to them strategically, and I tend to doubt they'll even bother extracting their robots before it blows. That means we have to act fast."

One combat shuttle could hold a whole platoon, but even so, Gamble had distributed the two he'd brought with him across four shuttles. Losing an entire platoon would do too much damage to the assault, and he'd wanted to spread out his risk.

A squadron of Pythons was keeping pace with the shuttles, trying to make sure they didn't lose any. The Progenitors weren't making that job easy, sending streams of Ravagers toward the transcripts. Two starfighters had gone down already, but so far the shuttles had remained untouched.

The Oneiri mechs shared in the credit for that. They were too big to fit through the shuttle airlocks, and they'd deployed straight from a *Vesta* flight deck, rocketing toward the orbital defense platform just as fast as the shuttles and giving it back to the Ravagers hard.

Accessing the shuttle's exterior sensors with his Oculenses, it wasn't hard for Gamble to tell that the mech pilots had had plenty of experience with Ravagers. They picked them off with astounding aim—probably with some computer assistance, too, Gamble assumed—and if the little devils got close enough, they simply ripped them limb from limb.

"The battle's happening on the east, so we're coming in from the northwest in a classic flank maneuver," Gamble continued over the wide channel. "Oneiri, you're taking the lead—I need you to start targeting down those Amblers as fast as you possibly can. Show us jarheads how it's done, and we'll do what we can to keep the Ravagers off your backs."

He accessed the exterior sensors again and saw that they'd nearly reached the platform, with some of its turrets picking off the last few Ravagers attempting to get at the shuttles. "Nearly there, Major," said Chief Haynes, right on time. "Prepare for a combat landing."

"Roger that, Psycho," Gamble said. "Don't make it too gentle, all right? I don't want my soldiers falling asleep on me."

"I hear you, Major."

With that, the shuttle connected with the platform's northern LZ, skidding to a stop with appropriate roughness. "Move, marines!" Gamble yelled over the wide channel. "Move your asses!"

As he waited for the shuttle's airlock to cycle through the usual processes, Gamble took another peek through the exterior sensors—just in time to see the Oneiri mechs crashing to the surface, using aerospike thrusters to soften their landing a bit.

Then he was outside, his R-57 clutched tight against his chest as he pounded across the metal deck of the platform, waving for his marines to follow. He'd had access to a full schematic download for the platform since before his shuttle departed the *Vesta*, but he hadn't bothered assigning individual squads anywhere, since the flow of battle almost certainly would have rendered his assignments obsolete by the time they arrived.

Instead, he directed his troops now, as they ran toward the robots' flank. Incorporating overhead sensor data from the *Vesta* along with on-the-ground intel forwarded to him by the platform's sensors, he deployed his troops accordingly. One squad to a guard tower. Half a squad each to stairwells flanking a broad passage that opened onto the expanse occupied by the enemy. One full platoon to charge through that passage, and two more squads to range around and hit them from the north.

As ordered, Oneiri team ranged ahead of them all, metal legs pumping as they charged for the passage Gamble had designated. They poured through without hesitation, establishing a position just past the far opening, which would allow the marines to entrench themselves in the passage mouth behind them.

Even with the limited view afforded by the passage, Gamble could see how much heat the mechs were drawing. Clearly, the enemy already knew to take them seriously. Running as fast as he could to back up the mechs, he used his Oculenses to open up a corner window where his vision was magnified.

Heavy fire peppered the area around Oneiri as Gamble watched Ash Sweeney—whose teammates had nicknamed her Steam—retract her MIMAS' fingers to reveal twin rotary auto-cannons built into the forearms. Threads of light lanced from them, connecting with an Ambler's bulk.

Marco Gonzalez—Spirit—detached the heavy machine gun from his back, swinging it around to join his fire with Sweeney's. They'd succeeded in getting the Ambler's attention, and it turned to lumber toward them, a swarm of Ravagers rushing to join in the attack.

As Sweeney and Gonzalez focused on the Ambler, Beth Ar-kanian and Maura Odell—Paste and Moe—dashed forward, bay-onets extending from their arms. They charged unflinchingly into the Ravager ranks, becoming twin whirlwinds of steel and death, even as the towering Ambler ran past.

As impressive as the MIMAS mechs were, the alien mechs pi-loted by Jake Price and Rug were in a class of their own.

Heedless of the friendly fire, the Quatro sprang from the metal of the platform to plant both paws on the enemy mech's rounded torso. It went down, and a pair of javelins sprouted from Rug's shoulders as it did, running the Ambler through. The Quatro proceeded to shred the autonomous mech with foot-long claws that grew and shrank as needed.

Another Ambler joined the fight, and Price took on this one, sprinting to meet his new adversary while hurling blue-white blasts of energy at it all the while.

Just before he collided with the Ambler, Price—nicknamed Clutch—turned his mech's right arm into a massive broadsword, which cleaved his target almost in two. When Price withdrew, the damaged mech began stumbling in circles, internal circuitry sparking as it fired armor-piercing rounds in random directions.

A final energy blast put an end to it, and the Ambler crumpled to the platform, shivering and twitching.

I'm sure glad Oneiri's on our side, Gamble reflected as he ran through the passage and selected his first target.

CHAPTER 21

Adaptations

"Banshees away, sir," Tremaine said. "With a healthy dose of Gorgons and Hydras mixed in."

"Very good," Husher said. Since the start of the war, the Progenitors had been adapting to the reality of the IGF's Gorgon stealth missiles, as well as their Hydras, each of which split into eight separate warheads. The enemy ships had to be running constant active scans of the battlespace, given how much their success rate at neutralizing Gorgons had gone up. Not only that, they now took every missile seriously, with the knowledge that any of them might multiply by eight without warning.

That didn't come as a surprise to Husher, and he doubted it surprised any other military captain, either. *That's just war.* New technology had its greatest effect when it was first introduced. Following that, the enemy adapted, and eventually they adopted the tech as their own.

But that doesn't mean we can't adapt to their adaptations. For example, the Progenitors didn't know that IGF Command had signed off on a dramatic expansion of the *Vesta*'s missile arsenal, or that he'd ordered the inclusion of three times the usual number of Gorgons and Hydras in the current barrage.

Under his instructions, Tremaine had timed the barrage so that it seemed like a response to the waves of Ravagers the carrier had sent at the *Vesta* and her battle group. In part, it truly was a response, and many of the Banshees carried directives to neutralize the robots.

"A lot of the Ravagers are changing course to take down Gorgons, sir," Winterton said.

"Acknowledged," Husher said, still unsurprised. The enemy had also learned to have their Ravagers prioritize Gorgons, since the Hydras would simply split into eight the moment they were threatened. Hydras were also more difficult to distinguish from regular Banshees, and so the best bet was to weed out the Gorgons and then attempt to take down the entire remaining missile cloud with lasers and point defense systems, with the knowledge that the cloud would probably grow at some point.

"Captain, something just departed the carrier," the sensor operator said. "It appears to be a mech bearing a close resemblance to the one piloted by Seaman Price."

Husher leaned forward, squinting at a magnified visual representation, which still didn't show much detail at this distance. The mech's appearance *did* come as a surprise.

Suppressing a wince, Husher said, "Coms, tell Commander Ayam to launch the subspace-capable Python squadron now."

"Aye, sir."

He'd been holding the subspace fighters in reserve, hoping to keep from tipping his hand for as long as possible. He still hoped it wouldn't be necessary to reveal their capabilities, but he wanted to at least put them into play. It wouldn't be wise to risk holding them back, with a mech of unknown capabilities hurtling across the battlespace toward the *Vesta*.

"Have the *Hero* and the *Impulsive* direct a stream of all three missile types at that mech, Coms," Husher said. "And tell Ayam to harry it with a squadron of regular Pythons."

"Yes, sir."

Husher tried to relax, then—as much as the unyielding command seat would allow him to relax, anyway. It would be some time before the mech encountered the missiles coming its way, and longer for the Python squadron to arrive. Still, more and more detail was becoming evident as the alien mech accelerated closer, and as he studied it, Husher began to notice differences between it and Price's mech. This mech was more jagged, and its coloration more varied, with some patches as dark as midnight and others the blue-white of a clear day. The thing was half again the size of Price's mech, too, and it didn't take much of a leap to deduce it carried more artillery as a result.

It turned out he didn't have to wait as long as he'd thought for something to happen. As the mech neared the *Vesta*'s initial missile barrage, it began targeting down Gorgons with alarming efficiency.

Stealth missile after stealth missile exploded harmlessly in space, until the last one had been neutralized. With that, the mech began working on the Hydras, triggering their onboard AIs to split them into eight. By the time the barrage was passing the alien monstrosity, it had forced every last Hydra to separate, and it had gotten a good start on cutting down the barrage as a whole.

Worse, none of the missiles had been fed the mech's profile as a target priority—how could they have been? And so none attempted to retaliate as the mech blew them apart one by one.

More Ravagers got through because of the mech's efforts, and they threw themselves at the rockets fired by the IGF missile cruisers, protecting their much larger counterpart.

For its part, the alien mech rocketed toward the *Vesta*. When it encountered the squadron of Pythons Husher had sent at it, it made short work of the Sidewinders they fired, and it seemed to simply absorb their kinetic impactors with no adverse effects. That done, the mech fired a rocket apiece at a trio of Pythons, taking down all three at point-blank range.

Husher's gaze was riveted to the visual display as the mech sailed through the exploding starfighters, ignoring the remaining thirteen pilots, who used gyroscopes to swing their main engines around and give chase.

Shaking his head to clear it, Husher opened a private channel with Commander Ayam. "Commander, this is Captain Husher."

"I read you, Captain. Go ahead."

"I need you to take the subspace Pythons and accelerate toward that carrier with all possible haste. Order the transition to subspace only when absolutely necessary."

"Acknowledged, Captain...but if the carrier vanishes in time, it'll take intel of our new capability to the Progenitors. The same goes for the destroyer."

"I'm aware of that, Ayam. But right now I have a mech hurtling toward the *Vesta*'s hull, and I'm not confident I can stop it. Threatening its base ship might be our only chance to turn it back."

CHAPTER 22

The Sapient Brotherhood

With the help of the Ravagers rallying around it, the mech dispatched the latest round of missiles sent at it by the IGF ships. The little robots seemed perfectly willing to throw themselves on the missiles, ripping them apart even though it meant disintegrating in the explosion.

All in an effort to get that thing to the Vesta. Once it arrived, Husher had no doubt it would tear through his hull like tissue paper, and who knew how many marines would die in the effort to put it down. *If they'll be able to put it down at all.* A vision of the mech laying waste to Cybele filled his head.

"Captain?" Tremaine said, the strain in his voice evident.

"Direct secondary lasers at the mech," Husher replied. "And have point defense turrets prioritize it."

"Yes, sir," the Tactical officer said, and a note of relief crept into his voice—probably for the mere fact he was doing something.

Beams lanced out from the supercarrier's forward secondary projectors, forcing the mech to jag to the left, then the right. The evasive maneuvers allowed the pursuing Pythons to catch up, and they lobbed more Sidewinders at it.

That got the mech's attention, and it turned to confront them, immediately taking out a fourth Python with a massive energy blast that engulfed the starfighter, incinerating it.

Husher grimaced. *At least we've slowed the thing.* That meant it must finally feel threatened on some level, but as it destroyed another Python, he knew it was only a matter of time before it continued its blistering progress toward his ship.

A glance at the tactical display told him his subspace-capable Pythons were just entering the enemy carrier's firing range. He returned his gaze to the view of the mech on his console...then looked back at the Pythons. They were the *Vesta*'s best hope, now.

The Progenitor carrier seemed to be ignoring them—until they started spraying kinetic impactors all across her hull. Then, it diverted some missile fire from the orbital defense platform to the oncoming squadron.

As ordered, the Pythons waited until the last possible second. Then, just as the missiles were about to make contact, each starfighter generated a spherical wormhole and vanished.

The missiles sailed harmlessly past, and then the Pythons reappeared, much closer to the carrier's hull. They loosed a volley of Sidewinders, then the fighters disappeared again before the enemy point defense turrets could shoot them down.

The turrets managed to deal with most of the Pythons' Sidewinders, but three got through, rupturing the carrier's port-side hull in a jagged line.

Then the squadron appeared on her starboard side, traveling in the opposite direction and unleashing an even bigger barrage of missiles before leaving the universe. They reappeared momentarily to add kinetic impactors to the mix, then vanished again.

With that, the alien mech about-turned, flying back across the battlespace toward the carrier, which moved laterally to meet it. Husher's subspace Pythons continued to flit in and out of subspace, dealing massive damage to the carrier's point defense systems, as well as the hull itself.

It wouldn't be long before the squadron managed to take out the entire ship, Husher knew. But the alien mech screamed into an open flight deck, and the moment it did, the carrier vanished. The destroyer followed seconds later.

Silence held sway inside the *Vesta*'s CIC, and Husher didn't break it. Yes, they'd defended Yclept—a hub system for the IU, with its three darkgates. But the attacking ships had once again flitted away before taking critical damage.

This is no way to fight a war. Not when our enemy's so nimble they rarely lose a ship.

"We're getting a transmission request from the planet's surface, sir," Ensign Fry said. "Video and audio."

"Accept it, and give everyone access."

Governor Gerald Russell appeared on the main display, his hard face topped by a wave of white hair that rolled backward across his head. "Captain Husher," Russell said. "I thank you for coming to our aid when we needed it most."

"Just doing our job," Husher said. "Besides, I should commend you for holding out as long as you did. Defending against two

Progenitor ships with just the defense platforms and your fighter defense group—that's remarkable enough on its own."

Russell beamed with pride, which Husher found charming...until he spoke again. "Did you know our defense group is made up of ninety-five percent human pilots?"

The side of Husher's mouth quirked downward, and he said, "Oh?"

The governor nodded. "This is how it used to be, isn't it? Humans working together with *humans,* to defeat an alien threat. I'm not sure why we abandoned that way of doing things."

"There are plenty of nonhuman crew aboard the *Vesta,* Governor. They played a vital role in the defense of your colony. I don't know what scenario you're trying to describe, exactly, but it isn't one that fits what just happened."

Nodding, Russell said, "I know you're right, Captain. We've thoroughly integrated with *them,* haven't we? But to what end, and at what price to humanity's noble culture, developed over millennia only to be sacrificed to the misguided cause of integration?"

Husher shook his head. "I don't think we're on the same wavelength."

"I understand, Captain, that you can't discuss this freely—not in front of your integrated crew. But know that the Sapient Brotherhood is on the rise, and soon, every human captain will be called upon to carry out his proper duty to his species."

"Governor, we're here under a directive from the Interstellar Union to help with the defense of this system. Nothing more. Husher out."

Gesturing to the Coms officer to cut the transmission, Husher studied the blank display, lips pursed.

The silence inside his CIC resumed.

CHAPTER 23

Trust

Flight Deck Sigma's airlock opened to admit Oneiri Team, along with the shuttles carrying the marine force that had helped them take the orbital defense platform.

Coming to as graceful a landing as the alien mech was capable of, Jake was about to exit it when he noticed Captain Husher, standing outside the flight deck's airlock with two more marine platoons arrayed around him.

The captain was glaring. "Get out of the mech, Price."

Jake glanced back at the rest of his pilots, who were using aerospike thrusters to lower themselves to the deck. He returned his gaze to Husher. "Why?"

"Because I'm not about to have this conversation with you inside it."

"Something happened."

"It certainly did. And if you have any interest in continuing to serve aboard my ship, you'll get out of that mech, *now.*"

The alien mech injected Jake with the antagonist of the sedative he'd used to enter the mech dream, then the front opened to form a ramp, its usual surface of ridged metal scales instead becoming a smooth surface for Jake to dismount. He did so, and the mech sealed up the moment he found his feet.

"Now, the rest of your team," Husher said, never taking his eyes from Jake's.

Turning his head sideways, Jake nodded. Only then did he hear the hiss of the MIMAS' rear ramps descending. He appreciated the show of loyalty, but they probably hadn't done him any favors by waiting for Jake to confirm that they should follow the captain's order.

Jake couldn't detect any resentment in Husher's face, though—just the same hard lines. "Now what?" Jake asked.

"Step away from the mechs, all of you. Then I want you to approach by yourself, Price."

The Oneiri pilots distanced themselves from their machines, corralled into a group by some of the marines they'd just worked with to take the defense platform. Jake did notice that the marines were at least treating his pilots with more respect than they'd given him on the day Rug was discovered inside a crate.

As Jake drew nearer the captain, his implant pinged to inform him he'd received a file transfer. Making the Darkstream implants compatible with the IU's Oculenses had been simple enough—that had happened within two days of Oneiri's arrival on the *Vesta*.

"I just sent you a vid," Husher said. "Open it."

Jake did. It showed an alien mech careening toward the *Vesta*, taking out missile after starfighter after missile with the help of an endless barrage of Ravagers. His pulse quickened, and he could feel a vein in his neck twitching. Hopefully the captain couldn't see it.

"Is there anything you can tell me about that thing?" Husher said.

"No, sir," Jake answered, suppressing the urge to swallow.

Husher advanced slowly across the flight deck, parade boots clicking on the metal. Behind him, his marines shifted nervously, as though Jake posed a threat to the captain's life even outside his mech. *I suppose I do, at that. I'm younger and I'm quicker. I might even be stronger.* Plus, he wore a sidearm in a holster on his waist.

Then again, there was also the fact that trying to harm the captain would be a colossally stupid move.

Husher must have known that too. He showed no fear as he crossed the rest of the distance between them, never breaking eye contact.

"You're lying," he said quietly, once their faces were inches away from each other. "And a lying subordinate, even a lying mech pilot, is more of a liability than an asset. Lie to me again, Price, and I'll know it. If one more falsehood leaves your lips, I'll put you in the brig until I can hand you over to the IGF. That's a promise."

"Yes, sir."

"Good. Now, is there anything you can tell me about that mech?"

"It's piloted by a man named Gabriel Roach. At least, it was piloted by him. He...used to command Oneiri."

"What do you mean, it *was* piloted by Roach? Who pilots it now?"

Jake took a deep breath, every fiber of his being screaming at him not to keep talking. But he believed Husher when he said that he'd know if Jake lied, and he knew the captain would make good on his threat to put him in the brig. "No one pilots it. That isn't really the right word for it. Not anymore. There is no Roach anymore, and whatever his mech used to be, it changed, too. Roach merged with the mech, and now they've become something else—a third being."

"Merged?"

"It consumed him. Dissolved his body, all but his nervous system."

"Why in Sol would he agree to that?"

"He began using the mech because he was completely paralyzed from battle, and only able to interact through his implant—through the mech dream. Sir, the alien mech...it whispers to you. Tries to tempt you to meld with it, to gain access to even more power than it already offers. I guess Roach figured that, since he could never leave the mech anyway, he had nothing to lose. But the mech corrupted him. Gabriel Roach doesn't exist anymore. Just a monster that calls himself Roach. We thought we left him for dead in the Steele System, but apparently not. And from the looks of it, he's stronger than ever."

"What else does the mech tempt you to do?" Husher asked, his sapphire eyes boring into Jake's, as though attempting to pierce his soul.

Jake returned that stare for as long as he could. Then, he cast his eyes downward. "It tries to get you to turn on your allies. To turn on life itself. The thing tries to drive you insane, Captain."

"Why didn't you bring this to my attention? That I'd invited an unstoppable war machine onto my ship, piloted by a young man who could go mad at any moment?"

"I'm not going to go—"

"*Why didn't you tell me, Price?*" Husher yelled in his face, causing Jake to start.

Suddenly, Jake's anger spiked. "Because I don't trust you!"

"It's not about trust," Husher snapped back. "It's about following orders."

"It *is* about trust, though, Captain. Leadership is built on trust. You of all people should know that. When trust is lost, things fall apart. That's why mutinies are things that happen from time to time."

At the word "mutinies" Husher's eyes went wide, but Jake wasn't finished: "You need to give some thought about why those under you might or might not trust you. Most of your crew won't tell you, so I'll do you the favor: I don't trust you because you're willing to work with a government that's slipping into tyranny—a government that just got into bed with one that's been tyrannical for decades. By cooperating, you're not only endorsing their radical actions, but you're letting them push you into becoming more radical yourself."

Husher's face had reddened, but he no longer shouted. "I'm doing everything I can to defeat an enemy who wants to wipe out every sentient being in the galaxy. It's impossible for me to do that if I don't work with the current political order."

"You say it's impossible," Jake said, softening his tone as well. "And yet, you've already done plenty of things people said were impossible. Beating Teth the first time, not to mention his super-intelligent father. Keeping the IGF strong despite two decades of political pressure to weaken it. Singlehandedly winning the Gok Wars by defending the Arrowwood System against a force that would have bested any other commander." Slowly, Jake nodded. "I've studied up on your record, Captain. I doubt the word 'impossible' would have ever left your lips, during those times. But now you're saying it's impossible to win the war while making sure society keeps the things that make it worth fighting for. I say you need to figure out how to do both."

But Jake could tell that Husher was unmoved. "Let me tell you something, *Seaman* Price. You're lucky I'm so focused on winning this war, because it's the only reason I'm going to let you continue piloting that mech. Its power is too great for me to sideline it, no matter the risk. But I want you to report directly to Doctor Bancroft for a psychological evaluation, and I want you to do the same every time you step out of that thing. Is that clear?"

"Clear, sir."

"Good," Husher said, looking around at the soldiers gathered all around them. "Dismissed."

CHAPTER 24

Alarm Bells

"We can't fight an enemy who can vanish as soon as they're vulnerable," Husher growled, pacing back and forth across Ochrim's lab. As he did, he was forced to pick his way past boxes they still hadn't found a home for—supplies from the former Supplies Module.

He came to a stop facing the Ixan, who sat on a lab stool with his claw-tipped hands dangling between his knees. The Fins watched the exchange from their tank, though they didn't eavesdrop—not unless they could read his lips, which he wouldn't be surprised by, come to think of it. "The minute we start doing significant damage to the Progenitors' hulls," Husher went on, "they just leave the universe, probably to make repairs. Then they send in fresh ships. In the last engagement, their carrier even had an asset it clearly wasn't willing to leave without, and we still couldn't destroy it in time!"

"Captain," Ochrim said. "I'm going to have to ask you to calm down."

For a moment, Husher fixed the scientist with a wide-eyed stare. Then he realized his hands were balled into tight fists. He forced himself to take a deep breath. "I'm sorry, Ochrim."

"You have something on your mind."

"I have a million things on my mind, and the sense that I'm not making progress on any of them isn't helping very much. This war has barely begun, Ochrim. We can count on the Progenitors having a far bigger fleet than the handful of ships they've shown so far. Till now, they've only been poking us where we're weak, stirring the galactic pot to see what damage we'll do to ourselves. Teth said he expected me to win this war *for* him. What the hell does that mean?"

The Ixan sighed. "I can't begin to imagine. But I would caution against letting my brother get inside your head."

"Regardless, I need a way to follow the Progenitors wherever they're going—to chase them down and finish the job of destroying them. How can we win if we can't even reduce their numbers?"

"You need me to reverse engineer their method of travel," Ochrim said, weariness creeping into his voice.

"I know I'm asking the impossible. But it's what we need, to have even a prayer of winning."

Nodding, Ochrim said, "I understand. And...I think I know where we can start, at least."

"You think you know how they're skipping across dimensions?"

"Oh, I have uncorroborated theories about how they're accomplishing it. But that isn't what I meant. I think I have a way to find out how."

"Go on."

"Well, as you pointed out, we can depend on the Progenitors to flee as soon as they're in danger, and then to strike where they have better odds. That poses a disadvantage to us from a strategic perspective, but perhaps we can turn it into an advantage from an intelligence perspective. If we affix a tracking device to the hull of a ship that then departs the universe, there's a good chance we'll encounter that ship again. Provided that we do, and that the device is still in place, then it can transmit the necessary data to us."

"How are we supposed to stick a tracker to a Progenitor hull without them noticing?"

"Some deft sleight of hand will be necessary, to be sure."

"Any ideas for doing that?"

"Actually, yes," Ochrim said. "As you know, I'm far from well-versed in military tactics, but my idea was to modify a Hydra so that one of the eight warheads is replaced with a tracker, designed according to our needs and optimized for stealth."

Husher blinked. "That...that actually sounds like it could work."

"Then I'm happy I could help with that as well."

"All right, then," Husher said, nodding curtly, then heading for the ladder. Before ascending, he turned to face the Ixan again. "Thank you, Ochrim. You've helped me feel better. You, uh..." Husher cleared his throat. "You have a knack for that."

The Ixan nodded, and Husher began his climb.

Wanting to sustain the peace of mind Ochrim had helped him to achieve, he decided to go through Santana Park on his way back to the *Vesta*'s crew section, to enjoy the sculpted landscape there—tree-lined pathways, ponds that glistened in the artificial sun, and even Oculens-simulated wildlife.

As it turned out, his decision proved horribly suited for maintaining peace of mind.

A vaguely familiar baritone reached him from the park's southern end, and it took him a few seconds to realize that it was coming from the acre that Cybele's city council had briefly designated a human-free zone.

That sent alarm bells through his head. He felt certain today would go much smoother if he avoided the area altogether. But the familiarity of the voice tugged at him, along with the place it emanated from. *It sounds like a speech.* Almost against his will, his feet started taking him toward it. As captain, he needed to keep on top of what was happening on his ship as best he could.

The voice clicked into place just before a copse of trees fell away, revealing its owner: Corporal Toby Yung. *Lance Corporal, now.*

Yung was holding something pinched between his thumb and index finger, too small for Husher to make out. "These keep us enslaved," he told the thirty or so people gathered to hear him speak. "They provide a way for the government to show us only the world they want to see. A world of enforced diversity, enforced integration. We're ostracized for even *mentioning* the possibility of going out in public without them in our eyes. I say, who cares? I reject the propaganda. I reject the deception."

Oh, God. Husher's stomach roiled as he began to piece together what Yung was doing, here. *Oculens.* That was what Yung was holding, he realized—right before he threw it on the grass and stomped on it with a combat boot.

"Those who would enforce policies aimed at equality of outcome between all the species—they place group identity above all else. I say, fine, then. If the most important thing about a Winger is the fact he's a Winger, and the most important thing about a Tumbran is that he's a Tumbra, then the same goes for humans. But the similarities end there. They say humans have benefited from advantages that must be countered, but I say we *celebrate* human culture. Let's raise humans up, as they're meant to be raised. Yes, the most important thing about a human is the fact he's a human. Why? Because humans are smarter and stronger than other species. We dominated the galaxy for decades, and we can dominate it again. We *will* dominate it again. Never feel ashamed of being human. Feel proud. Feel *strong!*"

Most of the few dozen listeners took the cue Yung's pause was clearly meant to represent, and they raised their fists in the air, cheering.

"If they don't like human dominance, then they can go somewhere else. Human culture has developed over millennia, and we like it just fine, thank you very much. I'm calling for the peaceful deportation of all nonhuman—"

Suddenly, a woman rushed in from the nearby copse of trees and decked Yung in the face, sending him stumbling to the right, clutching his jaw. He whirled around to face his assailant, eyes ablaze, a trickle of blood running down his cheek.

"*Hey,*" Husher shouted, rushing to the front of the crowd with his hands spread toward Yung and his assailant. "That's quite enough!"

That was when he saw the woman's face. It was Penelope Snyder, former president of Cybele University.

CHAPTER 25

At the Expense of Peace

As the deputy sheriff listened to accounts of the incident, Husher could tell he felt about as enthused about the whole thing as Husher did—that is, not at all. The man rubbed his cheek as he listened, his expression carefully neutral.

Snyder's attack had been documented by at least thirty sets of Oculenses, so variations between her, Yung's, and Husher's accounts could easily be resolved. Still, it was worthwhile to get their accounts nevertheless, especially when it came to establishing motive.

In this case, the motive was pretty clear. "So you say Corporal Yung was spouting 'violent rhetoric,' Ms. Snyder, and that's why you hit him?"

"I answered violence with violence," Snyder said. "It's the only thing people like him understand."

The deputy leaned back in his chair, leaning away from his desk—and from the three people in his office. "I reviewed the footage of the corporal's speech, and while it was certainly politically charged, I don't believe it violates IU strictures against inciting violence. That's for a judge to decide, of course, should the corporal decide to press charges."

"I won't be pressing charges," Yung said, wearing the same self-satisfied smile he'd developed within a minute of Snyder's attack. His jaw had swollen substantially. Snyder was wearing a ring, which had done a fair bit of damage.

"All right, then. In that case, I think we're done here, other than for me to request that you refrain from punching people in the future, Ms. Snyder. If you think someone is guilty of inciting violence, I would ask that you inform a law officer rather than taking the matter into your own hands. That's considered vigilantism under IU law, and it's more likely than not that the next person will press charges."

"I understand your perspective, Deputy," Snyder said, which made Husher want to roll his eyes until only the whites showed. He was pretty sure he knew what her attack was really about.

The deputy sheriff, clearly lost for what to say next, stared at them. Husher cleared his throat, standing. "You heard the deputy," he said to the other two, his voice coming out somewhat hoarse. "Ms. Snyder, you leave first. I'll leave with the corporal in a few minutes. I want to have a word with him, and I want to make sure you both get on your way home, separately, without further incident."

Snyder stood, avoiding eye contact with Yung, and left the office.

"Thank you for taking the time to come here, Captain," the sheriff's deputy said. "I know you have much more important matters to attend to."

"Least I could do," Husher said, suppressing a sigh. *Though this might end up being more important than I'd like it to be.*

Once they were outside the sheriff's station, Yung turned to him, eyebrows raised expectantly. "You wanted to speak with me, Captain Husher?"

"Yeah. What the hell are you doing?"

Yung's smile, already insufferable, broadened. "Why, I'm doing exactly what you told me to do. I'm making something of myself, just like you said I should have done a long time ago. I've stopped assuming the world owes me something because of my intelligence, and I'm trying to use that intelligence to make a positive difference."

"Bullshit. You were giving a speech in a location chosen for its divisiveness, about how humans are superior to other species. And you were about to speak in favor of human-only colonies, weren't you?"

Tilting his head to one side, Yung said, "Through the efforts of the IU and the IGF, human culture has been diluted, until—"

"Ah, come *on,* Corporal! You know that isn't true. You fought alongside aliens. You *know* integration made the IGF a more formidable fighting force than the United Human Fleet ever was. Why don't you tell me what this is really about?"

At last, Yung's smile fell away, and he was silent for a moment as Husher's words took root. The ex-marine's shoulders rose and fell with deepening breath. "I'm just doing what the IU leftist radicals taught me to do," Yung said at last, his tone of false levity replaced by one dripping with venom. "They wanted to take my job because of my species identity, and in the end they succeeded.

I say, fine. They want to make identity the foundation of every-thing? I can play that game, too. I say I'm *more* entitled to be where I was because of my humanity, not less. They took away a job I loved, Captain. They don't get to do that without conse-quences."

"So this is about getting revenge on the IU. At the expense of beings you fought alongside, and at the expense of peace and sta-bility aboard my ship."

Yung's jaw muscles tightened visibly. "If that's what it takes."

Shaking his head, Husher suddenly felt incredibly weary. *Here we go again.* "I'm sure this won't steer you away from what you've resolved to do, but I hope you know your personal vendetta is go-ing to take away from the war effort. The more division you sow on my ship, the less able I'm to fight the Ixa."

"Maybe I don't think this society is worth saving," Yung said, even more bitterly. The way his words echoed Price's made Husher stare at him longer than he'd intended, his pulse quick-ening as the depth of the quagmire he was standing in became fully apparent.

"Besides, Captain," Yung continued. "There are plenty of hu-mans who agree with me. And haven't you heard? Next to Teth, they consider you their greatest champion."

CHAPTER 26

Pressure Cooker

Husher's daughter contacted him the day after the Yung-Snyder incident, asking that he make the arrangements necessary for her to pay him a family visit inside the *Vesta*'s crew section. But considering she hadn't even spoken to him during the meeting with her mother, somehow he doubted the actual purpose of Maeve's request was to visit her father.

That became apparent the moment she closed the hatch to his office and marched over to his desk, planting both hands on the desktop. "You need to do more to crack down on radicals," she said.

That almost made him burst into laughter, but considering this was the first time his daughter had been willing to speak with him since the day she learned she was his daughter, he decided that probably wasn't a good idea. "Radicals on the right or on the left?" he said instead, unable to stop a small smile from forming on his lips.

"On the right, of course."

Husher tilted his head to one side. "So there aren't any groups on the left I should 'crack down' on in equal proportion?"

"That doesn't even make any sense. Why would you want to crack down on progressives?"

He shrugged. "Oh, I don't know. What about progressives who attack people unprovoked?"

"People like Toby Yung need to be punched. Penelope's a hero for what she did."

"So they're saying on the narrow net." The various videos from Santana Park had, of course, been making the narrow net rounds since yesterday. "I've seen a lot of calls to give Snyder her old job back."

"They should. She deserves it."

"Don't you think that might have been her intention all along?"

Maeve shook her head, clearly already dismissing Husher's viewpoint. "I don't care what her reasons were, to be honest. Human supremacists get punched. That's how it works, now."

"So you consider violence an acceptable way to answer people whose views aren't in line with yours."

"What?" his daughter said, squinting. "I didn't say that. Yung's views are poison, and poisoners need to be attacked."

"If you support unprovoked violence against one person, you support it against everyone. It doesn't matter who they are or what their views are. You can't have it both ways, Maeve. Either unprovoked violence is fine in all contexts or it's unacceptable in any context."

Maeve stared at him for a long time, eyes wide, and he readied himself for another tirade. But to his surprise, it never came. "Okay. You're right. I'm willing to concede that."

His eyebrows crept upward. "You're willing to concede that what Snyder did was wrong?"

"Well-intentioned, but misguided. Yes. Wrong."

"Well, then. All right."

Maeve took the seat opposite the desk, folding one leg over the other and fixing him with her gaze once again. "But as captain of the *Vesta*, you need to do more to stop people like Yung from spreading their hate."

"I can prosecute crimes committed by my crew, and I can support the Cybele justice system in prosecuting crimes committed by citizens. But I'm not about to impede anyone from freely expressing their ideas."

Hand flicking into the air in exasperation, Maeve said, "See, this is exactly why people think you're right there with the Brotherhood. And why so many far-right people name you as a hero."

"Right. About that. I've been hearing that claim a lot lately—yesterday, most recently. So last night, I went onto the narrow net when I should have been sleeping, to see if I could find my legion of Ixan-sympathizing supporters. I found four posts that could reasonably be said to fit that bill."

A brief pause, and then Maeve said, "Four is a lot!"

"Maybe, but not on a starship carrying almost sixty thousand people, including crew. I also saw thousands of posts from much more moderate people, who are just tired of all the identity politics—from *both* sides of the spectrum."

"So what are you trying to say?"

"I'm saying this claim that I'm a Sapient Brotherhood icon or something is overblown. And I'm beginning to realize why it's been overblown."

"Listen, Vin, I know you don't actually support those things. But failing to do anything about them is as bad as supporting them. They're taking to the streets, now. How much farther are you going to let this go?"

"The right to protest is supposed to be available to everyone, under IU law," Husher said. "If I understand you correctly, you're asking me to censor or suppress the views expressed by Yung yesterday. But honestly, even if I wanted to do that, there's not much more that can be done. The narrow net 'content filters' are already sophisticated enough to take down most 'sensitive content' seconds after it's posted. And what has that achieved? By suppressing ideas we consider undesirable, we only place them in a pressure cooker, until they blow. Have you considered that people like Yung are only taking to the streets because they have no other way to communicate their ideas?"

"You sound like you're defending him," Maeve said, her mouth twisting in disgust.

"I'm trying to tell you that you've been going about your activism all wrong. If you work to suppress views you don't like, you only empower them. You romanticize them, making them taboo and forbidden—you give them their own dark appeal that they wouldn't have had otherwise. But if you're truly confident that your ideas are superior, then you should show that through open discussion. Not censorship. That's how persuasion is supposed to work. The best ideas are supposed to rise to the top, as a result of open debate. And by censoring the people you disagree with, you prevent them from showing the galaxy who they truly are."

His daughter had nothing to say to that, but he got the sense that her silence was a lot closer to "rancorous" than "thoughtful."

Oh, well. I doubt she likes me any less than she did. "Everything your side has done so far has played right into the hands of people like Yung," he added, to make sure he was getting his point across.

At that, Maeve rose to her feet, fixed him with a final glare, and left his office without another word.

CHAPTER 27

Nothing if not Entertaining

"**B**ronson."

A boot nudged his ribs through the ragged garments he'd arranged around himself for warmth. He groaned, more out of annoyance than actual pain. The boot had only nudged him, after all. It was just that he'd been in a deep sleep. His sleep had been getting deeper and deeper, lately.

He peered up, blinking into the Imbros morning, at the silhouette standing over him. "You look like shit," it said.

"Warden," he croaked.

Eve Quinn's sardonic smile materialized as Bronson's eyes adjusted. "I came to find you. Wasn't hard. I've been tracking your little odyssey through the city streets. Kind of hard to watch, in a hilarious way."

"What do you want?"

"Nothing I'm about to discuss in a damp alleyway." She jerked her head back toward the street. "My ride is waiting. Shall we?"

He heaved himself to his feet, his legs complaining as he trudged after her to the idling two-door sedan.

Quinn slipped into the driver's seat—a term left over from when road vehicles hadn't driven themselves—leaving Bronson to let himself into the passenger side. The driver's side still had all the important controls for the car, such as setting the destination for instance, but Quinn didn't do that yet.

"There's no point in bringing you anywhere until you've agreed to the proposal," she said. "So it's my job to bring that up with you, too."

"Where will you bring me?" he asked. "The prison?"

"No. Somewhere where you can have a shave, first. And a bath," she added, wrinkling her nose. "Then, to a spaceport. You're going to Tartarus Station."

Bronson glanced in the side mirror, where he glimpsed several inches of unkempt facial growth. A twinge of embarrassment made him frown. "To do what?" he asked.

"The Union is interested in learning more about the implants Darkstream designed since leaving the Milky Way, and the ways the company used them to spy on everyone. It can't be the only tech you used, and if you can help us mimic whatever surveillance infrastructure you had set up in the Steele System, your value will increase. We'll start feeding you regularly, for one. Maybe buy you some clean clothes."

Bronson paused. "You're not really a prison warden, are you?"

Quinn smiled. "You got me. I actually was, once. That's how I got scouted for my current job—I took a keen interest in experimenting with how we monitor prisoners and keep them from bad behavior, or punish them when they indulge in it. But no, I'm not a warden anymore."

"Who do you really work for?"

"It's an intelligence agency, and one we've managed to keep concealed from the public so far. I certainly won't be telling you our name until after you've agreed to help us. So tell, me Bronson: are you going to share your secrets or not?"

"Who's saying we spied on people?" Bronson asked, stalling for time more than anything else. He knew where this was going, but he wanted to make sure he knew what to do when they got there.

"No one said it. You didn't have to. The obvious backdoor you included in the implants was one glaring sign. But that's not all—the board members' implants had plenty of personal data on high-priority surveillance targets, which we scraped through that same backdoor without them even noticing. They weren't nearly as diligent as you when it came to concealing all the compromising data you guys were hoarding."

Fools. He'd always thought of the Darkstream board as stubborn sheep in need of herding, which he'd tried his best to do. This proved they were sheep. Clearly, they'd never had the basic wherewithal even to properly cover their own asses. They'd just bleated at him obnoxiously, demanding that he do everything for them, and blaming him for their own shortcomings.

Well, they're gone now, for a long time. And I'm still here. Even during his stint on the streets, he'd never lost sight of his own greatness, never stopped believing in his own triumphant destiny. The fact that the IU had freed him from his cell at all had been the first indication that they understood his significance, at least in part. And now, here Quinn was. Asking for his help.

Delicious.

"May I ask why the IU has a sudden interest in mass surveillance?" he said. "And don't try to tell me it's merely academic, because I'll know that's bull. If I'm going to help you spy on hundreds of billions of beings, I'm going to know why."

Quinn raised her eyebrows, which she paired with the ghost of a smile. "Never lost your balls, did you Bronson? Not even out here, sleeping in alleyways. I'm offering you the opportunity to be a player again. To have consistent food and shelter, at the very least. And yet you're already making demands."

"That's right," he said.

She chuckled. "The Interstellar Union's come to realize how important 'societal harmony' is to its survival. They want to detect points of disharmony and deal with them before they become a problem."

What a load of bureaucratic doublespeak. "The Union wants to know whenever people disagree with them."

"That's about the long and short of it, yeah. As far as I can tell."

"All right, then. If I'm going to help, I have certain conditions, and they go quite a bit farther than three square meals a day."

Quinn chuckled again. "You're nothing if not entertaining, Bronson." She studied him briefly. "I'm not supposed to take you to the spaceport till you've agreed to help, but I've already told you enough that they'll probably kill you if you don't agree. I might as well take you now."

"Fine." The prospect of death didn't scare Bronson. Not after everything he'd been through. He was playing for keeps—for all the chips. And given the power of the Progenitors, who he was actually working for, failure would probably be about as bad as death anyway.

He'd serve the IU's interests for as long as it served his own to do so. The same went for the Progenitors.

CHAPTER 28

A Calculated Risk

Husher was asleep when his com emitted a high-pitched beeping from near his head, indicating a priority message. Snatching it up, he saw it was from his XO. The interruption to his rest wasn't exactly welcome, but at least he knew that Fesky wasn't likely to abuse her ability to send him urgent messages.

She was in the command seat right now, but he wanted full details on this right away. So he called her.

"Fesky," he said when she answered. "You have something for me?"

"A com drone just came through the darkgate from Alder," she said, her voice almost a whisper. "The neighboring system is under attack from the Progenitors. The system's current defenders are mostly Quatro ships, and according to the transmission they should be able to handle it."

"Right." It was protocol during wartime for systems under attack to notify nearby systems, even when an emergency hadn't been declared. "I'm coming to the CIC."

"Captain," Fesky said. "Are you planning to take us there?"

"Yes."

"But we've been assigned to Yclept."

"We'll leave our battle group here. But the *Vesta*'s going. This is important."

"You just got back into the IU's good graces, Captain. Is it wise to defy them again, so soon after the president granted you a pardon?"

Husher grimaced. "Who are you, Kaboh?"

"Well, with him gone, there aren't many left willing to question you to your face."

"I'm not getting into the details of this over com," he said. "I won't take the chance, however small, that a Progenitor agent is listening in. But you already know why I'm taking us to Alder. Do you really think we should let this opportunity pass us by?"

"No," Fesky admitted. "But someone has to play the part of Kaboh, now that Kaboh's decided he can't be part of what we do, here. If that means playing devil's advocate to keep you on your toes, then it's devil's advocate I'll play."

"Okay, Fesky. You do you." He ended the transmission and opened the wardrobe, where several changes of uniform hung, already neatly pressed. Having finally tired of Fesky's constant admonishments about his appearance, he carved out an hour or so each week to iron several changes of uniform, to make sure he always had one ready to go.

"Have the battle group captains been notified of our plans?" he asked as soon as the CIC hatch slid open to admit him.

"They have," Fesky said, rising from the command seat.

"Did they raise any concerns?"

"No, sir. I'm sure by now they know better than to interrupt you while you're going against Command's orders."

Husher glanced at his XO askance as he settled into his seat and she settled into hers. Talking so frankly about his decision to transition into Alder despite what the IU wanted...well, it was unorthodox, much like his decision to defy the IU.

I'm sure Fesky knows what she's doing. There's no hiding it from the crew that we're going off-script. Might as well make light of it, I guess, and relieve some of the tension.

"What about Governor Russell?" he asked. "Has he been notified?"

"I left that particular task to you, Captain. If you care to execute it."

Husher nodded. "The people of Juktas deserve some kind of explanation. Coms, get the governor on."

Soon enough, Governor Gerald Russell was on the main display, blinking at Husher rapidly. "You're saying you're leaving us defenseless to go help a bunch of Quatro?"

"Currently, those Quatro are defending a system with significant populations from all four Union species, including humans. I'm sure you agree it's important for us to make sure that system doesn't fall."

Russell sniffed. "Sure, but I thought the com drone said they don't need any help."

"We have a specific, classified mission in Alder, that's related but not critical to its defense." That wasn't entirely true, of course—it was only classified in that Husher was keeping it a secret from almost everyone.

"But the IU ordered you to remain here," the governor said.

"I thought you didn't like the IU."

"Even they're right sometimes. This is one of those times."

"That's why we're leaving our battle group in formation around your colony, Governor. Believe me when I say that our trip to Alder is a calculated risk, one that could turn the tide of the war in our favor. Beyond that, I can't tell you anything. Thank you for your understanding, Governor."

Husher nodded at his Coms officer, who cut off the transmission with evident relish.

The rest of the voyage out of Yclept was uneventful, but soon after transitioning into Alder, the tactical display became populated with five Quatro warships and two IGF cruisers, as well as three Progenitor destroyers and two carriers.

Husher frowned. "Whose projection was it that the Quatro needed no help with this system's defense? Theirs or the IGF's?"

"Hard to say, sir," the Coms officer said. "The message was signed Captain Penney of the *Simon*, but it doesn't mention who conducted the analysis."

"Right. Well, unless the Quatro ships are much more powerful than I've been led to believe, this looks like an even fight to me. In fact, the Progenitors might even be slightly favored to win."

No one commented on his diagnosis of the situation. Not that he'd expected them to. "All ahead toward the engagement, Helm."

CHAPTER 29

Optimize for Speed

Husher's analysis quickly proved more accurate than he would have liked. Shortly after the *Vesta* transitioned through the darkgate, Winterton reported that a Quatro destroyer and one of the IGF cruisers had been neutralized in quick succession, infiltrated with Ravagers and then torn apart from the inside.

This is good for our self-assigned mission, at least. Not so good for our prospects of winning the war. The plan was to plant trackers on multiple Progenitor ships, if they could. That would increase the likelihood they'd encounter one of them again. *It also increases the chances of one of the trackers being found, and once that happens, they'll all be scouring their hulls for the things.*

It was a trade-off, to be sure. But a calculated one.

The term "trackers" didn't really describe what the devices did. They weren't capable of sending signals interdimensionally, so no actual tracking would occur. *Not in real-time, anyway.*

Instead, Husher and Ochrim planned to scrape the data from the devices if and when they encountered them again, in the hopes of figuring out how to travel between the various universes themselves—and also how to reach the Progenitors' home dimension. The devices were research aids more than anything else.

He turned to his new Nav officer. "Noni, devise a course that takes us past the enemy formation, coming to a stop well beyond them. The delayed deceleration will shorten the window the Progenitor ships will have to react to our missiles. Tremaine, once Noni's done that, I need you to work with her to find the optimal timing for firing our barrage, given our current course and acceleration. Optimize for missile speed."

"Aye, sir," Tremaine said, hard on the heels of Noni's "Yes, Captain."

"I trust our forward tubes have already been loaded with our preplanned volley, Tremaine?"

"Yes, sir," the Tactical officer said. "And the second volley is ready for loading immediately after. In total, fifty-five Banshees, sixteen Gorgons, and nine Hydras, four of them modified. The modified missiles will be fired with the second barrage."

"Very good." If this went flawlessly, four Progenitor ships would leave the universe with trackers on their hulls. "Coms, tell Commander Ayam he'll be launching Pythons soon: the entire Air Group, including the subspace-capable squadron."

"Aye."

He hadn't wanted to reveal his Pythons' new capabilities back in Yclept, but now that he had, it was time to hit as hard and as fast with them as he could. There was a decent chance that these Progenitor ships hadn't received the intel about them yet, but they would. Now was the time to press the advantage.

"First missiles away," Tremaine said after a tense period of waiting. "Second volley being loaded into the tubes now...firing."

Husher nodded, pleased at the coordinated efforts of his crew and the *Vesta*'s automated systems.

As expected, the enemy ships were too busy dealing with the distributed missile strike to bother Husher's supercarrier very much as she sailed past their formation, decelerating.

Still, if everything went his way, this wouldn't be war.

"Two of the four tracker segments have been neutralized, sir," Winterton reported. "Ravagers got to the Hydras carrying them, they separated, and then point defense turrets mowed down all eight partitions."

"Acknowledged, Ensign," Husher said, trying not to sound as pissed-off as he felt. The trackers had been designed along the same principles as Gorgons, with stealth in mind. But maybe that had been a mistake. By now, the Progenitors knew to expect eight warheads from Hydras. Perhaps seeing only seven was too glaring a warning sign that something wasn't right.

I need to take their minds off the anomaly, if I can. "Tactical, send a dispersed spray of kinetic impactors from our aft rail guns, before we reach our allied ships. It doesn't need to be precise, it just needs to happen now."

"Yes, sir," Tremaine said, his voice tight as his fingers flew over the console.

"Helm, we're deviating from Noni's course. I want to execute an emergency braking procedure, immediately." The stress wouldn't do his ship any favors, but this was too important. "Coms, tell Ayam he's launching ahead of schedule."

His orders delivered, Husher monitored the tactical display as they played out. The kinetic impactors had prompted some hasty repositioning from the enemy fleet, but the *Vesta* missiles' guidance systems were smart enough to readjust, tracking their targets.

As Pythons shot out of their launch tubes toward the enemy ships, squadron by squadron, Winterton turned toward Husher, wearing an uncharacteristic smile.

"I'm receiving signals from the two remaining trackers, Captain. They've both successfully landed on enemy hulls, a destroyer's and a carrier's, with no sign they've been detected."

"Excellent," Husher said as his CIC erupted into cheering. "Supply Ensign Fry with which ships have been tagged, Winterton. Fry, transmit the designations to Commander Ayam and tell him to pressure the most vulnerable enemy ship that isn't one of those two."

Both officers answered in the affirmative, and Husher returned to monitoring the tactical display. As he did, his mood continued to improve. Watching the subspace Pythons flit in and out of reality in response to immediate threats—it was a beautiful thing to behold. Almost as beautiful as watching the destroyer they targeted go up in flames.

The cheering picked back up, then. The destruction of Progenitor ships was rare enough to buoy Husher's officers even further, and he wasn't about to tamp their spirits.

The Progenitors seemed just as shocked as they did. Seconds after the destroyer went down, the four remaining enemy ships vanished from the Alder System.

But when it came to fostering joy, war did not make for fertile ground. A com drone arrived from the Yclept System, even as the other IGF and Quatro captains were thanking Husher and his crew for the assist.

The system they'd abandoned was under attack by a Progenitor destroyer and three carriers.

CHAPTER 30

Stellarpol

Today is just full of surprises.

Protocol called for transitioning through darkgates at a measured speed, but learning of the attack on the system they were supposed to be defending had made Husher less concerned with protocol than with the pit of guilt that sat at the bottom of his stomach. *You made your choice with full knowledge of what might happen,* he'd told himself. *You knew it was important enough to take the risk.* Unfortunately, his self-talk hadn't accomplishing much.

But after the *Vesta* tore from the Alder-Yclept darkgate at a speed well above regulation, and the tactical display populated, they saw that another capital starship, the *Eos*, was already there and contending with the Progenitor threat.

With her own battle group as well as the *Vesta*'s backing her up, not to mention Juktas' orbital defense platforms and its fighter group, the *Eos* was mounting a vigorous defense.

"Nav, devise a course that pairs full engine power with the system's gravity well to get us to that engagement as quickly as possible," Husher said. Despite the relief he felt at the *Eos'* presence, he had no desire to lose even a single ship to the Progenitors. He knew that losing an entire crew after he'd chosen to leave his post would never leave his conscience.

Thankfully, that didn't happen. Instead, the Progenitor ships vanished just before the *Vesta* entered missile range, clearly un-interested in getting flanked by two capital starships.

"We have a transmission request from the *Eos*, Captain."

Husher nodded, not expecting to enjoy this. The prospect of taking the transmission in his office popped into his mind, unbidden. *No.* He wouldn't allow himself that reprieve. *We make our decisions and we live with them.* "Put in on the display, and give everyone access," Husher said.

"Captain Husher," said the graying, thin-faced woman who appeared on the display. "Where were you?"

"Hello, Captain Norberg," he said. Husher knew all the capital starship captains, and Katrina Norberg was perhaps the least likely to take nonsense lightly. "We've just come from aiding in the defense of the Alder System."

"I'm told Alder needed no help with its defense," Norberg said, her lips a flat line.

"We were told the same, though that assessment proved some-what inaccurate. Two allied ships were lost within ten minutes of our arrival."

Norberg nodded. "It's a good thing you were there, then. But even so. You were assigned to Yclept. Why leave, when your intel told you Alder was safe? If it hadn't been for our arrival, things might have turned out quite differently today."

"I understand that. All I can say is that we made a calculated risk. I'm not able to tell you the nature of that risk, because it's classified." He'd decided it was easier to treat the trackers they'd affixed to the Progenitor ships as classified than to say he simply didn't trust anyone enough to supply them with the information.

Norberg was studying him closely, clearly not fully buying his account. "Well, I have no authority over you, Captain Husher. The IU does, however, and so does the admiralty. I hope you don't expect me to conceal anything about your actions from them."

"Of course not."

"All right, then," Norberg said, though her expression remained just as hardened. Not that that was much of a departure from her usual demeanor.

"Can I ask why you've come to the Yclept System, Captain?" Husher asked. "Given your intel told you it was protected by the *Vesta?*"

"We're following orders that come straight from Galactic Congress, or so Admiral Iver told me," Norberg said. "We're here to arrest Governor Russell. Indeed, my marines are planetside right now, assisting Stellarpol officers in apprehending him. We have a few more stops to make after this, and then we're heading back to Caprice."

Husher lowered his eyebrows. "Do your other stops involve arresting people?"

"I see no reason not to tell you that they do indeed. My orders aren't classified."

"What crimes did Governor Russell commit?"

"Crimes against IU's nonhuman member species, I'm told."

"What crimes?"

"Fomenting resentful attitudes against nonhuman beings. That's the official wording, anyway."

Slowly, Husher asked, "So, he was inciting violence?"

"That's not what the charges say."

"What does 'fomenting resentful attitudes' mean, then?"

Norberg sighed. "I'm a starship captain, not a politician, Husher. I know you've dipped your toe into that pool more than once, but I just follow orders. As far as I understand, the IU has enacted special wartime powers to make sure the galaxy stays stable when we most need it to be. We don't just need tolerance, at times like these. We need unity. Anyone working against that is being removed from the equation. That's the best explanation I have for you."

Husher could feel how wide his eyes had grown at Norberg's words. A creeping coldness spread across his stomach as he realized that the Union was only doing what he had been doing for much longer: whatever they thought would increase their chances of winning the war.

CHAPTER 31

Crowd Control

Ochrim didn't respond to Husher's messages as he walked through Cybele toward the Ixan's residence, and when he called, he didn't answer. It took ten minutes of standing on the step and ringing the bell to finally summon the scientist, who opened the door and blinked lethargically at him.

"You were asleep," Husher said, a note of surprise creeping into his voice. He knew Ochrim ran himself ragged, but it wasn't like him to sleep in.

"Yes."

Husher nodded. He hated to pull Ochrim out of a slumber the Ixan so obviously needed. On top of devising an exoskeleton for Ek and her children as well as trying to figure out the Progenitors' method of interdimensional travel, inventing a tracker with which to fit modified Hydras had taken an outsized toll on Ochrim.

Unfortunately, none of that mattered. Only defeating the Progenitors truly mattered, now.

Ochrim stepped back, making room for Husher to enter before closing the door behind him. "To what do I owe the pleasure?" he said, which made Husher do a double take. Sarcasm was *highly* uncharacteristic from Ochrim.

This war is taking from everyone. "When it comes time to chase down Progenitor ships, I need to know how big a vessel you think we'll be able to send through the dimensions."

"Right," Ochrim said, blinking some more as he apparently tried to work out how to answer. At last, he did: "That will be exceedingly difficult without knowing how the Progenitors are transitioning through the dimensions in the first place."

"I understand that."

"Do you?"

"Yes, Ochrim. But if we're going to implement the tech we're hoping to develop within a meaningful timeframe, we're going to need some idea of—"

Someone hammered on the door behind Husher, causing him to exchange glances with Ochrim. "Who's that?" Husher asked.

The Ixan's gaze went distant—no doubt he was checking the exterior camera via Oculens.

"It appears to be the young commander of Oneiri Team."

Lips tightening, Husher turned toward the door. "He must have followed me here. I'll deal with him." He paused. "I know I'm asking the impossible, Ochrim. But what else is new? Get some more rest, if you like. After that, I need you to make a start on what I've asked."

"Very well," Ochrim said as Husher palmed open the door.

"Back off, Price," he said before the seaman could speak. "We're not doing this on a civilian's doorstep." Price stepped aside to let him through. "Do yourself a favor and tread lightly," he added as he walked by, and Price fell in beside him, almost vibrating with tension.

"Sir, how can you stand by while the IU turns into a mirror image of the Assembly of Elders?"

Cybele was the last place he wanted to have a confrontation with a seaman, but he also wanted to get it over with. *If it wasn't for the IGF's policy of encouraging every subordinate to speak their mind, I wouldn't have to deal with this in the first place.* Staring straight ahead, he said, "For one thing, I still have no evidence that the Elders are what you say they are."

"Okay," Price said. "Forget the Elders. Are you going to tell me you agree with these arrests the Union is making now?"

Husher paused to gather his thoughts. "What would you have me do, Seaman?"

"Oppose them!"

"I'm busy opposing the Progenitors."

"And while you are, the Union's turning galactic society into something unrecognizable."

"I'm not a politician." *No matter what Captain Norberg says about me.*

"No, but you're a soldier. And the galaxy's about to go to war with itself."

Husher peeled his eyes from the streets ahead and stared at Price. "What are you talking about?"

"You haven't heard? It's all over the narrow net. The Sapient Brotherhood responded to the arrests by calling for every human to recognize the IU as their true enemy and to turn against them. Just before they put out their call, they liberated a large IGF battle group from the Lilac System—those ships are under Brotherhood control, now. They kicked off all the nonhumans at gunpoint. Packed them into escape pods and jettisoned them."

Husher came to a stop. "What are you saying my line of action should be, exactly?"

"I already told you. The galaxy's going to war with itself. It's time to pick a side."

"And you're saying I should side with the Brotherhood?"

"The Union *created* the Brotherhood. The more radical they got, the better the Brotherhood started to look, for more and more people. And so they became more powerful. I know I don't have to tell you that. You've been experiencing it here on the *Vesta*."

Husher had nothing to say to that. He just stood there in the street and stared into Price's fiery gaze.

"Pinochet just shot up in the polls," Price went on. "The election's still two years away, but he's skyrocketing now that the Union's doing what they are. Though with the way things are going, I have my doubts they'll even allow any more free elections."

Pinochet was the only nominee in the long-running race to become galactic president who'd openly expressed support for the Brotherhood. On a few occasions, he'd also dropped what many interpreted as subtle praise for certain Ixan policies.

"I'm going to ask you again," Husher said. "Are you saying I should side with the Brotherhood?"

"I'm saying you should do what needs to be done. Surely *you* understand that, Captain?" Price stormed down the street before

Husher could answer, unless he wanted to chase after him, shouting.

When he returned to his office, Major Gamble was waiting in the corridor to see him.

"Major," Husher said, opening the hatch and gesturing toward the office's interior. "Please, after you."

"Thank you, sir."

"Have a seat," Husher said, circling the desk. "What can I do for you?"

The major sat. "I think we may have a problem."

Husher studied Gamble's face as he lowered himself into his desk chair. "What sort of problem?"

"A Cybele problem."

That's my least favorite kind of problem. It was true—he could blow Progenitors clean off a battlespace, but Cybele problems twisted his brain into knots. "Out with it."

Gamble sighed. "Members of the Sapient Brotherhood are planning a rally in front of the Skyward Mall. There's a counter-protest already brewing. This...could get ugly. The sheriff's requested our help making sure it doesn't."

Resisting the urge to lower his face into his palm, Husher opened his mouth to say something, then closed it. He didn't like the idea of involving the military in civil matters, but then, if the protest turned to riots, and the rioters managed to damage the ship herself, that could prove catastrophic to everyone.

At last, he said, "You've kept up your crowd control drills, I trust?"

"Of course, sir. We're ready."

"Do nothing to impede protest or free expression of ideas, on either side. But if things turn violent, you'll need to contain the unrest."

"I understand, sir."

CHAPTER 32

Lucid

Jake called a meeting with Oneiri Team inside lucid—all except for Rug, their latest addition. Either an implant or a headset was required for going lucid, and neither of those had been invented for Quatro, yet. Rug didn't use the mech dream to pilot her mech. Instead, her suit amplified the innate superconducting ability wielded by every Quatro, which normally was very weak at regular temperatures. Inside the suit, though, her magnetic nudges were translated into powerful movements.

Jake didn't like excluding Rug, but the dream was the only place they could be sure no one with either the IGF or the IU would overhear them. As far as he knew, neither had any knowledge of the tech, making it perfect for talking in secrecy.

"What are we going to do?" Ash said. "The protests are sure to turn ugly."

"I'm not convinced we should do anything," Marco said, drawing a sharp look from Jake. "What? I'm sure the protests will turn ugly too, but what are we going to do about it? Mechs are great for pummeling an enemy into oblivion, but I don't think they're very well suited to crowd control."

"Do you think the demonstrators could get out of control?" Ash said, turning to Jake. "Like, really out of control—breaking into the crew section, taking over the ship?"

He hesitated before answering, chewing his lip. "No," he admitted at last. "I think Husher has a better grip on his ship than that." *I'll give him that much.*

"Still," Ash said, shaking her head. "This galaxy's falling apart. It's nothing like I expected. I just hope it's not too far gone."

"Husher needs to do something," Jake growled. "He needs to make tough decisions, ones that'll taste bitter. I'm not sure he has it in him."

"This is exactly what happened in the Steele System," Ash said. "Everyone turning on everyone else, and it all ends up serving the Progenitors."

"Maybe we should just leave," Lisa put in, and everyone turned to look at her.

"Leave?" Jake said.

"Yeah. As in, leave the Milky Way again, or at least find some corner of it where we can entrench ourselves. We're Oneiri Team—I'm sure we could commandeer a starship if we really wanted to."

"That's not how we do things," Jake answered slowly. "And it's never been how you've done them, either. What about our families? And what about what the Progenitors did to us in Steele? Are we going to leave the people here to suffer the same fate?"

"Seems like they deserve it, to me. As for our families, if we can find out where they went, we can take them with us. They may have even already found somewhere safe."

Jake shook his head. "I won't sign off on abandoning people to fight the Progenitors on their own, Lisa."

She shrugged and fell silent, but Jake noticed Andy looking thoughtful.

CHAPTER 33

Lines of Attack

"I can't believe they're carrying those flags," Gamble muttered, to no one in particular.

Lance Corporal Roux was standing beside him, and she nodded. "It's ridiculous, Major." She wore full riot gear, as he did.

The flags Gamble meant featured the triple stripe—black, white, and red—of the Ixa. Or rather, the faction that had taken power a few years before the First Galactic War; the faction that had agitated for the extermination of every Ixan who was the result of inter-species breeding. They'd nearly succeeded with their genocide during the first war, and before the second even began, they'd completed it.

That was what the Sapient Brotherhood members and sympathizers were supporting today. Right in front of his eyes, on an IGF starship. In an IU city.

But as revolting as he found the imagery, it wasn't Gamble's job to take sides. It was his job to make sure two groups of demonstrators, currently on a collision course, didn't devolve into violent chaos.

It hadn't been hard to figure out what the Brotherhood was planning, and the same went for the counterprotesters. Neither had made any effort to conceal their strategizing, and a cursory narrow net search had told Gamble and Cybele's sheriff everything they needed to know.

The Brotherhood, who'd gathered in front of the Skyward Mall to organize themselves into ranks and pump themselves up with anti-nonhuman chants, were now marching through the entire city, intending to end with a final rally on the Starboard Concourse. The counterprotesters had positioned themselves one-third of the way along that route, and they didn't intend to let the Brotherhood pass. Unlike the Brotherhood members and sympathizers, the group of counterprotesters included beings from all four Union species.

The Union had always prided itself on providing the broadest protections possible for free speech and expression while keeping the limits on that expression as slim as possible. Incitement to violence and libel weren't allowed, though where the line lay on that had been the subject of years and years of case law.

Of course, all that was before the IU had started arresting people, apparently for having views that matched those of the Brotherhood—or, less generously, for having views the IU *said* matched the Brotherhood's.

None of that mattered to Gamble. The captain had made it clear that he intended to follow the law as it had been interpreted and implemented before the arrival of the Quatro Assembly of Elders. And while hearing some of the Brotherhood chants and reading their signs made Gamble's stomach roil, his main task remained preventing and containing violent conflict. He knew that if the protesters directed slurs at individuals, then that was legally problematic. But it fell to the target whether to press charges or not, not to Gamble to sort through decades of case law in his head in order to make the call of whether to arrest someone or not.

As he scanned the crowd of marchers, his eyes fell on the whip-straight Lance Corporal Toby Yung. Yung stared back at him, a wide smile sprouting on his face. Gamble held the man's gaze until the ex-marine looked away.

He raised his com to his lips. "Sergeant Williams, what's the situation on your end?"

"As expected so far, Major," Williams answered. "The counterprotesters are chanting, interspersed with the occasional speech. Seems like every second speech is being given by the woman who used to be university president."

"I'm not interested in who's speaking," Gamble said. "I'm interested in making sure the situation's contained."

"It is so far, Major," Williams said, with no hint that the admonishment had affected him. The mark of a good soldier, in Gamble's eyes. "We're still in the process of erecting the barrier between the Brotherhood marchers and the counterprotesters, but it should be completed well in advance of their arrival. They can shout at each other from a safe distance."

"What about the alleys that permit access to and from the counterprotesters' flanks?"

Williams paused. "We talking lines of attack, here, Major? You really believe they're thinking on that level?"

"Emotions are running high. And the Brotherhood did just steal a battle group of warships. So yeah, at least someone is thinking on that level."

"All right. I'll post marines in every alley that could be used that way. Two marines per?"

"Should do it. I have four platoons leapfrogging from side street to side street all along the marchers' route, making sure they don't veer off to anywhere we don't expect."

"Everything seems textbook to me, Major."

"If it is, I'll buy you a beer at the lounge tonight."

"Deal."

"Gamble out." The marines around him were already preparing to depart this side street and double-time down a road parallel to the marchers' route. The next side street they blocked off would also be the last—it was right next to where the counterprotesters had situated themselves.

As soon as he arrived, Gamble threw a pair of microdrones into the air: one to monitor the marchers from above, and one to watch the counterprotesters. Immediately, the drones' feeds popped into his Oculens overlay.

As he observed the crowds from vantage points just underneath Cybele's artificial sky, it occurred to him that the *Vesta* marines would likely get accused of favoring the counterprotesters, since they were effectively helping them stop the Brotherhood from advancing. But that was happenstance. Their aim was to prevent violence between the two groups, and if it had been the counterprotesters marching, Gamble still would have had his people take these actions.

If the Brotherhood somehow managed to persuade the counterprotesters to move out of the way, then Gamble would order his marines to move, too. Somehow, he didn't see that happening.

At last, the Brotherhood marchers reached the blockade, and it was like someone turned up the volume. Both sides chanted and screamed at each other, and after a few minutes of that, something arced through the air from the Brotherhood marchers to the counterprotesters, drawing Gamble's eye. Flame blossomed amidst the tightly packed demonstrators as he realized what the projectile had been: a Molotov cocktail.

CHAPTER 34

Flying Wedge

Screams filled the air as the crowd of counterprotesters *bulged*, surging in every direction—into the marines' barricade and against the buildings bordering the street, but mostly back, away from their attacker.

Even so, there was nothing orderly about the retreat, and Gamble saw several protesters go down under the stampede.

He wrenched his focus away from the drones' overhead view and back to the situation on the ground, where he stood with a platoon of marines blocking a side street facing the Brotherhood protesters, at least one of whom had just become a rioter. He brought his com to his mouth again. "Viper, Chimera, Dragon, and Roundhouse," he said, naming the platoons who'd leapfrogged from side street to side street to keep the marchers corralled. "Surround the Brotherhood group and look for anyone holding a Molotov or showing any other signs of becoming violent. As soon as you've located them, start using flying wedges to break through the crowd and snatch out the troublemakers. The sheriff has mobile cells on hand—get them locked up and on their way as fast as you can."

Gamble sent a quick message to the Cybele fire chief, then he donned his riot helmet, intent on leading one of the wedges himself. "Form up behind me," he barked to four marines nearby. Someone handed him a riot shield, and using the drones, it wasn't long before he spotted one of the Brotherhood lighting a Molotov nearby. He lit the guy up using his Oculenses, sent the designation to the four marines with him, and shouted, "Go!"

The others kept batons at the ready as Gamble raised his shield, rushing into the crowd and knocking aside anyone who didn't scramble out of the way. The rioter throwing cocktails was near a street lamp, and Gamble used the shield to shove him against it.

"Get him, too," he ordered the marines through their earpieces, nodding at a short man nearby wearing a bandanna and holding a fresh Molotov. Two marines seized him, and the other two grabbed the rioter Gamble had pinned. That done, they pulled them back through the crowd and into a waiting van.

"Good work, marines. Let's find our next marks."

It quickly became apparent that Gamble's wedge was pulling the most rioters, and he realized a big reason why: his access to the drones' feeds. Once he made that connection, he patched the feeds through to all the other wedge leaders.

The counterprotesters were finally starting to figure themselves out, and the area on the other side of the marine barricade was quickly emptying of beings. That didn't deter the rioters, though—they simply turned their attention from the fleeing protesters to the surrounding buildings.

"We need to work faster," Gamble shouted over a wide channel. "A blazing Cybele is the last thing the captain needs."

A fresh wave of distant shrieks reached him from the counterprotesters' side, and Gamble ordered the drone to investigate.

He'd been about to plunge back into the crowd of Brotherhood supporters to snatch another rioter, but what he saw on the drone's feed made him draw up short: a second group of rioters, roughly equal in number to the first, had swept in from the opposite direction to engage the departing counterprotesters. Fistfights were breaking out along the front between the two groups, and Gamble saw more Molotovs being lit and hurled—into the counterprotesters and into the nearby residences and businesses.

They tricked us. Gamble wrenched his com from its holster and raised it. "There are more rioters sweeping in from the opposite side—somehow, they managed to organize a second group without our knowledge. I want the barricade between the first group and the counterprotesters dissolved. It's no use to anyone now. The marine platoons stationed there, it's up to you to follow the counterprotesters and shut this thing down. Things have gotten way out of hand. Marines on side streets, we've got the first group of rioters. I'm authorizing the use of immobilizing foam, rubber bullets, Active Denial Systems, and baton charge tactics. Baton charges should only be a last resort. And remember, never shoot for the head with rubber bullets. Get this city settled, marines. Oorah!"

Gamble lined up next to one of the supply trolleys until it was his turn to collect a riot gun. He checked the action, loaded up with ammo, then turned to confront the roiling mass of Brother-hood members, more and more of whom were turning violent.

He took aim at a tall man wearing a ski mask, who was winding up to throw a Molotov. Gamble's rubber bullet hit him center-mass, and he went down, clutching his rib cage. Scanning the crowd with the muzzle, Gamble saw someone wielding a baseball bat and approaching a marine from behind. Down he went. *Two for two.*

His Oculenses flashed red twice for a high-priority call, and he patched it through to his embedded ear piece. "Gamble here."

"Major, this is Sheriff Reynolds. It looks like this thing is way bigger than we expected."

"How do you mean, Sheriff?"

"Pockets of Brotherhood members are springing up all over Cybele. This wasn't just in response to the recent arrests the IU have been making, Major. That's becoming pretty clear. The Brotherhood's been planning this for a long time, and there are a lot more of their members on board the *Vesta* than we thought."

Damn it. "I'll call in the rest of the *Vesta*'s marine battalion. We need to quell this before they can do much more damage."

"Roger that. It's gonna be a long day, Major."

CHAPTER 35

Quantum Engine

Husher walked through the great hold that held Cybele, where the air scrubbers were working overtime to clear the smoke and circulate in fresh oxygen. Fesky walked beside him, her beak clacking softly every so often.

"At least this should kill the idea that you're some sort of hero to the Sapient Brotherhood," Fesky said. "Look what they've done to your ship."

"I wouldn't be so sure about that. I don't think this was necessarily targeted at me. It was targeted at the IU. Cybele's an important city to the Union, and the *Vesta* remains one of their starships, after all."

Fires had sprung up all over Cybele, one after another, until Husher had been forced to make the call to turn on the overhead sprinklers, with the knowledge that the moisture would cause a lot of damage. After that, the Molotovs lost their effect, and the marines focused on containing the riots and making arrests.

"What will you do with everyone detained by the marines and the sheriff's deputies?" Fesky asked.

"Someone will have to review all the footage, which is going to take a long time. But it will need to be done. I want the rioters off my ship. If they were defending themselves, well and good, but if they were inflicting unprovoked damage on people or property, they're going to federal prison. If there's no federal prison handy, I'll dump them on a remote rock somewhere. They're not going to be a liability on my ship anymore."

"Have you checked on your daughter?"

Husher nodded. "She's fine, thank God. She was with the counterprotesters, but she wasn't hurt."

"I'm glad to hear it. What about Yung and Snyder? Do you know whether either of those participated in the violence?"

"No. I've already had someone review the footage we have on them from during the riots—they were both careful not to be caught rioting." As he and Fesky passed another charred ruin that was once a residence, Husher winced. "Seven dead, thirty-nine injured. They've used my ship as a battleground for their ideologies, Fesky. Cities on starships should never have been permitted to exist. Least of all on a warship. And yet, I was one of the ones who made it happen."

"The alternative was barely any military at all, as I recall. You did what you had to."

"Thank you, Fesky. But with the way things are going, I have to wonder whether the outcome won't be the same."

Husher knew at least two of the injuries were third-degree burns that had resulted from Oculenses lying to their users about there being no fires. After learning that, he'd contacted the company that made the things, and they'd assured him the probability of it happening again was extremely low. *But it happened twice in the same day. When overlays start erasing authentic threats, we have a problem.*

Those injuries had happened on the counterprotesters' side, he knew, since most of the Brotherhood sympathizers had taken out their Oculenses, seeing them as tools of IU propaganda. But Husher didn't think removing Oculenses would help either the Brotherhood or the counterprotesters to see clearly. Their ideologies themselves were overlays, and they concealed so much of reality they might as well be blind.

He and Fesky reached Ochrim's residence, which thankfully hadn't been torched, and Husher rang the bell. The Ixan opened the door for them remotely, and Husher led the way to the trapdoor at the rear of the house, where they descended the door to Ochrim's lab.

Thank goodness the Brotherhood didn't have the presence of mind to target this place. Few knew about it, but it was still a lot less secret than it had been. If something had happened to Ek and her children, Husher doubted he ever would have been able to forgive himself. And at this point, losing Ochrim would likely be a deathblow to the galaxy.

But fortune had favored them, not once, but twice: Ochrim believed he'd discovered how to emulate the Progenitors' mode of interdimensional travel, even before encountering one of the ships they'd tagged with trackers. If the Ixan was right, then those ships only had one thing left to tell them: how to reach the Progenitors' home universe.

Fesky crossed the lab, wings tucked neatly, to stand in front of the Fins' great tank. Ek swam through the extension, surfacing at the top and regarding the Winger with her eternally calm eyes.

"Fesky. It is good to see you."

"Hello, Honored—" Fesky seemed to catch herself, beak clacking softly. "Ek," she finished.

That brought a smile to Ek's face. To Husher, that smile looked weary. *She must be so tired of living inside that glass prison.*

He turned to Ochrim. "Tell me what you've come up with. Just try to go as light on the physics as you can."

Ochrim nodded, and to his credit, he didn't seem to balk too much at the prospect of discussing quantum physics with Husher. "Do you recall my idea that interdimensional travel might be enabled by firing a photon at an atom whose spin and path are aligned, along the entire path integral? That is, in infinity directions?"

"Yes, actually." *Maybe I was paying more attention than I thought.* "But you couldn't think of a practical way to pull that off."

"I still can't. However, I'm beginning to think it may not be necessary. I believe that firing only one photon may be sufficient, as long as the action is executed within a decoherence-free space. That is, subspace."

"But if you travel to another universe from subspace, you'll no longer be in a decoherence-free space. How would you get back?"

"Exactly," Ochrim said, his eyes lighting up. "That's another issue, and one I think I've overcome. Of course, just as with your first voyage to subspace, my theory involves a lot of assumptions that are only testable by sending a sentient being to test them. If that person manages to return, then they can tell us that it worked."

"Right," Husher said, sighing. "Hit me with it, Ochrim. Tell me what you need me to do."

"My main assumption is that each universe will be structured the same way—that is, a series of interconnected branes, subspace being one of them. If that's true, then a quantum engine can be devised in such a way that it exists in both subspace and realspace simultaneously. That involves setting up the engine so that, once programmed, it's unobservable by the pilot until each command can be executed. The spherical wormhole that sends the engine to subspace must also be concealed—you see, for the quantum engine to work, whether or not the wormhole is generated must depend on a quantum event that has a fifty-fifty chance of occurring within a given timeframe, much like Schrödinger's famous cat. And if the pilot is able to observe the engine or the wormhole, the event will simply resolve one way or another, which won't work for our purposes. For this to work, we need the engine to reside in realspace and subspace simultaneously."

"I'm lost. But continue."

"At the moment the wormhole does or doesn't appear, the engine will fire a photon at an atom in the necessary configuration, along a preprogrammed trajectory. Because the engine exists in both subspace and realspace, it takes advantage of subspace's decoherence-free nature while transporting the ship located in realspace into another realspace. That is, another universe. It's my belief that every trajectory on the path integral corresponds to a different universe, and also that the universes loop back on each other. It's quite likely that you can return to our dimension from almost any other."

"But with infinity possible choices, wouldn't it take an eternity to map out?"

"Well, I'm not convinced there are infinity choices. A lot of the trajectories will likely lead to different coordinates within the same universe. It's possible there are only a handful of universes accessible using this method, and that trillions of the possible trajectories point to the same one. That would explain how the Progenitors are able to reappear at several points in the same system, after mapping it out."

"But how do they map those points so quickly? There's still the issue of reappearing in the same general location within a universe. Universes are big."

"So they are. But I'm assuming that all the trajectories corresponding with a single universe likely cluster together. Still, as you point out, we would need an engine that cycles through this process extremely quickly, collecting data all the while. It would need to be an automated process. We can install the engine with an AI intelligent enough to handle the task, but galactic law still forbids using one that would be smart enough to test my theory for us. As for the engine itself, I know it's possible, because I've already built it."

Husher raised his eyebrows. "So now you just need a volunteer." He nodded. "All right. I'll do it."

"You can't," Fesky said.

Husher turned to face her. "Why can't I? I already risked myself testing Ochrim's theories before."

"You weren't captain of the *Vesta* then. Kaboh managed to get you removed from command, and risking yourself was your only option for getting it back. That's not the case, now. This ship can't afford to lose her commanding officer."

"Who, then? There's not many I would trust with this, Fesky. Even the knowledge we might be on the verge of interdimensional travel is far too sensitive to risk getting into the wrong hands."

"I'll do it."

Husher shook his head. "I can't lose you, Fesky. You're my XO."

"You can find another XO if I don't return. Like you said, there's no one else we can trust with this, and it's too important not to test. I'll do it, Captain."

She's right, he realized. He turned back to Ochrim. "How big a ship do you think we can send?"

The scientist paused. "One roughly as big as the *Vesta*'s lifeboat, I should think. But I recommend starting with a starfighter, to test the theory. I don't think a Condor will cut it, this time—they don't have the energy capacity to ensure Fesky will be able to return to us. But a modified Python might."

Might. So much was uncertain about this, and losing his best friend was another thing Husher doubted he'd ever recover from.

But he also wouldn't recover from the Progenitors laying waste to the galaxy.

"All right," he said. "We'll start working on one of our reserve fighters."

CHAPTER 36

Every Parallel Fesky

"The engine is programmed according to a few of my theories about how the various dimensions are related," Ochrim told Fesky. "As soon as you leave this universe for the next and take the measurements I'll need for future calibration, you can simply give the AI the command to begin executing the first preprogrammed subroutine. It will then attempt to start honing in on the route for returning to this universe. If, after an hour, you still haven't reached a point in this universe that's near enough to the *Vesta* for you to fly back to her, then you should execute the second subroutine, which operates under a different set of assumptions. If that doesn't work, try the final subroutine."

"And if that still doesn't get me back?" Fesky asked.

"You're on your own. Feel free to test any other theory you might have about how the multiverse functions."

"I don't have a theory."

"Well, then." Ochrim cleared his throat.

The Python they'd spent the last week modifying sat in the center of the hangar deck. There was nothing left to do, and hesitating wouldn't serve anyone. Fesky strode toward it.

"Fesky," Husher called from where he stood near the bulkhead, hands folded behind his back. He approached her.

"Don't say anything that sounds like a goodbye," she said.

He stopped, then put on a smile that didn't look very enthusiastic to her. "Okay. Good luck, old friend."

"Thank you, human." With that, Fesky pulled herself into the cockpit and punched the button that would seal it around her.

She'd flown a Python during the Battle of Arrowwood, which had ended the Gok Wars. That had been the first time Pythons were deployed, and their advanced electronic warfare capabilities had dominated the engagement—the Gok sensors had been woefully inadequate for dealing with them.

After that, she'd only piloted a Python in a handful of training exercises. But she had decades of experience flying Condors, and many of the same principles applied. True, Pythons used Oculenses instead of the old tactical displays, but the new way had proved much more effective in combat, even if she wasn't altogether fond of it.

You're stalling, aren't you? As soon as she made the realization, she sent the command to Ochrim's quantum engine to isolate itself from the rest of the ship's systems in order to perform the feat that would place the engine in realspace and subspace simultaneously.

Here goes nothing. Husher had told her that when he'd first entered subspace, he lifted the Condor from the deck, to prevent the spherical wormhole from taking a chunk out of it. That wasn't necessary for Fesky, since it was only the engine that would—or wouldn't—be enveloped in a wormhole.

Husher had also told her that when he made the transition into subspace, he'd been surrounded by an infinite number of Hushers, stretching in every direction.

That didn't happen to Fesky. Indeed, there was barely anything to mark her transition at all, except that sensors told her the Python was no longer inside the hangar bay.

Switching to visual, she saw distant stars in the void, missing the trademark twinkle they would have had, viewed from within a planet's atmosphere. Here, they were static.

"I guess I made it." She told the computer to begin taking the readings Ochrim needed, some of which were designed to check whether physics operated in the same way here. Other tests would evaluate the color as well as the brightness of the stars she could see. Any occultations would be noted as well—when a planet or other body passed in front of a star, it said a lot about the planet's size, shape, and atmospheric properties.

If the physics of any of the universes Fesky visited *did* differ from her native universe, it was probable the atoms of her body would no longer be able retain the structure that made her a functioning organism. Ochrim had told her that. *He's just full of comforting news.*

According to the Ixan, he didn't expect that to happen. He said his theoretical "universal brane cosmology" should also mean physics would remain constant across the universes she visited. Possibly, that had just been his way of convincing her to test the theory. The conversation hadn't brought her much comfort either way.

At last, the readings had all been taken, and Fesky instructed the Python's engine to execute the primary subroutine. After a few long moments, it responded, flitting from universe to universe, working under the assumption Ochrim considered most likely—that the potentially trillions of trajectories that led to the same universe would cluster together. If that was true, it would just be a matter of mapping which "regions" of the path integral corresponded to which universes.

Easy.

She tried to watch the visual sensors as the engine worked, but she soon had to stop. The constant flickering—from starlight to no starlight, from the middle of a star system to stranded deep in the void—proved too much for her visual cortex to process.

So she shut off visual and didn't bother consulting the other sensors.

Not for the first time, it occurred to her that if Ochrim's quantum engine brought her into the middle of a star, or attempted to occupy the same space as a planet, she would die. He'd said that was extremely unlikely, since space tended to be overwhelmingly empty, but she found herself dwelling on it all the same.

After what seemed like an eternity, the engine stopped, leaving her on the periphery of a star system, in who knew what universe. She checked the elapsed time—fifty-six minutes.

Why did it stop?

She waited almost another hour, and she was about to execute the second subroutine when lidar and radar sensors began to populate her display with more data:

This was the Yclept System. And there was the *Vesta,* in formation with her battle group over Juktas.

I'm back.

It would take her the better part of a day to fly down to meet them, but she wasn't about to chance traveling through the universes again just to find a closer spot. She began the journey.

When at last she neared the supercarrier, she sent a transmission request directly to Husher's com. He answered immediately.

"Fesky?" Excitement filled his voice.

"Captain. Is that really you, or did I return to the wrong universe?"

"I think we're going to have to operate under the assumption that I'm really me, and you're really you."

"You're sure this isn't just a parallel universe, and you're not your twin?"

"All I know is that you left the *Vesta* twelve hours ago, and now you're back. As long as every parallel Fesky returns to a parallel Husher, then what's the difference, really?"

"Thinking about this is making my head hurt." Fesky said, brushing her talons through her crown feathers.

"Then why don't you come aboard. Ochrim's eager to examine the readings. If it turns out we really did succeed, we're leaving Yclept again, for longer this time. I'm planning to call on an old connection in Feverfew—the IU won't like us leaving again, but I intend to let them know about it this time, so they can send more ships here. If my Feverfew connection cooperates, then hopefully we can get the modifications made in time to implement this new tech soon."

"Who's your connection?"

"Do you remember Calum Ralston?"

Fesky paused. "Now I'm sure I'm in the right universe."

"Why do you say that?"

"Because the idea that there might be more than one Calum Ralston is too horrific for me to accept."

CHAPTER 37

Reporting for Duty

Chief Calum Ralston hobbled into the living room carrying a metal tray in shaking hands. "Want some tea?" he asked in a heavy Scottish accent, placing the tray on a circular table in the center of the room.

Husher counted the mugs. There weren't enough for everyone, even leaving out Fesky, whose beak didn't interface well with mugs.

"I can't believe you still live in the same house, Calum," Husher said, foregoing the tea so everyone else could have some. *Everyone able to drink it, anyway.*

Ralston shrugged. "Why change things up? I don't like change."

Fesky laughed, drawing a glare from the veteran. "Sounds kind of odd, coming from the man who helped topple the Commonwealth."

Snorting, Ralston said, "That was a bit different, what with them and Darkstream being about to destroy the universe and all, wasn't it? Anyway, I like change now even less than I did then. That happens when you get older. You'll see." Ralston sniffed, then turned his glare on Husher. "Wait a minute. You don't want me to help take down another government, do you? If that's why you're here, you can go fly, you bastards."

Tremaine spit his tea back into his mug, having just taken his first sip. That earned him a glare from Ralston, too.

"Don't like your tea?" the aging Scot said, volume rising sharply on the last word.

"No, it's just—well, it's ice cold."

"What?" Ralston snatched up a mug for himself and took a sip. "Oh," he said, replacing it on the tray. "Seems I forgot to boil the water."

Ochrim, about to drink from his mug, also placed his tea back on the tray, as quickly as he could. Probably, he was trying to be discreet, but Ralston didn't miss much.

"No government needs toppling," Husher said, in an attempt to move thing forward. "At least, if one does, we're not asking for your help in doing it."

"That's a relief," Ralston spat. "What do you want, then?"

"We need some pretty major modifications made to the *Vesta*'s lifeboat. I could file a request with the IGF, and they could seek approval from the IU, but the galaxy would likely be reduced to rubble by the time it got approved. I'm here to ask if there's anything you can do to speed the process up a bit."

"What's in it for me?'

Husher fought the urge to fix Ralston with a glare of his own. "Hopefully, the mods will help us beat the Progenitors, and you'll continue having a galaxy to live in."

"Ah. So you're appealing to my better nature."

"We're appealing to your will to live," Fesky snapped, her patience having apparently run out. *Which isn't the most surprising development.*

Ralston ignored her. "Well, the veterans we got together to take down President Hurst have kept in touch, for the most part. And a few of them do work in the Feverfew Shipyards. They're at the end of their careers, of course—a lot of them are overdue for retirement, if you ask me, even though they still choose to work. But they're high up in the ranks, by now. Might be I can ask them to make something happen."

"Thank you," Husher said.

"I'm not doing it for you," Ralston said. "I'm doing it because Senator Bernard would have wanted me to. She spent her career trying to build something, and I'm keen to help preserve what she helped build. It was your father that shot her, so I'm a bit hesitant to help you out at all. But the senator liked you, for some reason. I'll help you for her."

Husher felt his face heating. "My father was under the influence of the Ixa when—"

Putting up a hand, Ralston said, "Don't push your luck, Captain. I said I'd help. Now go back to your ship. Leave me with the mods you want done, and I'll let you know when the arrangements are made."

"Very well," Husher said, standing. The others stood, too. Before they left, he forced himself to speak again: "Thank you, Chief Ralston."

Back on the *Vesta*, he ordered his crew to start making the necessary preparations for the supercarrier to enter dry dock.

It took the better part of two days to make the arrangements—confirming clearance measures with the dry dock manager, clearing out the compartments that would be affected by the modifications, and a thousand other things. But at last, Husher settled into the command seat to work with Chief Noni to guide the *Vesta* into dry dock.

He opened his mouth to give the order to start moving toward the Feverfew Shipyards when the CIC hatch opened and a being entered. The figure was clad in strange, midnight armor with overlapping plates that cascaded downward to its feet, with a broad tail that swept the deck behind it.

The faceplate, however, was transparent—and the face that stared out at Husher seemed to be engulfed in water.

"Reporting for duty, Captain," Ek said.

CHAPTER 38

Face the Music

Captain Vanessa Harding sat at her desk with her hands clamped to the sides of her head, pulling her features backward as she poured over the reports her implant showed her. As was her habit, she'd had the device project them onto the surface of her desk, which acted as a screen. Scrolling through them was a matter of brushing her finger against the desktop.

She was responsible for fifty-five ships—keeping them running and feeding their occupants. Morale throughout the mostly civilian fleet had been high after they'd fled Hellebore and made it through Feverfew without the IGF apprehending them. But it hadn't taken much of drifting aimlessly through depopulated systems for morale to plummet back to the depths it had occupied ever since the Darkstream fleet had returned to the Milky Way.

We can't run forever. That was the realization that had quickly swept every ship. With no connections and nowhere to resupply, they had to stay on the run or turn themselves in. Rationing their food across the fleet would last them for three months at most, and the phrase "restricted diet" certainly didn't do much to cheer anyone up.

The other problem was that the darkgate network only extended so far. Yes, they'd evaded capture till now, but that would only last as long as the IGF was otherwise occupied. A concerted effort to hunt them down—to corner them in a dead-end system—would work. Vanessa knew that. The IU had apparently developed warp tech since Darkstream had fled the galaxy twenty years ago, which had enabled them to expand well beyond the darkgate network. But she didn't have access to that tech, and so she was trapped within it.

An alert told her that Plank, who captained the sole Quatro ship in the fleet, was hailing her. "Plank" was the name he'd chosen back on Eresos, to facilitate communication with humans.

"Hello, Captain," Vanessa said, trying not to sound as weary as she felt. She tried to avoid saying "Captain Plank," since it sounded a bit funny to her.

"Captain Vanessa Harding," the Quatro said, the deep timbre of his voice an antidote to any thoughts of humor, just as their situation was. "We walk the path of hopelessness and ruin. We must choose a new one."

"Yes," she said, nodding. "Things do look kind of bleak."

"I know nothing of this galaxy, and my ideas are limited for putting the fleet on better footing. But this was your home. Surely you know of an alternative to this predicament."

Vanessa hesitated. "I do," she admitted. "Though it's not one I'm eager to turn to."

"Why not?"

She sighed. "Not all of Darkstream fled the galaxy. Some employees were fine remaining, and many were low-level enough that they escaped prosecution for the company's crimes. But even some executives stayed, to face the music. I caught wind of one of those executives back while we were waiting in Hellebore, an old friend. Apparently he did five years in prison, got out, and landed a job with an interstellar shipping company almost right away."

"And you believe making contact with your friend might be of some benefit?"

Slowly, she nodded. "Maybe. He could keep us informed about what's going on in the galaxy at large—with the IU, and with the war. He might even be able to give us a lead on where we can resupply." *Though I fear the answer to that question is likely to lead down Pirate's Path.* Negotiating with criminals was not something she felt eager to involve tens of thousands of civilians in. *That said, I suppose I'm a criminal now, too.*

"I sense your reluctance in this matter," Plank said.

"Yes. As far as I know, my friend is working in an office station in the Quince System, which is more populated than it once was. Going there would be very risky. It might be best for me to take a smaller craft, with just a few others. In the meantime, I'd pass command of the fleet to you."

"Waiting for your return would be trying for everyone," the Quatro said. "Especially if it runs longer than expected."

"Yes."

"But we must do something. This is worth the risk, I think, Captain Vanessa Harding. You have my blessing in this."

I was afraid you'd say that. "All right, then. I'll start preparing for the journey now."

CHAPTER 39

Spire

Sitting around for the month it took Feverfew shipwrights to complete the work on the *Vesta* was one of the hardest things Husher had ever had to do.

Com drones entered Feverfew almost every day about new systems getting attacked by the Progenitors. They also contained rumors of more arrests made by the IU—of individuals with views they considered harmful to galactic security.

According to information he'd gleaned from the com drones, the IU had deployed more ships to the Yclept System, to cover for the *Vesta* leaving. No rebuke had arrived for abandoning his post, either by com drone or otherwise.

Surely they must know where we are. He supposed the government might just have too much occupying them to bother with reprimanding him right now. That said, he *did* pilot one of their seven remaining capital starships, and they seemed to have plenty of time to arrest people who held views they found distasteful, so it was strange they hadn't taken the time to contact him.

Oh well. Husher certainly wasn't bored while he waited. The Cybele city council welcomed his help in effecting the necessary repairs after the day of rioting, not to mention relocating citizens whose homes had been affected by the fires, whether scorched or reduced to cinders. Hundreds of crewmembers had volunteered to double up with others in order to make room for displaced citizens in the *Vesta*'s crew quarters. Far more bunks were offered than were needed, which made Husher quietly swell with pride.

He wasn't only waiting on mods, in Feverfew. He'd also ordered all the *Vesta*'s sensors recalibrated, along with a full hull integrity check, with any damage patched up. At last, the day came when the dry dock manager messaged Husher to inform him that the mods and repairs had all been made. Husher left the *Vesta* to inspect them, walking the mammoth hold with Fesky, Ochrim, Tremaine, Ayam...and Ek.

In her new exoskeleton, Ek towered several inches over even Ayam, who was otherwise the tallest among them. To allow her to control it, Ochrim had expanded on the Oculens technology that read brain waves, distributing it throughout the suit's helmet so that Ek could control it by thinking, in a way she said felt quite natural. So she could communicate, the helmet also featured sophisticated sensors that picked up on sound waves traveling through the water, cleaned them up, and output them as clear speech through speakers on the suit's exterior.

But the main reason for developing the suit had been to prevent the space sickness Ek had almost died from, twenty years ago. To do so, Ochrim had filled the suit with water that had high enough salinity for Ek to perpetually float, even as she walked around the *Vesta*—and now, the shipyards. The suit was a lot closer to her natural environment, and as long as she spent enough time in Ochrim's lab, performing calisthenic exercises in the large tank there, the Ixan said she should be fine.

For Husher, the upshot was that now, he would have access to Ek's keen perception in real-time. He'd already decided to confer the rank of commander on her, which he was sure Keyes would have done twenty years ago if it hadn't been for the United Human Fleet's restrictions on nonhuman personnel.

It felt good to get off the *Vesta* for a bit, even if only onto another space-locked structure. It felt even better to take in the modifications they'd made to his ship.

"Along with topping up our missile arsenal after the engagements in Yclept and Alder, the main modifications were made to the *Vesta*'s lifeboat," he told his officers. "In short, she's not a lifeboat any longer. She's a detachable craft capable of authentic interdimensional travel, and she's been fitted with a railgun and missile tubes. She also has a full sensor suite and a warp drive."

"I'm all for it, sir," Tremaine said. "But don't you think the IU might have a problem with us messing with their lifeboat? They seemed to think it was pretty important for their effort to attract new residents to the starship cities."

"I think that ship has basically sailed, Chief. So to speak. The rioting will prevent our city's population from increasing anytime soon, if you ask me." Even since reaching Feverfew, Cybele's population had been plummeting. As far as Husher could tell, everyone who wasn't a hardline ideologue and who could afford to leave had left. When you added in all the radicals he'd kicked off his ship, that represented a sharp decline. "Besides, the Union has a problem with many things I do. This isn't too bad, comparatively.

Technically, the detachable craft could still be used as a lifeboat. It'll just be a little more cramped in there, with all the new equipment."

"What are you going to name her?" Fesky asked.

"Actually, I thought I'd leave that job to you," Husher said. "Since you're going to be the one to captain her."

Fesky's beak opened and closed, and her feathers stood at attention. "Captain, I...I don't know what to say."

"You don't have to say anything. Come up with a name, and send me some proposals for who you'd like to take as your crew."

"I'll call her *Spire.* After the homeworld Wingers shared with Fins." Fesky's gaze shifted to Ek, who nodded.

"Very good." Husher met each officer's eyes in turn. "A new chapter in this war has just begun."

Toward the end of his watch, Husher found himself in the command seat, working with Noni to carefully guide the *Vesta* out of dry dock without damaging anything. The tedious process took almost a half hour, and as soon as they were out in open space, Ensign Fry spoke.

"Sir, a recorded transmission just came in from a com drone that recently entered the system," she said. "It's addressed to you."

"Play it, Ensign."

President Chiba appeared on the main display. "Captain Husher. It pains me to have to record this message, especially after granting you a presidential pardon for the crimes of which you've been found guilty. Betraying my trust as you have isn't much of a repayment. It's come to my attention that you're harboring aboard the *Vesta* a Quatro fugitive, who's guilty of breaking several of their laws. If you're at all interested in staying in command of your supercarrier, you will bring that Quatro to the Roundleaf System with all possible haste, where Quatro authorities will be on hand to arrest her. That is all."

The president vanished from the main display, and a tense silence settled over the CIC as Husher weighed his options.

At last, he realized there was only one thing he could do. "Nav, set a course for Roundleaf, via the Feverfew-Thistle darkgate."

CHAPTER 40

I'm Not Going to Ask

"You can't do this," Price told him, his voice tight as he stood over Husher's desk, hands balled into fists.

"First of all, you need to address me as 'captain' or 'sir.' Second, I can and will do whatever I decide is best for this ship and best for the galaxy."

The young pilot's eyes narrowed, but he said nothing.

"Sit down."

Slowly, Price sat.

"Rug is only one being," Husher said. "Do you really expect me to enter open rebellion against the Interstellar Union over one Quatro—a Quatro you sneaked onto my ship without my permission?"

"It's wrong whether it's one Quatro or a thousand," Price shot back. "You know her arrest won't be legitimate. You've seen the reasons the IU is arresting people for, lately. The Assembly of Elders' reasons will be even less legitimate. They're tyrants, obsessed with their own power. They only want Rug because she defied them."

"According to Rug."

Price's jaw tightened. "So you're planning to hand her over, then? Just like that?"

"I didn't say that."

"What are you saying, then, sir?"

Husher drew a breath. "Maybe the IU can be reasoned with. I managed to bring them around to waging this war in the first place. Maybe I can get them to back off on this."

"No way. The Elders won't allow it. God, you really are becoming just like a Union politician, aren't you, Captain? Trying to negotiate with people who have no interest in negotiating with you."

"Better that than have the galaxy fall apart, making us easy pickings for the Progenitors."

"Better to have the galaxy fall apart than let it become as hellish as the Elders made their own galaxy."

"I don't believe that."

"I do." Price's eyes were locked onto Husher's. "If you give them Rug, Oneiri leaves this ship."

"You can't leave. You're under my command."

"We agreed to follow your orders. We can just as easily decide to stop following them."

"That would make you insubordinate."

Jake laughed. "You wouldn't know anything about that, would you?"

Husher opened his mouth to deliver a retort—something about how he ought to throw Price in a cell—but he closed it again, as he'd been struck hard by déjà vu. This conversation was just like several he'd had with Captain Keyes back on the

Providence, except that he'd been in Price's position, and Keyes had been where Husher was now.

He'd often questioned Keyes's decisions, sometimes in what he knew was an inappropriate manner. But Keyes had needed him, just as Husher needed Price.

"I'll make my decisions to the best of my ability," he said at last. "And you'll make yours. That's all we can do."

Husher's com buzzed, and he picked it up from the table, finding a message from the second watch coms officer: "Sir, we're currently passing through the Dooryard System, and we've just received a transmission request from the *Marblehead*. Should I route it to your office?"

The *Marblehead*. That was one of the ships the Brotherhood had stolen from the IU, before kicking off all nonhuman crew.

"Put it through," he messaged back, and when it came, he instructed his Oculenses to play it on a blank section of the office wall, right next to the photo of the *Vesta*. He gave Price access to the conversation, via his implant. The mech pilot looked surprised at that, but he said nothing.

Captain Anthony Flores appeared on the wall, wearing a tight smile. "Captain," he said, glancing at Price before turning again to Husher. "How fortunate that the *Vesta* would be passing through the very system the Brotherhood has chosen as a gathering place."

"Define fortunate," Husher said.

"I mean the word in the sincerest way possible. Though they are not currently visible to your sensors, every ship we have commandeered from the IGF is in this system, concealed behind moons, planets, and asteroids. But we mean you no harm. Quite the opposite—we would like to meet with you. It's our belief that we stand to benefit each other greatly."

"How?"

"It would be remiss for me to get into details during this conversation. I don't speak for the entire Brotherhood, and our whole leadership should be represented in any such discussion. Will you meet with us, Captain?"

Husher studied the man's face for a long time, trying to get a read on his intention. Was this a trap, or did he really have a proposal? And if he did, should Husher be interested in anything he had to propose?

Price spoke up, then. "Captain, this is how you can do the right thing and refuse to hand Rug over to the IU. With the backing of a second large battle group, how could they demand anything of the *Vesta*, especially while they're busy fending off the Progenitors?"

Husher didn't answer. He continued to study Flores's face.

"It costs nothing to meet with us," Flores said. "Nothing except time, and I can promise you that it will be time well spent."

"All right," Husher said at last. "Send a single shuttle, and know that if my sensors pick up any of your warships trying to maneuver against us, I'm not going to ask before firing."

"Of course, Captain Husher," Flores said, though his smile had left his eyes.

CHAPTER 41

Best for the Galaxy

A knock came at his office hatch, and Husher pressed a button on his desk. "Come in," he said through the intercom.

The hatch opened, and his daughter entered. She closed it behind her, then walked to the chair and sat down.

"You're meeting with human supremacists," she said flatly.

"Yes."

"I'm not sure which surprises me more—that, or the fact that you want me at the meeting."

"They control eleven warships, Maeve. As I'm sure you've heard, at the end of our current voyage, the IU wants me to hand over the Quatro, Rug, to the Assembly of Elders. I'm not sure it's the right thing to do."

"Well, I'm sure an alliance with the Brotherhood isn't the right thing to do either. Why don't you hear the evidence against the Quatro, and then decide whether to give her to the Elders?"

Husher nodded. "That's what I plan to do. But having eleven more ships at my back will give me a much better bargaining position if I decide not to do it."

His daughter leaned forward, and for a moment, he was sure she was going to explode at him. But then, she didn't. Instead, she leaned back in the chair and studied him.

"The last time we talked, you showed me that I was being inconsistent when it came to silencing or even attacking Brotherhood supporters. That's why I got so angry—because you made me feel like a hypocrite, and you were right to do that. If I support unprovoked attacks on Brotherhood members, then I support them against everyone. I get that, now."

Husher opened his mouth to respond, then realized he had nothing to say. *Wow. That was unexpected.*

Shaking her head, Maeve said, "Listen, I know you think a lot of my generation has gone astray. And I know you really are trying to do the best thing for the galaxy. I get that, too, though I didn't before, and a lot of people still don't. But whatever you think about young people, they do own tomorrow. There's no getting away from that. So if you want to make a case for your way of doing things—for tradition, honor, order, or whatever you want to call it—then you'd better not be a hypocrite. Because young people can smell hypocrisy a mile away, and if they see you betraying what you claim to believe, you're done. You'll be written off before you even realize it's happening. And if the young really have gone astray, then you'll only make them more astray."

Husher nodded slowly. "Okay. Which of my beliefs do you think I'm betraying?"

"You say you want to do what's best for the galaxy, and like I said, I believe that. But you're focused on winning the war to the exclusion of everything else. That's a short-term solution, Vin, and if you sacrifice everything that's important to achieve it, then what's the point?"

He smiled at her. "You've given me a lot to think about. So you'll be at the meeting?"

Eyes narrowing, Maeve said, "You still plan to meet with them?"

"Yes. I do."

CHAPTER 42

The Table of Power

Husher met the Brotherhood leadership at their shuttle, with a squad of marines at his back. The Brotherhood had brought their own armed escort, who exited the airlock first to array themselves on either side of it.

Next, Captain Flores stepped out, wearing a jet-black uniform. He saluted Husher, who returned the salute.

"This way," Husher said, motioning to the hatch that led to the corridor. "We'll have our discussion in the conference room. My officers are waiting there."

"Thank you for coming personally to welcome us," Flores said as he fell into step with Husher. "Many would not have shown us that much respect, and the fact you did speaks to your honorable reputation."

Husher nodded. "Of course." He doubted everyone in the IU would use the word honorable to describe him, but he didn't feel like getting into that.

When they reached their destination, Husher took a seat at the far end of the conference table, at the head. The seats nearest the door had been left empty for the Brotherhood, and Flores settled in opposite from Husher. It was Husher's custom to give guests the seats closest to the hatch, to make them feel more at ease.

He noticed his daughter staring at him, from where she sat next to Commander Ayam. Inclining his head toward her, he turned back to Flores. "Let's waste no time. One way or another, the IU expects the *Vesta* in the Roundleaf System soon. What have you come here to propose?"

Flores spread his hands. "I know you want what's best for humanity. I want the same. I—"

"I want what's best for the galaxy."

"Isn't it the same thing?"

"There are other species in the galaxy."

Flores smiled wanly. "Yes. Let's get that matter out of the way, shall we? I know we both hold views the other finds distasteful. Please rest assured that we would not make any alliance between us conditional on you expelling nonhumans from your ship. I understand that you value them, and we don't seek to oppose that."

"Well, that's a relief," Husher said flatly.

"Be at ease," Flores said, nodding. "Now, as I've already alluded, I'm here to propose an alliance. A partnership. We both know the IU has not been conducting themselves in a rational manner. They've been violating their own principles left and right, and they've leapt into bed with a government that's even worse. These unjust arrests are only the latest example of their tyranny, but they won't be the last. Are we in agreement so far?"

"Basically, yes," Husher said.

"Good. We are both rational people, Captain Husher. That's the difference between us and the IU. They pose a clear threat to both of us, and to the war effort as well. I think you know that. And so I would put it to you that a partnership would grant us both security. Together, we would have greater leverage over the IU, and if things came to blows, then we would be better positioned in that regard as well."

Husher folded his hands on the conference table. "You said that you wouldn't ask me to kick out my nonhuman crew. But surely you would want to make an alliance conditional on something."

"You're very perceptive. You're right, there is something we want, but I doubt it's anything like you're thinking. Captain, we don't expect the Union to last very much longer. Their own corruption and rot renders them barely able to win this war, let alone survive its aftermath. All the Brotherhood wants in return for lending you our aid is a seat at the table in whatever society takes shape after the war."

Husher paused. "You're not referring to just any table. You want a seat at the table of power."

Faltering for just a second, Flores said, "Yes."

With that, Husher began to contend with what he'd known all along, on some level. By entering an alliance with the Brotherhood, he would bolster them. Lend them legitimacy. And even though he condemned their views, by aligning himself with them, he would be tacitly endorsing them.

Maybe allying with the Brotherhood was the only path to victory through the thicket of brambles this war had become. But if it meant helping the Brotherhood shape the society that came after, it wasn't worth it to him.

"I support you having a seat at the table," Husher said. "By which I mean, I will defend your right to express your views, however repugnant I find them." He glanced at Maeve. "But I won't help you win a seat at the table of *power.* So my answer is no, Captain Flores. I've heard you out, and I've made my decision. There will be no partnership between us."

A brittle silence fell over the conference room as the Brotherhood leaders in attendance stiffened in their chairs. For their part, Husher's officers seemed to relax in theirs. He may have just consigned them all to defeat and death, but even if he had, they would die with clear consciences.

Flores rose to his feet. "You will come to regret your decision," he said, and he left the conference room, the other Brotherhood members filing out behind him.

Husher turned to the pair of marines stationed near the hatch. "Take the rest of your squad and see them to their shuttle," he ordered.

The marines both saluted. "Yes, sir," they said in unison.

"All right, everyone," Husher said to his officers. "The show's over, and we have a meeting with the IU to make. Before that, we might even have an engagement on our hands, depending on what Flores meant by his statement that I'll regret my decision."

The officers stood, saluted him, and left.

With that, only he and Maeve remained. They both rose to their feet and headed for the hatch.

Before Husher could leave, she wrapped him in an embrace, pressing her head against his chest.

"Thank you, Dad," she said.

CHAPTER 43

One Way or Another

The shuttle's airlock cycled through its usual processes, and the inner hatch opened, admitting Anthony Flores and the rest of the Sapient Brotherhood leaders. Their armed escort followed soon after.

In silence, Flores made his way to his crash seat halfway down the shuttle's port side. None of the other leaders spoke either. No doubt they were contemplating the implications of what had just happened.

Once everyone was aboard, the pilot lifted off from the *Vesta*'s flight deck, heading for the airlock, which was big enough for shuttles and starfighters to pass through.

"Do you think Husher will try to stop us from reaching our ships?" Captain Reggie Butler asked.

"No," Flores said. "I meant what I said about his honor."

"He's an honorable fool."

"Time will determine the veracity of that statement. But for us, our decision is made clear. We gave Husher the chance to save himself. We turned to a member of our own species, and he spurned us. No matter. We have been loyal to humanity every step of the way, and we will remain loyal—but in a way that will prove more painful than it could have been."

Butler nodded. "To save the species from the IU...we know what we have to do."

"We must take Teth's offer."

"Yes," Butler said, nodding, and the gesture was mirrored by the other Brotherhood leaders in the shuttle.

"The Interstellar Union will fall," Flores said. "One way or another."

CHAPTER 44

Political Prisoner

"**T**ransitioning into Roundleaf now, Captain," Winterton said.

"Acknowledged, Ensign."

Fifteen minutes later, Winterton had more news for him: "There are two capital starships in orbit around Thebes, along with their respective battle groups and five Quatro warships."

"Wow," Tremaine said. "That's quite a welcoming party."

"Indeed," Husher said. "Nav, set a course that takes us close enough for real-time communication, but no closer."

"Aye, sir."

Husher shifted in his command seat, his discomfort as much to do with his inner struggle as with the unyielding chair. *They've certainly gathered together a lot of muscle to greet us with.* Clearly, the IU had anticipated that he might have reservations about handing over Rug.

The *Vesta* proceeded down the Roundleaf System's gravity well, her battle group maintaining a dispersed V behind her. It was a stately arrangement, and whether it was considered a formality or a battle formation would depend on how paranoid whoever you asked was feeling.

At last, they reached real-time communication range, and a transmission request came in from the *Eos.* Husher told his Coms officer to put it on the main display and to give everyone access to the conversation—not just everyone in the CIC, but everyone in the battle group, fleet member and civilian alike.

Captain Katrina Norberg appeared, fixing Husher with her hawklike gaze. "Captain Husher."

"Hello, Captain Norberg. Can I ask the reason for such a large military presence in this system?"

"Roundleaf's sensor web has been getting the strange readings we've come to recognize as precursors to an attack."

"I see." Husher happened to know that the IGF and Quatro ships had been here before they'd started getting those readings, but he didn't reveal that.

Norberg seemed about to speak again when she did a double take at the XO's chair.

"Captain Husher, is that…what is that sitting in the seat meant for Commander Fesky?"

"This is Ek," Husher answered. "She's a Fin."

"I know who Ek is. But…*this* is Ek? How? And what manner of suit is she wearing?"

"It's a long story, and I'm sure we have other matters to discuss."

"Yes," Norberg said, recovering her composure. "We do. Such as where your lifeboat might be. It appears to be missing. Did you have cause to evacuate Cybele on your way here?"

"No. The few citizens still interested in living in the city are there now."

"Then where is your lifeboat?"

"Never mind that."

"Captain Husher, I *demand* to—"

"You'll be making a lot of demands on behalf of the IU today, Captain Norberg," he said. "I think you should pace yourself. Let's get to the reason I was called here. I'm called on to turn over the Quatro who I have aboard my ship to the Assembly of Elders. Before I do that, I want to know why. I'd also be interested in knowing how the IU knew she was on the *Vesta*." The only time Rug had deployed from the supercarrier had been to retake the orbital defense platform over Juktas, and that didn't seem like the type of colony to willingly share intelligence with the IU.

Norberg scoffed. "We're not about to reveal our source to you. As for why we're demanding you turn the Quatro over, it's because she's a fugitive."

"Okay, but for what reasons? What crimes did she commit?"

Norberg continued to meet Husher's gaze unflinchingly, but even that told him something—her eyes were too wide, for one. "That Quatro and her cohorts violated multiple laws designed to preserve the peace and keep the Quatro public safe."

"Okay. What were the laws?"

Norberg continued to stare at him, not answering.

"Were they laws that prohibited disagreeing with the government? Laws that required unquestioning obedience from Quatro citizens? Because I don't consider laws like that to be good ones."

"I'm not familiar with the exact laws the Quatro violated, Captain. All I know is that she's a criminal."

Husher laughed. "I think you are familiar with them, Norberg. I think you know exactly what laws, and I think I've already described them accurately. If you didn't know what laws she broke, you could simply check with the Quatro in the ships nearby and get back to me. We've got time. But you're not doing that, because you know I won't agree with your reasons for wanting to give Rug to the Elders."

"Rug?"

He ignored the question. "How do you think this is going to end, Captain?"

"I'll tell you how it's going to end. You're going to give us that Quatro, or you'll be forced to."

"That's what I thought. And the answer's no."

Norberg's posture grew even more rigid. "Very well. Captain Husher, on behalf of the Interstellar Union, I hereby relieve you from duty."

"I don't accept that, either," he said, and he motioned toward his Coms officer with a cutting gesture.

Ensign Fry terminated the transmission.

"Put me through to the entire battle group, Ensign."

"Yes, sir. It's done."

"Captains of the battle group and crew. Right now, you are no doubt being contacted with orders to turn on me. If you decide to follow those orders, that's your prerogative. The forces aligned against us are powerful, and it's possible you disagree with my point of view. But before you make your decision, I'm asking you to hear me out. Hopefully our service together will move you to give me that much.

"The Sapient Brotherhood approached me proposing an alliance, and I turned them down because I won't support their goals. You already know that. But I want you to know that I've decided not to support the Interstellar Union's goals either. I can't support them. I can't stand by as they arrest people merely for holding beliefs they consider undesirable. Today, I'm being asked to hand over a being as a political prisoner. If I agree to that because it's convenient for me to do so, then what will I be asked to do tomorrow? What will *you* be asked to do tomorrow, if you turn on me now? I refuse to live in a society that condones the things the IU has done, and I'm willing to fight for what the IU was supposed to be in the first place."

He nodded at Fry, who stopped the broadcast. That done, they waited, for what seemed like an eternity. Meanwhile, on the tactical display, both the IGF and the ovoid Quatro ships were creeping closer while spreading out to surround the *Vesta*.

"The *Hero* has confirmed their support of you, Captain," Fry said. "Captain Hall of the *Resolution* just followed suit." She paused, staring at her console. "The other two captains support you as well."

"Good," Husher said. It wasn't much—not against the forces arrayed against them. But it was something. He turned to his Tactical officer. "Tremaine?"

The man nodded. "Prepping the first barrage now, Captain."

CHAPTER 45

Under Heavy Fire

"Captain Norberg likely will not expect the *Vesta*'s battle group to side with you, Captain," Ek said from the XO's seat. "I recommend striking at once, with ferocity."

"I like the way you think, Commander." If Husher could use the element of surprise to neutralize one of the capital starships, it would go a long way toward evening the odds. "Coms, order our battle group ships to load every forward tube with missiles and fire them at the *Promedon* at once."

"Aye, Captain."

"Missiles away, sir," Tremaine said, and Husher watched on the Tactical display as a mix of Banshees, Gorgons, and Hydras left the *Vesta* to scream across space toward the *Promedon.*

Promedon's battle group moved to intercept the barrage with missiles of their own, but the Quatro ships flanking it did nothing. Likely, they saw no need.

Then the two destroyers and two missile cruisers on Husher's side loosed their barrage.

That sent the enemy formation into a panic. The Quatro warships sped forward, lasers lancing out to intercept the incoming rockets.

That's right. Use up your capacitor charge.

Together, the *Promedon*, her battle group, and the two Quatro ships managed to cut what began as a nearly four hundred-strong barrage down to around seventy, and most of those were mopped up by the *Promedon*'s point defense systems, supplemented by secondary lasers.

But not all of them. Seven missiles made it through, blowing a massive hole in her prow.

"Let's twist the knife," Husher said. "Fire our primary laser into that breach, Tremaine."

"Yes, sir. Firing laser."

Seconds later, the already jagged metal began to twist and warp even more. Massive explosions began to cover the area as the beset capital starship backed away at speed.

Her battle group sprang forth, launching a volley of Banshees at the *Vesta*, supplemented mightily by the *Eos*. That forced Husher to redirect his attention to defending his supercarrier, allowing the *Promedon* to pull back and lick her wounds.

He'd wanted to destroy her completely, but taking down a capital starship wasn't so easy, despite the mighty blow they'd dealt. The *Promedon* was still in the fight, but her crew would no doubt be suffering from a serious case of nerves.

"The *Eos* is launching Pythons, sir," Winterton said. "According to the last reports we received from Command, we know one of their squadrons to be subspace-capable."

Husher nodded. *Thank God none of the Promedon fighters have gotten the upgrades.* "It's about time we scrambled our own Pythons. Coms, pass the order along to Commander Ayam. Tell him missile defense is our main priority for now—except for neutralizing the enemy subspace fighters if at all possible."

"Aye, sir."

"When you're finished with that, tell our missile cruiser captains to start targeting down the Quatro ships, one by one. From what we saw in Hellebore, they have conventional weaponry, and their ships are designed to be multipurpose, meaning they're decent at everything but excellent at nothing. Heavy barrages from two dedicated missile cruisers should overwhelm them—especially if they mix in a healthy dose of Gorgons. None of the enemy captains are used to dealing with stealth missiles, so I expect Gorgons to have an outsized impact today."

"I'll pass that on, Captain."

"Very good. As for the destroyer captains, tell them they're on missile defense with us. We can expect to be under heavy fire from here on out, so for now, the missile cruisers represent our only offense. Tremaine, assign secondary lasers to assist with point defense."

"Aye, sir."

"Winterton, we also have no experience being targeted with stealth missiles. I need you to stay vigilant, conducting constant active scans of the battlespace. The second you detect an incoming Gorgon, send its telemetry over to Tactical. Tremaine, I want you to answer every Gorgon with two Banshees, and be sure to monitor their progress, staying ready to follow up if the Banshees get taken out."

Both officers acknowledged the orders, the tension in their voices evident. This engagement had a lot of moving pieces, and they'd rarely faced this much firepower since the war began.

"Rely on your backshops, everyone. Don't try to do everything yourselves. We can win this engagement, but only if we maximize every asset at our disposal."

The enemy Air Group darted forward, maneuvering much more aggressively than Husher would have expected, especially given how effectively the *Vesta* and her accompanying destroyers were blanketing the space around them with missiles and lasers. *They must be eager to put their subspace Pythons to work.* Maybe too eager. The problem was, Ayam wouldn't know which squadron was comprised of subspace fighters until they vanished.

"Tremaine, fire a spray of kinetic impactors at the enemy Pythons while we still have a clean shot."

"Aye, Captain."

Husher returned to his study of the tactical display. His carrier group was holding firm so far, but the first Quatro ship had yet to fall—that was taking longer than he'd expected. If they didn't start knocking down the enemy's numbers soon, the sheer weight of them would prove too much.

CHAPTER 46

Enemy Subspace Squadron

Ayam's Oculens tactical overlay was filled with red-tinged miniature representations of enemy Pythons. The opposing Air Group's aggression surprised him. *Looks like they want to end this quickly.* Probably by getting Gorgons close. Or their own subspace-capable squadron. Unopposed, that could quickly spell game over for the *Vesta*.

He'd kept his own subspace squadron at the rear of the *Vesta*'s Air Group, with full knowledge of exactly how valuable they were.

"Enemy Pythons seem focused on full-squadron and half-squadron tactics," he told the rest of his pilots. "That tells me they hope to get in some alpha strikes on the *Vesta* or on some of our battle group ships. I want all non-subspace capable Pythons to group into preassigned finger-four formations, and be ready to split into partner pairs. This is about outflanking the enemy squadrons and dismantling them with surgical strikes. Especially if you spot a squadron that's close to getting in position for an alpha strike."

A transmission came in from the CIC, then. It was Tremaine, the Tactical officer: "Commander, I spotted an incoming Gorgon too late to do anything about it. Nearby turret batteries are tied up with other things. It's going to fly near your subspace squadron—think you can take care of it?"

Ayam clacked his beak, not happy about putting subspace fighters on the line for missile defense. "I'm on it," he said, his speech clipped. Then he jumped on a squadron-wide channel. "We have an incoming Gorgon. I'll take care of it. Watch my six."

Although he'd selected his subspace pilots for their top-notch skills, Ayam wouldn't trust anyone except himself to go after the missile. The subspace Pythons were too valuable to entrust the job to anyone but the best.

He glanced at the missile's telemetry, which Tremaine had supplied to him just a few seconds ago. Then he engaged gyroscopes to angle his engines away from the missile and accelerate toward it.

It was going to be a near thing—the missile was already close by, otherwise Tremaine wouldn't have asked for his help. Kinetic impactors sailed from Ayam's main gun the moment he had a stable firing solution.

The Gorgon detonated just a few dozen meters from his fighter, leaving him no choice but to pass through its explosion, which dissipated fast, thankfully.

His vision washed red—kinetic impactors flashed toward him from an enemy Python squadron who'd caught him out of formation.

Ayam activated his spherical wormhole just in time, leaving realspace for subspace. He whirled his bird around, pointing the main engine in the opposite direction and executing an engine burn back toward where he knew his squadron would be waiting in realspace.

Before transitioning back in, he performed a quick scan of subspace's oppressive blackness. *Nothing.* He was alone in here, for now.

He reentered realspace in almost perfect formation with his subspace squadron.

"Fancy flying, Commander," said his second-in-command, Lieutenant Cyn.

"There's a lot more where that came from," Ayam said. "And we'll need every bit of it."

He'd kept an eye on the tactical situation as he'd spoken, and as he said the last word he noticed one of the enemy squadrons wink out of existence—right at the front of their Air Group.

Wow. Gutsy of them to expose themselves like that. Although, he supposed the enemy had put their subspace Pythons in the last place Ayam would have looked.

Fingers flying over the small console between his legs, he asked the computer for the enemy subspace squadron's vector and speed at the moment they vanished.

Bingo. He painted a point thousands of kilometers to the right of the enemy Pythons' exit point and forwarded it to his squadron's computers. Then he got back on the squadron-wide. "Make for the point I just marked, matching my acceleration. Do not transition to subspace until I say so. Go now."

With that, he punched it. His Python leapt forward, tearing across the battlespace. "Clear a path," he squawked after hammering his console to put him on an Air Group-wide channel.

Vesta fighters began peeling out of the way. It was still occasionally necessary to dodge Banshees and Hydra segments, but the subspace fighters had already accumulated enough speed that, as long as they avoided impact, the missiles wouldn't have a hope of catching up, whether they'd been programmed to prioritize Pythons as targets or not.

Ayam's sensors weren't showing any Gorgons, which could either be a good thing or a very bad one.

That question was answered immediately, as one of the fighters on the left side of his squadron blew up, followed almost immediately by another.

"Should we transition to subspace?" Cyn asked, voice strangled with tension.

"Not yet," Ayam grunted, flexing and unflexing muscles all over his body to fight the crushing force of increasing Gs. As if that wasn't bad enough, a Banshee flashed toward him, and when he edged his bird out of the way, he ended up in the path of another.

An enemy squadron of Pythons took notice of Ayam's fourteen remaining subspace fighters, their speed no doubt telegraphing to the enemy that they were doing something important, if not exactly what that thing was. Either way, the opposing Pythons accelerated toward them, letting loose with kinetic impactors, filling the space ahead of Ayam and his squadron.

"Commander?" his second said.

"Lay on more speed, now!"

To their credit, his pilots followed the order immediately.

"Get ready to generate wormholes on my mark," Ayam said.

They were almost at the impactor-riddled region of space.

"Commander!" Cyn yelled.

"*Mark!*" Ayam yelled back.

They transitioned to subspace—at least, twelve of them did. Another must have fallen to the impactor barrage.

He had no time to process that, as his calculations had been spot-on: the enemy subspace fighters were right in front of them, on a direct collision course.

"Impactors!" Ayam shrieked. "Blanket the area, and follow up with Sidewinders!"

His Pythons' guns blazed, taking out seven enemy fighters. The Sidewinders accounted for the remaining nine, with the last one going down right in front of Ayam's fighter. Shrapnel battered his Python's hull, sending tremors throughout the entire structure, and his vision washed red once more.

But he made it through. One of his missile launchers was damaged, and his nose was dented...but otherwise he was in fighting form.

His ears filled with the cheering of his subspace pilots as they realized what they'd done.

At the expense of three subspace-capable Pythons. He didn't like that, but he had to acknowledge that the trade had been an extremely good one. Taking out the entire enemy subspace squadron would have a big impact on this engagement. It could easily make the difference between survival and death.

"Let's press the advantage," Ayam ground out, refusing to let their victory distract him. "If we transition back in now, we'll be right in the middle of the enemy fighters. Let's pop back in, take some out, and pop out again. We're the only ones on this battlespace with subspace capabilities now, people. If we don't squeeze that for everything it's worth, we're idiots."

"Yes, sir," came the reply, from his twelve remaining pilots.

"Let's go now." They transitioned back into realspace, chose their targets, and fired.

CHAPTER 47

Filled With Fire

Captain Zora Sawyer watched the tactical display in disbelief as eleven IGF ships crossed the Larkspur System toward Thessaly, advancing on the colony's orbital defense platforms.

They used to be IGF ships, anyway. She'd read the reports about the Sapient Brother commandeering them.

But their presence in Larkspur, while disconcerting, wasn't the most surprising thing about their actions. It was the fact that they were moving toward a heavily defended Union core world as though they could reasonably expect to endanger it.

That wasn't very likely. Zora commanded the *Zeus*, a destroyer and the flagship of a ten-strong battle group of warships with fully stocked arsenals. Ten wasn't as much as eleven, but when you added in Thessaly's full complement of orbital defense platforms, as well as the top-tier fighter pilots that made up its planetary defense group...

...the Brotherhood didn't stand a chance.

"They're decelerating, ma'am," her sensor operator said as the approaching battle group crossed the halfway point between the

Larkspur-Shadbush darkgate and Thessaly. "At that rate, they'll come to rest just within range of this defense platform." He marked the one he meant on the tactical display.

Zora nodded, still pondering what the Brotherhood could possibly hope to accomplish. That they'd been able to commandeer eleven IGF warships was shocking; something she never would have predicted happening in today's society. But even their overgrown battle group was no match before the might of the IU.

"Coms, tell the other captains to move their ships up the planet and distribute them along the equator."

"Yes, Captain."

Despite her confidence, Zora recognized that eleven warships did pose a threat to a defense platform, if it wasn't properly supported. Should the Brotherhood launch an all-out assault on one, she wanted the other defenders to be ready to assist. *This is no time to suffer a hole getting blasted in Thessaly's defense.* It would take months to replace an orbital defense platform, and who knew when the next Progenitor attack might be? Larkspur had been one of the seventeen systems whose sensor web had recently detected the telltale anomalous readings, though so far it had remained untouched. Other systems hadn't been so lucky.

At last, the Brotherhood arrived at the destination her sensor operator had predicted. They immediately began throwing missiles at the defense platform.

Zora nodded. "Coms, tell the rest of our battle group to move up to support. Tactical, use Banshees to pick off what missiles we can, and send the defense platform operators your targeting data, so that we don't aim at the same ones."

Both officers she'd given orders to answered in the affirmative, and Zora monitored the tactical display as the besieged orbital platform defended itself.

Eleven ships did indeed pose a threat, but even so, she wasn't overly worried. Since defense platforms had no need for locomotion, all the mass that would otherwise have been devoted to engines, fuel, and supplies was devoted to a massive arsenal instead. It would take time for the Brotherhood to overwhelm that arsenal—time they didn't have, as nine IGF ships converged on their position and began lobbing missiles of their own at the Brotherhood's stolen ships.

Seeing that, Zora actually began to feel glad that the Brotherhood had decided to attack Thessaly. The thought that she might be responsible for putting an end to them was doing a lot for her mood, and when the Brotherhood ships started pulling away from the concentrated attack, she knew what to do.

"Coms, order the other captains to give chase, in battle spread formation. The enemy ships are in disarray. We can start targeting them down, one by one." If she could neutralize the entire battle group, or even secure their surrender, then this would be a productive day indeed.

She watched the nine other IGF ships move in for the kill, crossing the tactical display like lions stalking prey.

Then her Coms officer turned toward her, the color draining from his face. "Ma'am," he whispered.

"Yes, Ensign? What is it?"

"An orbital defense platform on the other side of the planet is under attack. They're relaying their sensor feed to us in real-time."

Eyes locked on the Coms officer's face, Zora spoke slowly: "Patch the visual through to the main display."

As she watched the defense platform's feed, it felt like an iron fist had gripped her stomach and squeezed.

Five Progenitor destroyers had appeared underneath the platform, and four of their carriers were suspended above it. All nine ships were unloading on the unsupported platform, their savage robots pouring across space by the hundreds.

"Temperature readings show superheating in three places along the bottom surface of the platform," her sensor operator said. "It's—"

Before he could finish, fire filled the visual feed, which went dark.

CHAPTER 48

Act as Turrets

Jake burst from Flight Deck Omicron's airlock, finding his first target by feel more than data from any sensor. Or maybe the alien mech merely wove the sensor data into a tapestry of emotion.

It didn't matter. Intention sprang from his body like an arrow, and he pointed two cannons that way, firing. Twin energy bursts leapt into space, headed toward nothing. But seconds later, an enemy Python occupied their path, and it exploded.

One down.

Oneiri surged from the airlock behind him, forming up.

"Don't stray far from the ship," he told them over a team-wide channel. "The fighters we faced back in Steele almost did us in, and there were only eight of them. Today, we face hundreds. Be ready to fall back on my command. Let's go!"

Oneiri surged into space, rockets streaming forth in all directions. Two more Pythons went down, and with that, the enemy Air Group began to take notice of them. A squadron changed course, screaming toward them through the void in a wall formation.

"Disperse," Jake barked. "Let's not offer them a cluster of targets."

Oneiri spread out, neutralizing the initial wave of Sidewinders the Pythons sent at them.

Kinetic impactors were next, but even the MIMAS sensors were sophisticated enough to zoom in on each Python and track where its gun was pointing. Jake's mech dream used scarlet to paint shifting lines of fire across space, and he maneuvered laterally to avoid them all. The others did the same.

The problems started when the Pythons split their formation, half of them braking to stay ahead of the mechs while the other eight screamed past to get behind them. Suddenly, Oneiri was boxed in, caught in the crossfire of sixteen pilots gunning for them hard.

Now is the moment, Jake's mech whispered to him, as it so often did since the day he'd claimed it, back on Bronson's destroyer. *Merge with me, or you and your friends will be lost in this storm.*

For a moment, the mech's whispers rang like truth in Jake's ears, and he reached toward it like a drowning man reaches for passing driftwood.

Then, he clamped down hard on himself. *No. If I do that, we'll all be lost anyway.*

"Follow me," he yelled over the team-wide instead, rocketing up to escape the canyon of death the Python squadron had created.

The others responded immediately, though the dream washed out Marco's mech, all in red. The MIMAS was taking heavy fire, and it couldn't handle any more.

Jake's world narrowed, until it consisted only of the three starfighters shooting at Marco's mech. Time slowed as he fired once, twice, three times—a trio of energy blasts, all following completely different vectors.

Three Pythons were consumed in fire.

"Cover Marco!" he screamed as time resumed its normal flow. Oneiri banded together at the top of the Pythons' canyon, picking off the starfighters one by one, until the remaining seven fled, covering their own retreat with impactors that sailed past Oneiri, toward the supercarrier. Two more Pythons went down before they escaped.

"The starfighters' agility trumps ours in space," Jake said. "Back to the airlock, everyone. We'll remain on the hull around it and act as turrets. We're going to keep the outer airlock door open—be ready to duck inside it the moment you're taking heavy fire."

Oneiri arranged themselves as he'd instructed. "Not you, Spirit. Your MIMAS is toast if it takes any more hits."

The MIMAS' head swung toward him. "But Jake, I—"

"I was giving an order, not opening a line of dialog. Go inside and get repaired. We don't know how soon it'll be till we need you again."

Without another word, Marco went inside the airlock, closing the outer door long enough for it to pressurize and admit him.

Jake selected his next target and fired. Another Python went down, which satisfied him. Revenge was a harmonious song, sung to him by the alien mech.

CHAPTER 49

Something Has to Give

"The enemy subspace squadron still hasn't emerged back into realspace?" Husher asked in disbelief.

"It hasn't, sir," Winterton said. "Unless they experienced some unknown malfunction, it seems likely Commander Ayam and his squadron managed to neutralize every enemy subspace fighter."

"Hmm." *That would have been nice to know.* Although, he wasn't about to chastise Ayam for failing to share the information with the CIC. The Winger had been quite busy since reentering the battlespace, taking out enemy fighters by the dozen with near impunity. The CAG made use of the ability to flit in and out of subspace like he'd been doing so for his entire career, instead of just a few weeks. And now, the *Vesta*'s subspace squadron was nearing a Quatro warship, which was scrambling to respond, filling empty space with kinetic impactors—no doubt trying to anticipate where the fighters would reappear.

So far, the missile cruisers in Husher's carrier group had only managed to take out one of the five Quatro warships. The other four were still in play, along with both capital starships' battle groups, and the *Eos* herself.

"Take heed, Captain," Ek said. "the *Promedon* prepares to reenter the fray."

Husher returned his gaze to the tactical display, grimacing. The wounded capital starship did seem to be rallying. It was edging around the battlespace, no doubt to fire on the *Vesta* from a distance and add to the mounting pressure being applied to her.

As if on cue, Winterton said, "The *Promedon* is scrambling her own Air Group, Captain."

"Acknowledged," Husher said, trying not to wince. Even with all the enemy fighters Ayam's squadron had managed to take out, the *Vesta*'s Pythons would still be heavily outnumbered.

He monitored the tactical display as Ayam and his subspace fighters closed with the Quatro's ship, vanishing whenever threatened by its ordnance and reappearing in unexpected locations. Husher knew that doing so would require abrupt reversals of vector—meaning intense G forces bearing down on the pilots' bodies. *They have to be getting fatigued.* Yet, they showed no sign of slowing.

The subspace fighters appeared again, speeding along a vector the Quatro captain clearly hadn't anticipated. They executed an alpha strike—and the enemy ship blew up.

Husher's fist clenched in victory, and some of his other officers looked grimly satisfied, but no one cheered. The Quatro ship's destruction was too insignificant in the face of how many warships were still attacking the *Vesta*.

Our subspace squadron can't destroy all those ships in time. Even if they could, the demanding maneuvers required of the pilots had to be exhausting them. Soon, they would start getting sloppy, start making mistakes, and when that happened, Husher doubted even their subspace capability would save them.

With the damaged capital starship and her Air Group reentering the fray, it was difficult to see how he could win, as things stood.

Husher's entire battle group was now using secondary lasers to supplement point defense, their capacitors draining steadily. Even the missile cruisers, who'd originally been focused mainly on offense, were now devoting most of their missile fire to preventing enemy rockets from making it to their hulls. The same went for the *Vesta*'s Air Group—they remained near the warships' point defense systems, doing everything they could to take down incoming missiles and enemy fighters. But with the second enemy Air Group approaching, anyone could see it wouldn't be enough.

Something has to give.

Then, something did—but not in the way Husher had hoped. The *Eos*' laser lanced across space, striking the missile cruiser on the *Vesta*'s port side square on her prow.

The cruiser maneuvered laterally to escape the beam, but two enemy fighter squadrons swept in, pincering the warship.

Two clean alpha strikes, and the *Hero* exploded.

A coldness spread through Husher's chest as he contemplated the very real possibility that everything he'd worked for could fall apart, today. Whether it was the Progenitors slaughtering everyone in the galaxy or the Interstellar Union growing increasingly tyrannical—it didn't really matter, did it? Either outcome would mean Husher had failed.

Come on, Fesky...where are you?

CHAPTER 50

Exploit Viciously

"How much longer?" Fesky squawked at her Nav officer.

"It's difficult to say, Captain," Chief Devar said. "I don't recognize this route."

Fesky felt her feathers stiffening at that, and she attempted to calm herself by breathing deeply. "It didn't take this long when we mapped the Roundleaf System for entry points. I thought the AI was supposed to optimize for the quickest path through the universes."

"It is, ma'am. I think that may be the problem. We left our own universe at a different point from our original departure point, when we first mapped Roundleaf. That meant we entered a different universe, or maybe a different region of the same universe. Either way, the computer thought it saw a way to shorten our journey, but I think it calculated wrong."

"What? How can it be wrong?" Fesky realized she was shrieking, and she focused on her breathing again.

"Ochrim's theory of how the universes are spatially related may have some kinks that need ironing out. It could be that timing plays a part—I'm just guessing, here. Either way, once the computer finds a path it recognizes, it should get back on track."

Clacking her beak, Fesky fell silent, her chest tight with worry over what the *Vesta* might be facing right now. She checked the mission time and saw that they were now officially overdue to arrive in Roundleaf to back up the *Vesta* and her battle group. *Damn it!*

She turned to her sensor operator. "Get me a visual of some of the universes we're passing through."

"Yes, ma'am," the Winger said, bending over his console.

At least you have something to do. As they flitted through the dimensions along preset routes they'd fed to the computer, Fesky and her small crew had very little to occupy themselves with.

"I've just sent a collection of snapshots to your console, ma'am."

"Very good," Fesky snapped, downloading the images from the console to her Oculenses.

She'd had Ochrim modify *Spire*'s visual sensors so that they took a still image of every universe the ship passed through. The Ixan had been willing enough to do it, since it gave him more data for his research.

Shuffling through a few of the images taken of various universes, she compared them with her memory of those they'd passed through during their initial scouting mission. Her Nav officer was right, it seemed—she didn't recognize any of them.

A universe filled with a greater density of stars than she'd ever seen or heard about. Then, another with barely any. A dimension made up of red-tinged nothingness—probably, they'd appeared in the middle of an interstellar cloud.

"Ma'am, we're back on track!" the Nav officer said. "The computer seems to have found a route it's familiar with from our recon run. We should appear in Roundleaf in ten minutes."

"Excellent." Hopefully, the engagement hadn't shifted far from where Husher had expected it to occur. Otherwise, *Spire* would pop back into their native universe too far out of place to help.

Although emulating the Progenitors' interdimensional travel was a huge step forward, it wasn't hard to tell that *Spire*'s quantum engine wasn't capable of traversing the dimensions with anywhere near the speed the Progenitor ships managed. The enemy flitted in and out of a battlespace in a matter of moments, whereas Fesky and her crew had been underway for the better part of an hour. Even accounting for the detour their computer had taken, the disparity was substantial.

"Tactical, double check that our missile barrage is prepped and ready."

"Already on it, ma'am."

Fesky nodded. The process of loading missiles into tubes was mostly automated, but it did require some oversight to make sure everything ran smoothly and efficiently. As such, Tactical had a small backshop just below the CIC.

She turned to her sensor operator, Yvan. "The moment we reenter Roundleaf, feed me all sensor data. I want as complete a picture of the engagement as possible, as quickly as you can give me it."

"Aye, ma'am."

Nav spoke up on the heels of her sensor operator: "Captain, we've just arrived!"

Feathers stiff, Yvan bent over his console, no doubt compiling all relevant sensor data as fast as he could. Then, with a flicking motion across the top of his console, he sent Fesky what he'd put together.

This doesn't look overly promising. Where the *Hero* should have been, there was a spreading debris cloud instead, and a quick computer analysis told her that the *Vesta*'s Air Group had suffered heavy losses, too.

But none of that changed her mission. She needed to act with all possible haste, to maximize the element of surprise.

She noticed that one of the enemy capital starships was hanging back and firing on the *Vesta* from afar. Fesky soon saw why—Husher had managed to blow a massive hole in its prow, leaving it vulnerable.

None of the enemy warships seemed to have registered the *Spire*'s presence yet. No doubt their sensors were picking her up just fine—but the sensor operators simply wouldn't be watching for a vessel matching the former lifeboat's profile to appear off their sterns. It didn't fit their perceptions of what was and wasn't possible, and Fesky intended to exploit that viciously.

"Tactical, fire twenty Gorgons at that capital starship's damaged prow and nothing else. Meanwhile, I want fifteen Banshees and five Hydras launched at this Quatro ship, and the same number at this one too." She marked the ships she meant on their shared view of the tactical display.

"Aye, ma'am. Firing missiles now."

The Gorgons were already in the *Spire*'s forward tubes, and the other missiles she'd ordered were primed and ready for hasty loading.

It had been her idea to use stealth missiles immediately after *Spire*'s unexpected arrival. She was banking on the fact that the capital starship wouldn't anticipate *anything* coming from this direction, let alone twenty Gorgons.

The Quatro ships were closer, however, and they did seem to pick up on the Banshee and Hydra missiles before they struck.

It didn't matter. Their reaction was delayed, and the number of missiles Fesky had sent was too high to deal with in time—especially when five Hydras split into forty warheads.

The two Quatro ships went down as the remaining pair of alien ships turned to confront the *Spire*.

Before they could act, the Gorgons began landing on the *Promedon*'s hull. Or rather, they sailed through her prow, where her hull used to be, and deep into her guts.

The capital starship's entire bow exploded, causing a chain reaction of explosions that traveled down her immense hull. Within ten seconds, all that remained was the shrapnel that hurtled through space in every direction.

Her officers burst into cheering, but Fesky silenced them. "We can't stick around to celebrate!" she squawked. "Fire five Hydras each at the remaining Quatro ships, and follow with a dispersed spray of kinetic impactors. Nav, take us out of this dimension as soon as the ordnance is away."

"Yes, ma'am!"

CHAPTER 51

Staring at a Tactical Display

At Fesky's incredible success, the *Vesta*'s CIC crew broke into whooping and fist-pumping. While it was good to hear celebrating where only grim silence had held sway before, Husher couldn't bring himself to join in.

The *Promedon* was the second capital starship to go down in as many months. With each supercarrier that went down, the IGF grew weaker. As was often said, the capital starships formed the backbone of the IGF. How many more would it take to paralyze the Fleet entirely?

He supposed that, now, he was technically an enemy of the IGF, and maybe he should be glad. But he wasn't feeling as jubilant as his officers. Instead, a sense of dread threatened to overwhelm him. The words Teth had spoken in Hellebore echoed through his head: "I barely have to fight this war, Captain Husher. I have complete confidence that *you* are going to win it for me."

Winterton was the only one in the CIC who seemed of a mind with Husher, but then, the man could be counted on not to get excited under almost any circumstances. "Sir, one of the Quatro ships Commander Fesky targeted before departing has gone down, but the final alien ship managed to evade her attack and is moving in position to hit us again."

Husher nodded. "Coms, broadcast a repeating transmission across the battlespace encoded to Commander Ayam's fighter. Tell him that if he thinks his pilots are still flying tight and clean, I want him to focus on taking down the final Quatro ship. But *only* if he thinks the subspace pilots are up to it. Tell him I don't want to lose any more subspace fighters just because we kept the pilots flying for too long."

"Aye, sir."

With Ayam's squadron spending as much time in subspace as it did in realspace, it could be difficult to get a transmission to them, which was why Husher had come to rely on encrypted transmissions that repeated until receipt of message was confirmed.

His hope was that losing the final Quatro ship would deal a blow to enemy morale, at minimum. With any luck, it would make Captain Norberg reconsider this whole thing, especially given the threat of Fesky's reappearance at any moment. In truth, Husher had no idea when the *Spire* might make it back here, but Norberg didn't know that.

Before any of that could happen, Fry looked up at him from her work. "Sir, we're getting an unencrypted broadcast from a com drone that entered the system just sixteen minutes ago. It appears to be a vid recorded by Captain Zora Sawyer of the Thessaly system defense group."

"Play it on the main display."

Sawyer appeared, looking haggard. Husher knew her by reputation only, but his understanding was that she was a supremely competent captain. His first thought upon seeing her was that for her to look this bad, something had to be very wrong.

And indeed it was. "I'm sending this message via com drones to all surrounding systems. I only pray that they all arrive. Thessaly is under heavy assault by nine Progenitor ships, who have destroyed one of the colony's orbital defense platforms and who are now laying waste to the colony itself. The system's ten defending warships are moving to engage, but I fear it won't be enough." Sawyer paused, seeming to falter before continuing. "It's my fault the Progenitor ships were able to blow a hole in the colony's defenses. This all began when the eleven warships commandeered by the Sapient Brotherhood entered the system and began moving on the colony. I was overconfident, and I ordered all defending ships to engage them, with the intention of dealing with them permanently. It didn't occur to me that the Brotherhood might be working with the Progenitors. If you're listening to this message, I'm begging you—please come to Thessaly's aid."

With that, Zora Sawyer vanished from the main display, her words having crushed any positive sentiment the *Vesta*'s CIC officers might have been experiencing.

Missiles continued to fly across the battlespace, traded between the *Eos* and the *Vesta*, along with their supporting ships. Pythons continued to engage each other, with another one exploding every few seconds.

"Commander Ayam just succeeded in taking down the final Quatro ship, Captain," Winterton said, his tone neutral.

Husher drew a ragged breath. "Get me Captain Norberg, Coms," he forced himself to say. "She'll have gotten Captain Sawyer's message just the same as us."

As he waited for Fry to send the transmission request, more words sounded in Husher's head, this time from Captain Anthony Flores: "You will come to regret your decision."

At last, Norberg's hardened face appeared on the display, where Zora Sawyer's had been moments before. "Husher. What could you possibly have to say to me now? You've finished wiping out our Quatro allies' presence in the system, you've destroyed one of our sister capital starships, and you show no signs of remorse."

"It's hard to read remorse by staring at a tactical display," Husher said. "And I do regret having to do what I've done."

"You didn't *have* to do anything, other than simply hand over the fugitive."

He nodded. "That's what I'm getting at. You were just as willing to fire on IGF ships as I was, all because of a demand the Assembly of Elders made of you. I refuse to enable the IU's descent into tyranny, Norberg. We've been over this."

"Then why have you contacted me?"

"Didn't you just get the same broadcast I did?"

"Yes. I plan to lend aid to Thessaly as soon as I'm finished dealing with you."

Are you kidding me? "Captain Norberg, I think you're making that sound a little too easy. As you pointed out, we've already done serious damage to your forces, and if this continues we'll do even more. You've no doubt caught on to the nature of the modifications made to the *Vesta*'s lifeboat. We're calling it the *Spire* now, and she's going to come back, on an attack vector you don't anticipate. Next, it could be your ship that goes down."

"What are you trying to accomplish by threatening me like this?"

"I'm not threatening you. I'm offering a forecast of what will happen if this battle continues."

"How can it not continue? You're a threat, Husher. You've been a threat for a long time, and the orders have finally been given to put you down."

"A bigger threat than the Progenitors? Such a threat that you'll waste ships that could otherwise have been used to fight them? Captain Norberg, civilians are dying right now by the tens of thousands, just one system over. Captain Sawyer was concerned about her com drones making it to the surrounding systems—what if ours was the only one that got through? Are you willing to risk an entire system just to settle the IU's vendetta against me?"

Norberg pursed her lips and didn't answer.

"We can keep fighting," Husher said. "But it's exactly what Teth wants, and it will lead to our mutual destruction, whether today or someday soon. I'm proposing an alternative, Captain. I'm proposing we set aside our differences for the moment so we can go and deal with the real threat."

For a long time, Norberg continued to study him in silence. At last, her shoulders rose and fell with a deep breath, and she said, "All right, Husher. We'll work together. For now."

CHAPTER 52

The Price We Pay

Winterton announced the transition into Larkspur, and Husher braced for what he knew was coming.

"We're already getting signals from Thessaly's planetary net," Ensign Fry said as she sifted through them on her console. "None of them are of tactical significance, but..." The ensign swallowed, clearly struggling with what she was seeing. Her gaze drifted into the distance, the characteristic stare of someone watching Oculens footage. Then her eyes found Husher's. "Vids of Larissa being scoured from the face of Thessaly from above. Citizens running from Ravagers and Amblers, panicking, getting gunned down. Bodies littering the streets, people wandering aimlessly, shouting the names of family members." A tear slid down Fry's cheek.

Husher let her finish relaying what she saw. From a tactical perspective, he should have cut her off, so that they could turn to the task at hand. But this was important, too—so that everyone in the CIC knew exactly what the Progenitors were capable of.

Part of him wanted to tell Fry to forward the footage to Captain Norberg, but she would have access to it, too. He realized his body had tensed in the command seat, and he forced himself to relax. He was sure his CIC officers felt the same anger he did.

Which is fine, as long as it's controlled, and served cold.

"How are the planet's defenders faring, Winterton?"

"Thessaly's fighter defense group has taken a beating, and six of the original ten IGF warships remain, including Captain Sawyer's destroyer. The Brotherhood ships are still in the system, sir. They're headed for the Larkspur-Shadbush darkgate."

Noni peered at him from the Nav station. "Should we pursue, sir?"

"Negative." As much as he would have liked to blast those ships from space, they couldn't afford to withhold aid from Thessaly any longer. As long as the Brotherhood didn't stray from their course out of the system, he had to let them go.

"Coms, send Captain Norberg a transmission request."

"Yes, sir," Fry said, and seconds later, Norberg was back on the main display.

"We need to decide who will command our forces," he said. "We'll limit our responsiveness if we both try to call the shots."

"I could command mine, and you could command yours."

"I think that'll be limiting, too. It's much easier to execute a strategy with just one person giving the orders." He would have thought that was obvious, and it surprised him to have to spell it out. *Maybe Norberg just doesn't like agreeing with me.*

"I have more ships than you," she said.

"So you want to be the one in command," Husher said, nodding. It would be difficult for him to relinquish ultimate control over the *Vesta* and her remaining battle group ships, but he was prepared to do it. Just getting Norberg to join him in fighting the Progenitors had been a major accomplishment, and he'd known it would come at a price.

"Actually, no," Norberg said, surprising him again. "I think you should have the command. You have a lot more combat experience than me, Captain Husher."

He realized his eyebrows had climbed up his forehead, and he lowered them again. "Uh, thank you, then, Captain Norberg."

She nodded curtly. "Do you have any orders to give, yet?"

"I do. The planet's spin has taken the site of the Progenitor attack a little closer to our position, but the hole in Thessaly's defenses still faces away from us. We're still going to have to loop around the planet, and I think we should adopt a course that follows a wide arc through the system, so that we approach the planet perpendicular to its surface."

Norberg frowned. "I know I just handed command to you, but I would have thought it better to approach parallel to the planet's surface, so that we have the still-functional defense platforms backing us up."

"A valid thought, but that will also give us fewer viable firing solutions, and it will limit our ability to spread out—or to retreat, if it comes to that. The Progenitor ships are powerful, and not to be underestimated."

"Well, I'll yield to your judgment, Captain. As I agreed to. Is that all?"

"For now. I'll send over what formation I'd like us to adopt via my Coms officer. Oh, and I think it best if Commander Ayam is given command of all three Air Groups."

"Very well. Norberg out." With that, she vanished from the screen.

"Nav, I trust you heard me tell Captain Norberg how I'd like to approach the planet?"

"Yes, Captain."

"Good. Devise a course that follows my specifications." He turned toward the XO's seat. "Based on what you've seen so far, do you think my read of the situation checks out?"

Ek paused, presumably to consider the question. "Your usual caution is commendable. However, caution is your trademark, and the Progenitors will know that. It is always difficult to predict how thoroughly they will have anticipated our actions."

"Right," Husher said, and sniffed. "So, what's your prescription? Try to be more reckless?"

"I would advocate even greater caution than you are accustomed to."

"Okay. I'll take that under advisement."

Ek turned away, as though finished, but then turned back. "There is also the fact that, if any of our shots miss, they could hit the planet below."

Husher smiled. "Missile tech has advanced since you entered Klaxon's oceans, Ek. They're designed to self-destruct before they get close enough to a planet's surface to do damage." His smile faltered, then. "As for kinetic impactors, we'll try to go easy on them, and we'll angle our shots so that they'll hit depopulated areas if they miss. If they hit, though...yes, they'll cause significant damage. But the Progenitors are already laying waste to the surface. The most important thing now is that we stop them as quickly as we can, before they can move on to other regions."

Ek nodded.

Given the *Promedon*'s destruction, Husher and Norberg had been forced to find places for her Air Group wherever they could—mostly in unused hangar bays, where the fighters would be able to take advantage of the launch tubes there, but many of the starfighters ended up sitting on flight decks. They wouldn't be able to scramble with nearly the same energy as the other pilots, but it was better than nothing.

With two capital starships, three combined battle groups totaling eleven ships, as well as three Air Groups, Husher knew he'd be justified in calling their force a small fleet. Under normal circumstances, he'd feel quite confident in engaging just nine enemy ships, especially when he factored in Thessaly's fighter defense group, as well as the six IGF ships already fighting.

But with the Progenitors, nothing was predictable. As if to underscore that fact, as the *Vesta* and her allied ships closed in, an IGF frigate exploded over the planet, followed almost immediately by a missile cruiser.

And just as the *Vesta* entered missile range, the Progenitors neutralized the destroyer captained by Zora Sawyer.

Husher's grip on the command seat's armrests tightened. "Coms, tell Commander Ayam to scramble all three Air Groups. I'll let him decide how many to put on offense and how many to assign to missile defense, depending on how much the Progenitors send our way. But tell him to standby to prioritize any warship that's targeting one of ours with a particle beam. And let him know we'll be leaning heavily on his subspace squadron again."

As soon as the fighting with Norberg and the other IGF captains had ended, Husher had ordered the entire Air Group to get as much rest as possible before they reached Thessaly. Hopefully, it would be enough for the subspace Pythons to perform some more miracles. *We sorely need them.*

Unfortunately, the capital starship Fesky had destroyed had never been equipped with subspace fighters, and Ayam had taken out the *Eos'*. *The price we pay when we fight amongst ourselves, ignoring the real enemy.*

"Captain," Winterton said, and his voice wavered, which made Husher stare at him. A wavering voice from the sensor operator was equivalent to a bloodcurdling scream from anyone else.

"What is it?"

"Six Progenitor destroyers and three carriers just appeared ten thousand kilometers off our sterns. They're moving to hem us in."

Husher's jaw clenched involuntarily. *Eighteen Progenitor warships against our sixteen...and our ships are less powerful on average.*

Even as he thought it, another of the planet's defenders, an IGF destroyer, went down.

CHAPTER 53

Just Getting Started

Captain Katrina Norberg was on Husher's main display again, shouting. "We need a new plan, Husher, and we need it now!"

"Calm down," he said, though he felt far from calm himself. He couldn't get his daughter's face out of his mind, couldn't stop thinking of her somewhere in Cybele. Forty minutes ago, he'd sent out the warning that the *Vesta* would enter combat, and he hoped she was strapped into a safety harness. It had already occurred to him that if he survived this battle, Sera was going to kill him.

"For the moment, I'm giving you command over my remaining battle group ships—the two destroyers and the missile cruiser. I want you to take them, along with the other two carrier groups, and confront the Progenitor ships that just appeared. In the meantime, I'll take command of the three Air Groups, and together, they and the *Vesta* will engage the enemy ships closest to the planet. We should be able to help take some pressure off the planet's defenders."

Norberg shook her head. "Why not turn and engage the newcomers with everything we have, while the ones over the planet's surface are occupied?"

"Because the enemy's mechs are ravaging the civilian population, Captain," Husher said softly. "We need to make it a priority to get troops down to the surface, and that won't happen if we let the Progenitors maintain control of the skies."

"I don't like our odds as they are, Captain Husher. If we don't win, the civilians are doomed anyway."

"This could be our only window to help. I'm going to take it. Besides, if we abandon the planet's defenders now, they'll crumble. They're already crumbling."

"Very well," Norberg said, and the tightness in her voice told Husher she might be starting to regret giving him the command.

The display went dark again, and Husher turned to his Coms officer. "Ensign Fry, tell Major Gamble to prepare to mobilize the *Vesta*'s entire marine battalion. I want a total of six platoons to remain aboard—four to patrol the corridors and two in Cybele, as a precaution against Ravagers breaching the hull. The rest will deploy to Thessaly's surface."

Fry nodded. "Aye, sir."

"When you've done that, tell Commander Fesky to decouple the *Spire* and set an interdimensional course that takes her behind the newest group of Progenitor ships. I want her to see what damage she can do." Even though the Progenitors were well acquainted with interdimensional travel, they wouldn't be expecting the IGF to have access to it. Hopefully that would once again work in Fesky's favor.

Studying the tactical display, Husher saw that Thessaly's fighter defense group was battling valiantly to protect the remaining pair of defending warships, a missile cruiser and a corvette, from the stream of Ravagers being sent their way. Python after Python went down, either mowed down by kinetic impactors or latched onto by a robot and ripped apart.

Seeing that, Husher opened a two-way channel with Commander Ayam.

"Ayam here, Captain. All our birds are in the air."

"Commander, there's been a change of plans. I'm sure you noticed the latecomers to the party?"

"They're kind of hard to miss, sir."

"Indeed. Their arrival makes getting forces to the planet all the more urgent, since we may not be able to manage it for much longer. We have enough to assign a squadron to each shuttle of marines, and that's what I want you to do. Not only that, I want your subspace squadron playing sheepdog to the entire flock, hitting back at anything that tries to shoot my marines out of the air."

"I'm on it, sir. What about the rest of the fighters?"

"Deploy them as best you see fit to back up the planet's defender ships. We need to preserve every asset we can, and if we can keep those crews alive, it should go a long way. I plan to position the *Vesta* between the descending shuttles and the Progenitor battle group, to protect whoever needs it most."

"Sounds like a plan to me. Is that all, sir?"

"That's all. God speed, Ayam."

"You too, Captain. Ayam out."

Husher turned to Noni. "Nav, our shuttles will descend here," he said, marking a point over Thessaly's surface on Noni's overlay. "I want you to set a course that puts us equidistant between that point and the nearest enemy battle group."

"Yes, Captain."

"Tactical, let's start hammering them right away. As soon as we have an angle that won't hit the two IGF warships or the planet, spray kinetic impactors at their sterns. Prepare to fire our primary laser as well."

"Aye."

But they didn't need to hit the Progenitors to get their attention. A pair of destroyers and a pair of carriers were already coming about to face them, lines of Ravagers spewing from all four as they turned. Many of the robots would be caught up in the planet's gravity well, to plummet to the surface, but Husher was sure that didn't bother whoever or whatever was captaining those ships.

Briefly, he wondered whether Teth was aboard any of the attacking warships. His instincts told him no. *I barely have to fight this war,* Teth had said.

"Coms, tell Ayam to redirect six squadrons to providing missile defense for the *Vesta.*"

"Yes, sir."

At least we've taken some of the heat off the planet's defenders. They still faced down five Progenitor ships on their own, but their fighter pilots seemed well trained, and hopefully they'd help the warships hold.

"Captain, the approaching warships aren't stopping," Winterton said. "At least half of their Ravagers are sailing past us, toward our descending shuttles."

Husher nodded. He'd anticipated this. "Nav, set a course that takes us between the carrier and the destroyer that are clustered closest together."

Blinking at him, Noni said, "Sir?"

"Do it."

"Aye."

"Tremaine, have point defense systems redirect any fire not needed to hold Ravagers at bay—I want it sent at those ships instead. It looks like we'll be close enough to hit them."

The Progenitor ships sped forward, seemingly focused on the shuttles screaming toward Thessaly's surface. Husher could understand why. Their efforts today represented the largest, most concerted attack on a Union colony by far. Clearly, the Progenitors believed it would devastate public morale to wipe out a core world. *And it would.* So they were doing everything they could to make sure it happened.

It didn't take long for the enemy ships to enter range of the *Vesta*'s point defense turrets, which began pumping thousands of rounds into their hulls. They clearly hadn't expected the maneuver, possibly because they'd never encountered it from an IGF vessel before. Either way, the two ships immediately reversed course, heading back toward their fellows.

"Winterton, which enemy ship looks the most damaged?"

"The carrier, sir."

"Very good. Tremaine, dump our primary laser into the part of her hull that's suffered the most hurt."

"Firing laser now, Captain."

Husher toggled over to a zoomed-in visual display just as the carrier's hull began to twist and melt. The ship accelerated even more, and Tremaine switched off the primary, recalibrated his firing solution on the fly, and fired again.

The carrier's hull erupted, the fire consuming her entire frame before succumbing to the void.

"Excellent work," Husher said.

But Winterton didn't sound as impressed. "Two Progenitor ships made it past us, sir. They're attempting to overwhelm the shuttles with Ravagers."

Husher nodded, though he'd already been monitoring the tactical display, where Ayam's subspace fighters were flitting in and out of existence, dodging one wave of Ravagers, blasting through the next—weaving through both the enemy barrage and reality itself on their way to the target.

Seconds later, an alpha strike connected with the destroyer's hull, obliterating two turret batteries as well as three Ravager launch tubes.

The subspace squadron disappeared in time to dodge point defense fire, then reappeared off the destroyer's stern, still hurtling in the same direction. As a parting shot, they delivered another alpha strike, concentrating their fire on one of the warship's main reactors. It blew, and the explosion swallowed most of the stern. The rest of the ship soon followed.

"Coms, have three of the six squadrons helping us with missile defense redirect their efforts. I want them helping Ayam take down that carrier instead. Tremaine, let's offer up six Hydras, to speed it on its way."

"Aye."

Husher permitted himself a small smile as he watched the fighters and missiles converging on the enemy ship.

I'm just getting started, you bastards.

CHAPTER 54

Across the Battlespace

The Progenitor carrier went down—and so did three of the nineteen shuttles carrying his marines to the surface of Thessaly. That made Husher want to hammer the command seat's armrests with his fist, but he forced himself to convert his anger into cold determination.

Three platoons of marines, gone. It wasn't a total disaster, but it was far from ideal, either, especially given the forces the Progenitors had devoted to their ground assault on the colony.

It could have been worse, he told himself again. *Thanks to my Python pilots, it wasn't.* They'd managed to keep most of the Ravagers from ripping the shuttles apart, though they'd lost a squadron and a half in the process. Oneiri Team was with the shuttles too, but they hadn't been of much help. To be fair, Husher knew that orbital reentry tended to occupy all of one's attention, mech suit or no. Either way, the surviving marines were almost to the planet's surface.

Neutralizing three Progenitor warships had represented amazing progress, but it had also caused the enemy to rally, and now IGF forces were paying the price.

"Our second missile cruiser just fell, Captain," Winterton said. "And Captain Norberg just lost one of her battle group ships as well."

Damn it. He'd hoped giving Norberg superior numbers would help her keep the second Progenitor force at bay, but the enemy had just evened things up, meaning more IGF losses would surely follow.

"The marines have made it to the planet," the sensor operator continued. "Their Python escort is returning to join us." The man's frown deepened, however. "The nine enemy ships facing off with Captain Norberg are spreading out. It looks like they're trying to shepherd her forces toward the planet."

Of course they are. "They know if they can sandwich us between their two battle groups, we won't last long." Husher caught himself gritting his teeth, and forced himself to stop. "We need to throw everything we have at the six Progenitor ships remaining over the planet's surface. Coms, tell Commander Ayam to rally the Air Groups and advance on the enemy formation in a wide arc."

Husher turned toward the Tactical station. "This needs to happen quickly. Tremaine, I want twenty Hydras fired along firing solutions designed to blanket the battlespace with warheads. On the heels of that, fire forty-eight Gorgons—eight apiece for each Progenitor ship."

"That's a lot of our specialized missiles, Captain."

"I'm aware of that."

"Yes, sir." Tremaine bent to his work.

"I would caution against over-committing to this attack, Captain," Ek said.

He nodded. "I hear you, but we need to win the orbital battle before Norberg lets the Progenitors push her force to us."

"Captain Norberg just lost another ship, sir," Winterton said. "A corvette. They still haven't managed to destroy any Progenitor ships."

"Acknowledged, Ensign," Husher said, and the news made him feel even more resolved to follow through with his planned strike. Frowning at the tactical display, he zoomed it in on the region of space where Norberg and the Progenitors battled. An unending Ravager assault flooded across the battlespace, and it was everything the IGF ships could do it keep them from penetrating their hulls, with point defense systems supplemented by lasers. They were devoting Banshees to defense as well, he saw.

Maybe it was a mistake to take all three Air Groups with me. He refocused on his own battlespace. *As soon we complete this attack, I'll redirect some fighters to Norberg.*

Hydras and Gorgons crossed the void between the *Vesta* and the enemy ships, with over a thousand Pythons closing in behind. Husher found himself gripping his armrests. *This could turn the tide. There's no way this doesn't do major damage.* He expected to take down at least two or three ships, here, but he didn't consider it impossible that he'd destroy them all.

"The enemy ships are accelerating, Captain. I believe—I believe they're fleeing. But they won't be able to outstrip our missiles in time."

Holding his breath, Husher watched to see whether his gambit would pay off. The Progenitors weren't even bothering to try shooting down the approaching missiles. *They know there's too many.* Instead, they continued to flee...

...straight toward the remaining two IGF ships.

The six enemy ships belched a tide of Ravagers at the cruiser and corvette. The defenders did all they could to defend themselves, reversing thrust, engaging point defense systems, and using missiles to shoot down the approaching Ravagers.

It didn't matter. Hundreds of Ravagers lighted on their hulls, burrowing through and infesting them.

Seconds later, both ships became balls of flame.

Husher's vision blurred, and he fought to steady his breathing. *They're about to pay the price for that.*

But just as the Gorgons and Hydras closed with the nearest Progenitor ship, it vanished. So did the next-closest ship, and the next. Within seconds, all six warships had disappeared, and sixty-eight incredibly expensive missiles sailed harmlessly past, with nothing to connect with but the expanding cloud of shrapnel that had once been two IGF vessels.

A brittle silence descended over the CIC—which was soon broken, as it so often was, by Winterton:

"The six enemy ships have reappeared in a roughly spherical formation, sir. They're surrounding us."

CHAPTER 55

That's New

All around Jake, the MIMAS mechs' parachutes disengaged, whipping away into the air and leaving the pilots to descend the rest of the way using aerospike thrusters.

The alien mech Jake piloted needed no such assistance. He fired an energy blast behind him, to even out the angle of his trajectory. When he landed, the mech's legs accordioned flawlessly to absorb the impact, and he curled into a ball, rolling over and over with the momentum. Spikes sprouted from his body to slow his progress, and in seconds, he was back on his feet, skidding the rest of the way.

He turned to monitor the rest of his team's descent, and to cover them if need be. They'd yet to come under any fire from the ground, but he knew that could change in a heartbeat. Jake kept a close eye on Marco's MIMAS—*Vesta* engineers had patched it up as best they could, with their limited knowledge of the mechs. Marco had been present for the repairs, which had no doubt helped, but still...Jake would try to look out for Marco if he could.

Rug careened from the sky, crashing to the ground beside Jake and causing it to rumble. She too became a ball, tumbling forward and quickly arresting her momentum.

"How's your mental state?" he asked her, before the others could reach them.

"The machine whispers to me still, Jake Price," the Quatro told him in her deep, resonant tones. "It speaks to me of the power we could bring to bear on our enemies, if only we joined as one."

"You're still able to resist?"

Rug paused. "So far."

The others landed, then. All around them, shuttles filled with marines were touching down on the grassy plain as well. They were a few miles out from the valley that held Crete, the city the Progenitor mechs had just begun attacking. The enemy had already laid waste to Larissa, the capital, but Crete had an even greater population.

This is a beautiful world, Jake reflected, casting his gaze toward the horizon, drinking in a lush oasis surrounded by a vast expanse of sand. Of course, most worlds looked beautiful after months spent on a spaceship. Still, it made him miss Eresos, back in the Steele System.

He eyed the black-and-brown scars that he and Rug had inflicted on the earth with their arrival. The mech dream painted the sky with the dark gray of regret. Then he remembered that the Progenitors would do much worse to this colony, if he let them.

The airlock of the nearest shuttle opened, and Major Gamble was the first to emerge, immediately jogging toward the group of mechs.

"You guys all made the descent all right?" Gamble said as he neared.

"Piece of cake, Major," Andy said, though he sounded shaken to Jake's ears. Andy hadn't performed very many orbital insertions, and they weren't for the faint of heart.

"Glad to hear it," the major said, turning to Price. "I'm sure it won't surprise you to hear that you'll be our forward assault force. This is that shock and awe we were talking about."

"Yes, Major," Price said.

"We aren't leaving these shuttles here. We only landed here so we could regroup with you and get our bearings. These are direct action craft. A few of them are designed to act as gunships, and the rest we'll use to place marines wherever we need them—to execute flanking maneuvers, take down valuable positions, you name it. And with their fold-out bulletproof barriers, the shuttles will also act as cover when we have none. But you won't be needing any cover, I'm guessing."

"Not really our style," Price said, his voice emanating from amplifiers on the alien mech's shoulders.

"I didn't think so. Like I said before, Price, I'll leave specific tactics up to you. All I ask is that you go in guns blazing while we rally around you. If anything changes, I'll be in touch."

With that, Gamble jogged back toward the shuttle. He didn't reenter it, though, and marines continued to pour out of every transport. Once they'd all deployed, the shuttles lifted off, hovering twenty meters or so off the ground while Gamble organized his marines into a sprawling formation that centered on Oneiri.

"Advance," came Gamble's command over a wide channel.

"You heard the major," Jake said, and Oneiri fell into the semicircular formation they'd discussed, with Jake and Rug at the apex and the six MIMAS mechs spread out to either side. This way, they'd have a good angle on any enemy forces they came across, without getting in each other's way.

It didn't take long for the enemy to emerge. Soon after the marine force poured through the pass and into the valley that held Crete, Ravagers began to emerge from between the buildings—first by the handful, then by the dozens. Eventually, a steady stream of the squat, bipedal robots was surging out of the city, followed by the appearance of at least a dozen Amblers. The great robots stalked forward on long limbs, towering over their counterparts. Together, the great mass of robots spread out in a wide arc, preparing to charge.

None of this came as a surprise to Jake. The mechs would have known in advance that the marines were coming, and it made sense to engage them out here, where they could try to push them back against the mountains. The pass was too narrow for a quick retreat, and if the Progenitors gained the upper hand, they could quickly turn this into a rout.

"At least we don't have to deal with any Gatherers," Ash said over the team-wide.

Gatherers had been Eresos' resource-gathering robots, and even though they'd served the humans living there for decades, it had turned out they belonged to the Progenitors. They'd become weapons of war themselves, in the end, and in the final battle for Eresos, which had ended with the fall of Ingress, the Gatherers had proved just as deadly as their larger fellows.

Without ceremony, the Amblers and Ravagers facing the *Vesta*'s marine battalion broke into a run, a vast tide of metal rushing across the plain.

"Rockets," Jake said once the enemy mechs came into viable range. At once, sixteen missiles left their tubes, hissing across the battlefield, only to be followed by sixteen more.

All along the Progenitor ranks, explosions ripped up the terrain, sending grass and dirt and metal limbs sky-high. Then the second wave hit, causing even more damage.

An Ambler was knocked back, though Jake couldn't tell whether it was out for the count or simply off-balance. The other Amblers slowed their advance, no doubt to steady their aim. Sure enough, seconds later, answering rockets sailed across the battlefield.

"Oneiri, disperse!" Jake yelled over the team-wide. "Evasive action."

For his part, he used the advanced telemetry readings available to him inside the alien mech to line up his own shot. As he aligned his arm with one of the rockets, that arm became an energy cannon, which he fired. A blast of blue-white energy shot forth, connecting with the missile and detonating it well before it found its target. He managed to take out another rocket—and then a third, one that had been heading straight for him. The remaining rockets struck home, some hitting empty terrain. But several landed at marine locations, and screams of agony filled the air.

That was one of the advantages the Progenitor mechs had. They never screamed.

Five combat shuttles soared forward, pelting Ambler and Ravager alike with high-velocity rounds. By now, Gamble's people had set up several heavy machine guns on tripods, and they came into play, too. Next, rockets of their own crossed the battlefield, slamming into the oncoming mechs.

Just like that, the plain was filled with smoke and fire and death. This was war, and it was all Jake knew, these days.

He waded into it.

Ravagers surged forward to meet him, engulfing him, trying to bring him down while tearing at his scaled metal hide. His arms became broadswords, and he whirled, slicing through bot after bot. When it became too much, with bots ripping at his head and shoulders and back, Jake exploded. Shrapnel burst from all over his body, cutting the Ravagers to shreds, and when he was finished, the pieces that had burst from him came cartwheeling back like iron filings to a magnet.

Two Amblers took notice of the display, stepping toward him across the battlefield, heedless of the smaller robots they crushed underfoot.

Jake didn't wait for them to make the first move. Instead, his broadswords became energy cannons, and he fired at one of the Amblers as he charged toward it.

The mech answered with armor-piercing rounds, but Jake leapt to the left, rolling with the momentum and coming up again to continue his attack. The maneuver had apparently thrown the second Ambler off as well, since no rounds hit him from that direction.

His target resumed fire, and a few of the rounds connected with Jake center-mass, but by then he was already upon the Ambler. In a flash, cannons reverted to broadswords, which he plunged into the enemy mech's torso, once, twice. Thrusters sprouting from his calves, he rocketed upward, taking the Ambler with him before releasing it. The thing slid from his blades to land on the battlefield, supine and motionless.

The other Ambler actually seemed to falter, as it appeared to reevaluate the power differential involved. *That's new,* Jake reflected as he landed on top of his fallen foe, morphing energy cannons once again to begin pelting the Ambler left standing.

Something collided with Jake from behind, sending him sprawling forward toward the Ambler, who immediately began hitting him with more armor-piercing rounds.

Jake focused on recovering, bounding to his feet and using his momentum to drive newly formed broadswords through the Ambler. The mech tipped back, and Jake went with it, coming down on the other side and twisting around to use it as a shield against whatever had hit him.

His attacker crashed into the makeshift barrier, sending both it and Jake sliding backward, sending streams of sand into the air.

His assailant was a mech that was almost identical to Jake's—its greater size being the main difference.

Roach.

CHAPTER 56

Fading Light

At last, *Spire*, reappeared in her native dimension—on time, unlike her last voyage through the universes.

"What do you have for me, Yvan," Fesky squawked, trying not to glare at her sensor operator. Interdimensional travel was a great thing, but entering combat with zero intel on the current situation sent her stress levels skyrocketing.

Yvan went rigid at his console, then started shuffling things around rapidly.

"What?" Fesky said. "What is it?"

"The *Vesta*'s alone, and completely surrounded, ma'am," the Winger said, his feathers standing at attention. "Six Progenitor ships are all around her in a sphere, hammering her with Ravagers."

Fesky clacked her beak softly. The sensor operator's news did nothing good for her anxiety.

"She does have the three Air Groups with her," Yvan added.

"Well, I'd call that pretty relevant information," Fesky said, her voice drenched in sarcasm. "Thanks for deciding to share it with me."

Yvan looked up at her, blinking. "Yes, ma'am."

Shaking her head, Fesky said, "We need to focus on the Progenitors we can actually affect. What's their posture?"

"There are still nine warships operational in the enemy battle group facing Captain Norberg. The captain is down to nine ships as well." Yvan's gaze flitted back to his console. "Uh, Captain, I think the Progenitors have spotted us. Two of the nearest destroyers are turning to engage."

If you hadn't wasted my time worrying me about something we can't affect... Fesky was beginning to think that maybe she'd made the wrong choice for her sensor operator.

"Tactical, fire the preplanned missile barrages."

"Yes, ma'am," Lieutenant Lambert said, sounding relieved to be doing something.

The sensor operator, probably sensing Fesky's displeasure, looked abashed. Nonetheless, he turned toward her again and spoke in almost a whisper: "Ma'am, Ravagers are already headed for us."

Cursing under her breath, Fesky glanced to her right. "Helm, full reverse thrust, now. We need time to fire all the missiles."

"On it, Captain." And she was—immediately, the *Spire* leapt backward, away from the oncoming robots.

"Be ready to transition back out of the universe on my mark, Nav. Tactical?"

"The last barrage is being loaded in the tubes now, ma'am."

"Okay. Good." Fesky watched the tactical display, focused on the stream of tiny blips representing the incoming Ravagers. Everything had happened so fast. The Ravagers were almost here—she wasn't sure Tactical would finish launching all the missiles in time.

"Engage point defense turrets, Lambert." The *Spire* had no lasers, so she had nothing to supplement their defense with.

The lead Ravagers neared her ship and were mowed down. That wouldn't last, though. There were too many.

"The last missiles are away!" Lambert shouted.

"Nav, get us out of here!"

"Yes, ma'am," Devar said, fingers flying over her console.

Fesky's eyes were glued to the visual feed, which showed the tiny gleaming dots that would become full-size Ravagers in a matter of seconds. Something connected with their hull—and then the universe disappeared, replaced by another, and then another. Universes flashed by in quick succession. They were underway.

But it wasn't over. Head bowed, her sensor operator spoke again without even looking at her. "One of the Ravagers made it through the hull, Captain."

Now, Fesky did glare at him. *No time for that. I have to do something.* "Where did it burrow through?"

"Near the missile loading bay."

"Okay. Coms, have Damage Control personnel seal off the section where the breach is, and alert the missile loading crew about the intruder." Fesky stood up from the command seat and rushed to the rear of the CIC, where she slapped a panel to open a compact weapons locker; a broad drawer that ejected and slid across the deck. As per regulation, every crewmember carried a sidearm, but they needed something with a little more punch to deal with the Ravager as quickly as they needed to—before it destroyed something vital, potentially stranding them in another universe with no means of returning to their own. Inside the drawer were two loaded R-57 assault rifles, nestled beside several extra magazines.

"Come here, Lambert." Fesky removed one of the guns, checked the action, then handed the other to her Tactical officer as he neared her. He checked his gun, too, then nodded.

"Let's go." She opened the CIC hatch, which let onto a three-way intersection—four, if you counted the entrance to the CIC. Down the corridor to the right waited the lift that would take them to the missile loading bay below.

Checking the other two corridors, Fesky nodded at Lambert, then jogged toward the elevator, assault rifle held at the ready.

The screech of rending metal reached her ears from behind, and she turned to find Lambert with his arms raised to protect his face from a shower of sparks. Then the Ravager was through, knocking Lambert to the ground and driving its tiny metal claws into his face again and again. With each blow, the claws became redder and redder.

Fesky opened fire on the robot, knocking it off Lambert. It scrambled against the deck for purchase, but she emptied the magazine into its torso, and that was enough to put it down for good.

She knelt beside Lambert. One eye blinked up at her through a mask of torn flesh—the other had been torn out completely. The tactical officer looked as though he was about to say something, but then the light faded from his remaining eye, and his body grew still.

Fesky stood, shaking as she made her way back toward the CIC. When she opened the hatch and stepped through, she found her officers staring at her expectantly.

"It killed Lambert," she said. "I managed to kill it before it got me."

"Who'll control the Tactical station?" the Nav officer asked.

Fesky lowered herself into the seat where Lambert had sat so recently. "I will." Before she'd taken command of the *Spire*, she made a point to give herself a rudimentary education in every station's operation. Tactical was one of the roles she was most comfortable taking over, thanks to her decades as a starfighter pilot. "Until a new Tactical officer can be appointed, I'll command *Spire* from this station while performing Lambert's duties. It's far from ideal, but it's the best we can do right now."

Casting her gaze around the CIC to see whether she met with any objections, she found that she did not. Her crew didn't appear at ease with the situation, exactly, but they obviously understood there was no other option.

As *Spire* continued to flit through the multiverse, Fesky brought her talons to the console's surface and began to work. She needed to prepare for their next appearance in the Milky Way.

CHAPTER 57

Back Down to Size

"**C**ommander Fesky's ship just vanished again, sir," Winterton said. "Though I believe a Ravager may have pierced her hull."

"She'll make it," Husher said through gritted teeth. Right now, he couldn't afford to accept that any other outcome was possible. They needed to focus on the six ships surrounding them, as well as the unending flood of Ravagers they were spewing at the *Vesta.*

I should have listened to Ek's warning. But it was far too late, now. The fact that the Progenitors had managed to reappear in such a formation showed their mastery of interdimensional travel. They'd clearly been refining the technology for a long time, whereas Husher and Ochrim were still fumbling in the dark.

"Ek, was this why you cautioned me against over-committing?" he said, turning toward his XO and gesturing toward his console.

"It was," the Fin said.

He drew a breath, fighting to prevent his mounting frustration from making him snap at her. "Next time you have a recommendation, I'd like your reasoning for it, too. Especially when you think my plan underemphasizes something important."

"I will, Captain Husher."

He returned his gaze to the tactical display, where hundreds of Pythons were working together with the *Vesta*'s point defense systems to defend her. Given that the three supercarrier Air Groups had never trained together, Husher was amazed at how well they were coordinating. The crucible of battle had quickly transformed them into a single, deadly weapon, and they took down Ravagers by the hundreds.

It wasn't enough, With each passing moment, the Ravager front crept closer, and more starfighters went down. The bots had clearly been programmed to reprioritize Pythons as targets the moment the opportunity presented itself, and despite the pilots' exquisite performance, the battlespace was simply too clogged with the robot-missiles to avoid steady losses.

Husher spared another glance at the tactical display, to check whether Fesky's efforts had paid off. Her Progenitor targets had succeeded in neutralizing all the missiles sent at them—the first wave, anyway. The ones that were visible.

The second wave consisted of a massive barrage of Gorgons, and while the enemy destroyers managed to take out some of them, they obviously hadn't anticipated the sheer number of stealth missiles. Both hulls blossomed with flames that rapidly engulfed them.

Buoyed by his friend's success, he turned to Chief Noni. "Nav, we need to break out of this death trap, and the only way we're going to do that is by taking some Ravagers on the nose. It's not what I'd call a desirable outcome, but it's necessary, and the longer we wait to do it the more starfighters we'll lose. So point us at this destroyer." Husher indicated the one he meant via Oculens. "Helm, the instant we're properly aimed, I want engines fired up to all ahead full."

"Aye, Captain," both officers said.

"Coms, tell Commander Ayam to keep his squadron with the other Pythons inside the sphere for now, standing by to engage whatever warship looks like it's going to pose the biggest threat. I also need a marine battalion stationed near our prow, to deal with the Ravager onslaught we know is coming."

"Aye."

"Tremaine...do we have enough charge to fire our primary?"

Husher held his breath while the Tactical officer checked the reading on his console. He wasn't sure this would work without the laser.

"Yes, sir. We're at sixty-five percent charge—more than enough to discharge the primary."

"Ready it for firing on my mark."

With that, everything started happening at once. Noni reoriented the ship toward their target, and Chief Vy brought the supercarrier's mighty engines to full power. They sprang toward the enemy destroyer.

"The prow is already getting perforated with Ravagers, sir," Winterton said. "The marines are going to have their hands full."

"Is it enough to justify diverting another platoon?" Husher asked the sensor operator.

"I would recommend it."

"Do it, Fry."

"Aye, sir," the Coms officer answered.

Winterton spoke again. "Sir, the carriers on our port and starboard sides are moving. Looks like they'll try to intercept."

"Acknowledged. Tremaine, hit the one off our port with a full broadside of Banshees. Coms, tell Commander Ayam to target the other carrier."

On visual, the destroyer ahead grew in size. It continued to spit Ravagers at the *Vesta*, and while most were mowed down by Pythons or turrets, more made it through. Husher felt a vein pulse on his forehead, and he forced himself to take a breath.

"Banshees away, sir," Tremaine said.

Winterton spoke up: "Commander Ayam is engaging his target already. If I can offer a tactical projection, I think our efforts should more than occupy both carriers."

"Very good," Husher said. "Tremaine, fire the primary laser."

"Firing primary, sir."

The great beam speared across space, striking the destroyer on its nose and causing it to warp. It began to maneuver out of the way, but before it could, its prow ruptured, prompting a chain reaction that consumed its whole hull.

The carrier they'd targeted with their broadside was managing to mop up the missiles, but moments after the destroyer's destruction, Ayam succeeded in neutralizing his carrier.

Husher could sense his crew's mood spiking, but before it could manifest in cheering, Winterton cut it back down to size: "One of our destroyers just went down. And Captain Norberg lost two of her own battle group ships."

Two of theirs, three of ours. Jaw clenched, Husher said, "Coms, order all Pythons to withdraw from the Progenitor formation and then form up around the *Vesta.*"

"Aye, sir."

CHAPTER 58

Hail of Bullets

Gabriel Roach was stronger than ever before—even since merging with the alien mech. It was everything Jake could do to dodge or fend off his attacks, and so far he'd barely been able to launch any attacks of his own.

Energy blasts ripped up the ground near his feet, and then one connected, sending him sprawling face-first onto the ground. He scrambled to regain his footing, then sprinted toward a nearby warehouse for some cover.

Roach had him on the run.

Just before Oneiri had left the Steele System, Roach had begged Jake to take him with them. He'd promised that he'd changed, that he'd learned to control the alien mech.

Jake had flatly refused. After Roach had killed Richaud, there was no way they could trust him again.

Either way, Roach had clearly shed his desire to rejoin Oneiri. He'd joined the Progenitors instead, who'd made him even more monstrous than before.

And more powerful.

Jake rounded the corner of the warehouse, but Roach simply crashed through the corner an instant later, obliterating it and knocking Jake to the ground, pinning him. A large metal fist crashed down into Jake's face—his mech's face, technically, but the mech dream made it feel like his. Sparks and shrapnel flew, and the pain made Jake bellow, his desire to kill Roach intensifying.

Roach raised his fist again, then paused. Absurdly, he began to chuckle. "If only you knew what I know, Price," he said, his voice barely recognizable. "They showed me the truth, and it's..." Roach shook his head, laughing some more. "Your new captain's in for a shock."

Jake twisted hard to the right, his left hand becoming a blade darting toward Roach's face. An arm raised to block it, but Roach recoiled at the same time, giving Jake the purchase he needed to shove him off and slip out from beneath him.

He ran.

"You should never have turned against Darkstream, Price!" Roach yelled, following up his words with an energy blast that sizzled past Jake's shoulder.

He's insane, Jake thought as he entered an alleyway just large enough for his mech. *Darkstream is gone.*

Forming energy cannons of his own, he turned once he made it halfway down the alley, ready to confront Roach. But he didn't appear. Instead, something crashed into one of the upper stories of the building on his right, just out of sight. Suddenly, Roach was hurtling at him from above, arms converted into javelins.

Jake ran backward, blasting Roach in midair, then ducked into another alley that opened on his left—its location sheer dumb luck. He spun around just as his assailant was crashing to the cracked asphalt. Roach turned to level his javelins at Jake once more.

Glancing back, he saw that this alley terminated in a dead end.

Jake's eyes lifted to the strip of sky above. *I can rocket out, if it comes to that.* Roach would try to intercept him, but it might be his only avenue of escape.

"Hey," someone called from the street they'd just left, and Roach turned toward the sound. "This is for Richaud!"

High-velocity rounds began to pepper Roach's mech, opening small craters in the scaled metal and forcing him to fall back a step. Then he rallied, charging into the hail of bullets.

Jake dashed to the intersection of alleys, rounding the corner just in time to see Roach impale Marco Gonzalez with one of the javelins meant for Jake.

Turning, Roach hefted the MIMAS, which flailed ineffectually. *Marco's still alive,* Jake thought, feeling more horrified than hopeful. Mostly, he felt numb, and through that numbness he again marveled at Roach's strength. Jake doubted his mech could hold a MIMAS aloft with such ease.

He charged at Roach, and everything seemed to slow. The hulking mech's other hand became an energy cannon, and he placed the barrel against the MIMAS' chest.

He fired, blowing a jagged hole clean through the machine.

Jake crashed into Roach, using thrusters to supplement his momentum. The **MIMAS** slid from Roach's weapon as they hurtled across the street and through a concrete wall.

They continued into a parking garage, connecting with a metal pillar that bent but didn't break. Roach worked the energy cannon's barrel between them so that it lay against Jake's stomach, and he twisted away, barely avoiding the blast. The cannon became a fist, and Roach stepped forward, twisting into the blow and sending Jake staggering backward.

He found his footing, but he couldn't help glancing over his shoulder toward Marco's **MIMAS**. He glimpsed it on the street outside, laying there, motionless.

Turning back, he barely managed to deflect the javelin Roach drove toward his head.

CHAPTER 59

With a Whimper

Major Gamble had left Sergeant Jeremy Peterson in command of the six marine battalions still on the *Vesta*, so that's who Husher contacted to check on their status, praying the man was still alive.

"Peterson here, Captain." Gunfire sounded in the background, and the sergeant seemed out of breath.

"Do you have the Ravager situation under control, Sergeant?"

"Working on it, sir. A lot of them made it through, and I've lost some good people to them. Hard to react in time when one of those things comes out of the bulkhead on top of you. But I have marines guarding all the vital systems, and we've fortified every exit from this area of the ship. We have the threat contained, Captain."

"I want it neutralized, Sergeant. Do you understand?"

"Yes, sir."

"Make it happen." Husher closed the channel. Peterson was a good soldier, but Husher needed those robots purged from his ship ten minutes ago. More were on the way.

"Captain Norberg just lost another ship, sir," Winterton said. "She's down to five now, including the *Eos.*"

"Acknowledged," Husher said, terser than he'd meant to. *If we can manage to deal with the four remaining ships confronting the* Vesta, *and bring the Air Group to Norberg...*

He realized it was past time to send Norberg some Pythons for backup. The Progenitors appearing around his ship in a sphere had delayed it, but he didn't need to wait any longer to send the other capital starship captain some help.

He opened his mouth to give the order to Coms, but Winterton spoke before he could. "Four more Progenitor ships just appeared off our port side, Captain."

"*Damn it!*" Husher snapped, and a couple of his officers jumped. That may have been the first time he'd ever cursed inside his CIC since taking command of the ship.

He immediately regretted it—his anger did nothing to help win this engagement, as Winterton's next words proved: "We're getting superheating near the bow. The lead destroyer is hitting us with its particle beam, and—"

A colossal explosion rocked the supercarrier, sending Husher hard against the command seat's right armrest.

"Tactical, answer with a Hydra broadside!" he shouted over the tumult, and Tremaine must have heard him, since he gripped his console and struggled to input the necessary commands in spite of the tremors. "Helm, full reverse thrust! Get us away from those ships."

At last, the rumbling subsided, and Husher turned to Winterton, who looked thoroughly shaken. "What was that?"

"One of our main capacitor banks, Captain. That one is always the last to discharge, and the particle beam hit it dead-on."

"But the shock-absorbent frames are supposed to prevent a catastrophic release of energy."

"Yes, sir. I know. If I were to speculate, I would say someone may have sabotaged the structure meant to cushion the capacitor. With all the fail-safes that are installed, I simply can't see this happening naturally."

"What's the damage?" On the tactical display, the renewed Progenitor battle group was giving chase as the *Vesta* sped backward, and Pythons were struggling to protect her from the Ravagers being dumped across the battlespace. Husher needed to do something, but first, he had to know what they'd done to his ship.

"Damage is extensive, sir. Every deck is at least partially exposed to space, top to bottom, and the damage runs from sections four to twenty-seven. A third of our port-side missile tubes have been disabled, and about as many of our point defense turrets. Initial reports give a death toll in the hundreds."

Husher wanted to put his face in his hands. Instead, he turned to his Coms officer. "Tell damage control to bring second and third watches on duty and start sealing off those sections. Then I need you to put someone on sorting through the personnel lost, to see which other departments need to call on extra crew, and how many."

"Yes, sir."

"The *Spire* just appeared on the far side of the eight approaching enemy ships," Winterton said. "She's already launched another missile barrage."

"Very good, Ensign," Husher said. *There's some positive news, at least.*

"Captain," Fry said, and her strange tone made Husher study her face. "We're getting an encrypted data stream originating from the hull of one of the newly arrived Progenitor carriers."

Husher's eyes widened. "The tracker," he whispered. Then, louder: "That's one of the ships we tagged with a tracker. It has to be. Forward all the data to Ochrim, Ensign, and tell him to contact me the moment he's run his analysis."

"I will, sir."

"Tremaine, prepare a salvo of kinetic impactors that cuts across the bows of the enemy ships, and share the firing solution with Commander Ayam once you have it." *We need to help keep them at bay.*

"Yes, Captain."

As he waited for Ochrim to get in touch, Husher studied the tactical display—Norberg's five ships, facing off with seven Progenitor ships, and he and the Pythons confronting seven more.

The enemy was too well-provisioned. Too powerful. For the first time in his career, he forced himself to accept that defeat was likely inevitable.

His Oculenses alerted him to an incoming call from Ochrim, and he accepted.

The Ixan didn't bother with formalities. "I've decrypted the data, and I can say with very high certainty that the carrier we tagged has been home. At least, it entered a universe where it encountered a very large number of Progenitor ships. That has to be their home dimension."

"And you were able to glean the route from the data?"

"Yes."

"Send it to Ensign Fry." Husher terminated the call and turned once again to his Coms officer. "Ochrim is about to send you a data packet, which I want you to forward to the *Spire.* For now, get me Commander Fesky."

Moments later, his old friend appeared on the main display. "Captain. I was just about to transition out again."

"I'm altering your mission, Commander. You'll no longer be participating in this engagement."

Fesky's head tilted to the right. "Why not?"

He drew a deep breath. "Because I'm no longer confident that victory is possible. In a moment, Ensign Fry will send you an interdimensional route that leads to the Progenitor homeworld. I need you to follow it there. Collect all the intel you can—on their defenses, their fleet, and anything else you deem important. I don't know how long you'll have before they spot you, so you'll need to be quick. The moment you're threatened, transition back to this universe and report to Admiral Iver. Give him everything you've collected, along with the tech for interdimensional travel. Hitting the Progenitors in their home is our only hope for winning this war, Fesky. Everything rides on this."

The Winger clacked her beak softly. "I understand, Captain."

"Good. Now go." Husher terminated the transmission. He had neither the time nor the emotional fortitude to bid his friend the final goodbye he knew the situation called for.

"Prep a mixed barrage of Gorgons and Hydras, Tremaine," Husher said. "If we're going out today, we won't be doing it with a whimper."

CHAPTER 60

Metal Giants

A half hour or so after Price fled into the city, hunted by the larger alien mech, Gamble's marine battalion finished breaking the Ambler and Ravager ranks.

The combined power of the gunships, the remaining mechs, and the marines' heavy artillery had gotten the job done, in the end. At some point, the mechs must have smelled their own defeat, and they beat an uneven retreat into the city.

Gamble hadn't hesitated to order his battalion to move in after them. The city was far from lost—there were still plenty of civilians holed up inside their homes, in underground shelters, in grocery stores, in shopping centers. He was going to save those people, or he was going to die trying. He couldn't see any other option.

Around twenty minutes ago, he'd gotten separated from his squad, and now he roamed alone with his Rk-9 sniper rifle, finding temporary hides wherever he could and picking off Ravagers. The Amblers, he left alone—the sniper rounds wouldn't do much to them, other than draw the giant mechs to Gamble's location.

He did alert Oneiri to Ambler locations, though, or the gunships if he thought they could get a good shot. Before entering the city, Gamble had taken all ten of the microdrones he carried with him and tossed them into the sky. Now, they gave him a bird's eye view of the battle, which he used to give orders over a battalion-wide channel. He was a one-man roving command post, and the Ravagers he took down were an added bonus.

The latest hide—the third story of an apartment building overlooking an empty intersection—netted him three of the metal devils, but when five minutes passed without him spotting any more, he decided to pack up and move to a more forward location.

He left the apartment, which he'd found empty with the door hanging open and a trail of clothes strewn through the hall and into one of the bedrooms. He made his way down the stairs, to the ground floor.

Outside, he hugged the building until he reached the intersection, checking in every direction before crossing.

The skittering of metal feet reached his ears, and he whirled to his left. A pack of Ravagers was pouring out of a side alley and sprinting down the road toward him. *Damn.* He'd been careless, and now he would pay the price.

Drawing his sidearm, he took aim at the lead Ravager, steadying his aim with his left hand. Five shots took down the lead bot, and he emptied the rest of the clip into the next. It didn't go down. Gamble fished out another clip, released the first to tumble to the pavement, and slammed in the fresh one before proceeding to finish off his target. He wouldn't get them all before they made it to him. Not nearly. There were at least thirty of them left. But he would get some.

Automatic gunfire hit the Ravagers from the right, coming out of an alley closer to Gamble than the one the robots emerged from. As one, the Ravagers turned to face their attackers, only for their entire front rank to get mowed down. The remaining robots charged toward the alley, but none of them reached it. Metal corpses littered the street.

Lance Corporal Jenkins stepped out of the alleyway, checking down the street both ways, his R-57 held at the ready. When his gaze fell on Gamble, a grin split his face ear to ear. "Major! Boys, it's the major!"

The rest of Teal Squad rushed out of the alley, jogging until they stood in front of Gamble. As one, they saluted crisply.

"We'd been tracking that pack of Ravagers for a while, looking to set a trap for them. Good thing we sprang it before they got to you, Major!"

"You boys have been hitting the sims," Gamble said, sounding as impressed as he felt.

Jenkins nodded, blushing a little.

"I do believe I owe you all a beer," Gamble said. "Now, let's go. We've got a city to take back."

The squad fell in around him, and Gamble could tell they were determined to protect him, without having to be asked. He supposed that was basically their job, but even so, the gesture warmed his heart, almost as much as Teal Squad's dramatic improvement did.

Gamble followed Teal—more specifically, he followed Corporal Jenkins as he led the way through the tangle of alleys they'd navigated while stalking the Ravager pack. Jenkins said the bots they'd just taken down had broken away from a larger group, back where most of the action was happening. Now, Gamble had to wonder whether the Ravagers had somehow gotten word of him moving from building to building, sniping their fellows. He didn't raise the prospect to the marines around him, but he considered it a real possibility, and an unsettling one too.

He glanced at the feed from one of his overhead microdrones and saw that they were approaching one of the city's circular central plazas. When he ordered the drone to telescope in, he saw that two metal giants were doing battle in that same plaza, and he raised his palm to signal a stop to the marines. They halted almost immediately, even Jenkins, who hadn't seen the gesture but must have noticed the absence of their footfalls. The lance corporal in particular continued to impress Gamble.

"Slow up, marines," Gamble said. "Price is up ahead, fighting that alien mech that's even bigger than he is. Looks like there's an alley ahead to the left, which also lets out onto the plaza. It leads to a main street on the other end, too, so if we're stealthy and quick, we can maybe execute a three-way flank on that thing. See if we can help Price even the odds."

"Oorah," the marines said, their voices barely above a whisper.

CHAPTER 61

Tattered

Jake's alien mech had the ability to rapidly self-heal—but not as fast as Roach was tearing it apart. As with their last duel on Eresos, the man-mech hybrid had the ability to absorb any pieces he managed to cut from Jake, adding to his already considerable mass.

During that fight, Roach had cut off Jake's arm, and he'd struggled to regenerate it during combat. This time, his adversary seemed intent on decapitating him.

Jake wasn't sure why Roach had suddenly become so fixated on that outcome, as thin blades as hard as diamond sliced toward his neck again and again. Who knew why Roach did anything? There was no doubt he was crazy. There also wasn't any doubt that if it was Jake's head he wanted, eventually, he would get it.

He stumbled backward, doing everything he could to fend off Roach's frenetic attacks. A fountain graced the plaza's center, which reminded him of one he'd seen in Plenitos, one of Eresos' major cities. Roach was forcing him back toward it, probably hoping it would mess with Jake's footing once he reached it. And it likely would, since Jake couldn't afford to take his eyes off Roach's swinging blades.

But as always, Roach had a surprise for him. Instead of slicing, he thrust at Jake's chest with one of his blades, and instead of stabbing the blade became a long-barreled energy cannon that shot a concentrated blue-white ball into Jake's chest. The force threw him back, and Roach leapt forward, never falling more than a few feet behind.

Jake's back connected with the lip of the fountain, and for the second time today, Roach landed on top of him. Both his forearms had become ultra-thin blades again. Roach spread them wide, lining them up with Jake's head as though about to prune a hedge.

Gunfire sounded, and Jake could hear it ricocheting against Roach's back. The great mech whirled around without hesitation, head whipping back and forth as he sought its source.

Jake should have taken advantage of Roach's diverted attention, but the shooting had taken him by surprise, too. Disgusted with himself, he pushed off of the fountain, getting to his feet. Even inside the mech dream, Jake was exhausted, and he staggered again as he regained his balance. *That's no excuse. Get it together. You command Oneiri—act like it.*

Roach raised newly formed tubes in two directions, and where Jake expected energy to emerge, rockets did instead. Given enough time, the alien mechs had the capacity to fabricate missiles from collected material, but Jake normally tried to conserve them, since they took time to make.

The gunfire was nothing more than a distraction to Roach, the bullets pinging off his metal scales like pellets from a boy's first gun. But it seemed to enrage him all the same, enough that he followed the first pair of rockets with two more.

Explosions blossomed, in an alley mouth and at an intersection where a street met the plaza. Jake rushed at his adversary, forearms becoming broadswords and feet becoming thrusters to propel him forward.

Both blades sunk into Roach's back to the hilt, prompting him to whirl around again. His strength was immense, and without feet to find purchase against the plaza's cobble, Jake traveled with the turn. He quickly addressed that lack, but too late—Roach's wounds were sealing rapidly, pushing the broadswords out of his back as they did. *Wow.* Apparently Roach's healing ability had received a lot of attention from the Progenitors as well.

Before his swords could be ejected completely, Jake withdrew them, turning them into rocket tubes of his own, which he fired point-blank at Roach as he turned around.

The explosion engulfed the larger mech, and Jake was close enough that intense heat washed over him too, enough to make him want to scream. He held it in, and when the smoke around Roach cleared, he was rewarded: the mech had been laid open, with circuitry gleaming darkly inside the cavity exposed.

"Price," a voice echoed inside the dream.

"Gamble," he said.

"I'm nearby, leading the squad that just fired on Roach. We've got a couple men down after those rockets, but we're still in this, and I just put out the call for a couple gunships to come back you up. A platoon of marines with heavy artillery, too, though they'll take longer to get here."

Roach was striding toward Jake again, his chest knitting itself back up as he did. *Damn. I should have let loose on that wound when I had the chance.* But his exhaustion from the long duel had rendered his brain barely functional, and he'd let Gamble distract him from the fight, even though he should have been able to handle both.

"I don't know how long I can hang in, here, Major," Jake said, slightly ashamed at how hoarse his voice came out.

"You don't have any other choice, son," Gamble said. "And that's an order. Who else is gonna take that thing down? The gunships are on their way. Gamble out."

"You can't defeat me," Roach said as he drew closer. "You know that. But why embrace death out of stubbornness?"

"What are you talking about?"

Roach raised his arms, which ended in hands, now. "Forget your ties to this world. Let go of those who would limit and bind you. That's meaningless content. Let it go."

"And do what?"

"Merge with me. Become the most powerful being this universe has ever known—the most powerful the *multiverse* has known. We can rise. Together."

"I'll never join the Progenitors."

"We can turn on the Progenitors. They will be our first target. And then we can rule. Wisely, and fairly. As long as lesser beings pay tribute."

Roach had almost reached him. With a titanic effort of will, Jake straightened, drawing his shoulders back and raising his head.

Unbidden, a memory surfaced of the training program Roach had subjected all the mech pilot candidates to. Except, he hadn't subjected them to it equally—certainly not on the day he'd knocked Jake to the ground in front of all the other recruits.

All because I questioned Darkstream.

Darkstream was gone, but Roach wasn't, and now, Jake let him stand for everything Darkstream had ever done. *Why not? He was always their obedient creature.*

"You'll always serve the Progenitors," Jake said. "You need a master, and now that Darkstream's gone, you'll serve them for as long as they're willing to use you."

Roach didn't answer...but his forearms were morphing, thinning out to become blades again. That was all the answer Jake needed. Roach marched forward, bringing the blades together as he did and scraping them against each other, generating a shower of orange sparks.

A whine sounded overhead, and Jake glanced past Roach's shoulder—the gunships. His mech wasn't capable of smiling, but Jake still felt a measure of satisfaction, and the mech dream played a harmonic chord for him, to mark the sentiment.

"You don't scare me, Roach," he shouted.

"That's irrelevant," Roach said, advancing.

"Yeah. Well, it was a lie, anyway. You freak me right the hell out."

Jake widened his stance, lifting his broadsword-arms in readiness. His adversary charged, thin blades whistling through the air.

An overhead slash was met with Jake's rising blade, and with his other he batted away a cut aimed at his side.

Then the gunships started in, hammering Roach from behind with their turrets, causing him to stagger forward on top of Jake, who used the break in the attack to plunge his blades into Roach's stomach.

He flashed back to Eresos, back to thrusting his blades into Ingress' city walls. His anger then had birthed a massive release of energy that had brought those walls down. Now, it was his determination to end Roach that did it—the sudden certainty that what Gamble had said was true. If Jake fell, so would everything else.

A tiny sun was born deep inside Roach, and it exploded outward, blowing out his entire left side and leaving him a twitching, mangled mess on the cobble.

But Jake knew that even this would only put Roach down temporarily. Indeed, his tattered body was already curling in on itself, seeking itself. It had begun the process of piecing Roach back together.

So Jake regrew hands and gathered the shredded from in his arms. Then, he rocketed upward. The plaza fell away, becoming a gray dot within seconds as Jake ascended rapidly through Thessaly's atmosphere.

The color drained from the sky, soon replaced by the inky, star-studded blackness of space. Discordant chords produced by the mech dream told him of potential danger to his right, and when he accessed the visual sensors in that direction, he beheld the light show produced by Captain Husher and the Progenitors battling.

He didn't move to join them. Instead, he veered left—toward the system's center.

The journey took hours. Long enough for Roach to become something vaguely humanoid, though his torso would require a lot more work to stitch itself back together.

Even so, the half-formed alien mech began struggling weakly in Jake's arms as he flew through space. Maybe it sensed what was coming.

Once he was near enough, Jake used his rockets to begin spinning. The frictionless arena of space allowed him to quickly begin rotating at high velocities, and the centripetal force taxed even the alien mech's grip.

At last, he released Roach, and his aim was true. The larger mech sailed toward the sun. Jake turned his arms into energy cannons, sending Roach off with massive energy blasts that caught up with him and ensured he couldn't repair himself in time to alter his course.

That done, Jake instructed the mech to telescope in, tracking Roach's progress until he became a small, dark chip against the sun's sea of fire.

When that chip disappeared, Jake knew it was over.

That was for Marco, he thought as he turned to rocket back toward Thessaly.

CHAPTER 62

Principled Stand

The massive barrage of specialized missiles that Husher had ordered succeeded in taking out two of the seven approaching ships. That was something, but it wasn't enough.

"Captain Norberg has lost another destroyer, sir," Winterton said.

"Acknowledged, Ensign," Husher said, his voice coming out almost robotic. He wasn't taking the fact of his defeat gracefully.

Think of Captain Keyes's sacrifice, he told himself. *Your sacrifice has to be just as meaningful, just as effective.*

But that was impossible. When Keyes had gone down, he'd taken an entire Ixan fleet with him, and he'd ended the war. Husher had no means of doing anything comparable. His death would be just one of many—and a precursor to the inferno that would soon consume the galaxy.

He just had to hope Fesky managed to make it to the Progenitors' home and report back with intel the IGF could use.

The enemy ships were circling the *Vesta*, angling to hit her forward port side, where the capacitor's explosion had taken out the point defense turrets. Husher had ordered the Helm to rotate the supercarrier, keeping it away from her attackers, but the Progenitors had simply split their ships.

Now, three ships were coming around the other way. Once they aligned themselves with the damaged area, they began to pour Ravagers toward the wound.

"Take us back, Helm," Husher said, feeling exhausted. "Full reverse thrust."

What remained of the three Python Air Groups descended on the incoming Ravagers.

"Use Banshees to try to staunch the bleeding, Tactical," Husher said. "Take some of the pressure off our pilots."

"Aye, Captain."

It was a temporary measure, Husher knew.

"Captain Norberg is down to five ships, sir," Winterton said. "She lost a corvette."

"Acknowledged."

"They just managed to take down a Progenitor carrier in kind. It seems as though—" Winterton broke off mid-sentence, his forehead creased as he stared at whatever his console showed him. "Sir, a wormhole just opened behind the Progenitor ships facing Norberg, and warships are pouring through."

Husher narrowed his eyes. "Who do they belong to?" As soon as he finished asking the question, he already knew the answer. IGF ships were no longer built with the capability to generate wormholes.

"They appear to be the Darkstream ships that fled Hellebore—that is, the old UHF ships, and the single Quatro vessel.

They're ripping into the Progenitors, sir. A destroyer just went down...and a carrier...and another destroyer!"

Husher watched in disbelief as the nine warships took the Progenitor force completely by surprise. They started in on another destroyer, pounding her hull with missiles—

—and without further ceremony, every Progenitor ship vanished from Larkspur.

Husher's eyes were glued to the tactical display, body rigid, as he waited for them to return. Around him, all his officers seemed to be holding their breath.

The Progenitors didn't return. It was over. Husher realized he'd been holding his breath as well, and he released it in a rush.

There was no celebrating inside the CIC. The cost of victory had been far too great. But they were alive.

"Coms," he said, "send a transmission request to that battle group's flagship. "I believe some thanks are owed."

Soon, a middle-aged woman appeared on-screen. Her face had a gauntness to it, topped by short-cropped blond hair. But she was smiling.

"Captain Vanessa Harding, at your service," she said. "I already know who you are, Captain Husher, so no introduction is required."

"Maybe not," he said. "But a thank you is in order, I believe, Captain."

Harding's smile broadened.

"Your employer and I have not always, uh, seen eye to eye," he went on. "I'm surprised you came to help me. Not to mention the fact that you used a means of travel that's wildly illegal."

Nodding, Harding said, "We don't consider ourselves part of Darkstream any longer, Captain. We've gathered that their star has fallen, and probably rightly so. Many of us disagree with the things they did back in the Steele System, but there, they were the only game in town. For many, the choice was to work for them or starve."

"And the wormhole?"

Harding shrugged. "We heard that you were facing down a Progenitor fleet here and decided to come to your aid. We actually did poke our heads in through the darkgate—that was just before our arrival through the wormhole, and sensor data showed us you weren't likely to survive long enough for us to cross the system under conventional means. So we broke the law. It's up to you how you want to handle that, Captain, but I understand that you've had your own woes with the IU, recently. It's still unclear how they're going to handle you."

"Is that why you decided to help?"

"Well, we recognize your importance to the war effort, Captain Husher. Yours, your ship's, and your crew's. We recognize the value of keeping galactic society from being wiped out. But most of all, we know that you refused to hand over the Quatro on your ship to the Assembly of Elders. Our Quatro friends have told us about the horrors the Elders have committed. We were impressed by your principled stand, and we've decided to cast our lot with you."

"I appreciate that. And I hope you won't come to regret it."

"Personally, I won't. No matter what happens. And I believe the same goes for most of the beings in our tiny fleet."

"There were dozens of civilian ships with you, weren't there? Are they safe?"

Harding nodded. "They are. We'll reveal their location once we've received assurances they'll be taken care of."

"Very good." *Price and Sato will be glad to know their families are well.*

CHAPTER 63

Sidearm

"There are certain things I'll stand for," Husher said, looking around at those gathered inside the Cybele's City Council chamber, "and certain things I won't."

Many groups were represented inside the chamber. Looking around, his eyes fell on Jake Price, Lisa Sato, and the rest of Oneiri Team. Captain Vanessa Harding was here, and Ek. President Chiba had sent high-ranking Union officials representing all four member species to meet with them—though notably, the president hadn't come himself. The city council was here as well. And Maeve.

Husher had also invited Penelope Snyder and Toby Yung, who'd seated themselves on opposite ends of the council chamber.

"If we're going to have a hope of surviving the onslaught that's coming, we can't have any more fighting between us. That's what the Progenitors want—indeed, I believe they've tried to actively encourage it. We've allowed the fires of ideology to be stoked so high they nearly consumed us, and if we don't get our act together, they still might."

His eyes fell on Yung, then on Snyder. "Our society has fragmented into two polarized camps—the far left and the far right. Each side sees themselves as the righteous saviors of the galaxy, but you're both wrong. You're its executioners."

Husher let that sink in before continuing. "The fact is, we need each other. All of us. Liberals need conservatives, and vice versa. For a balanced society, we need both. If we didn't, the various species never would have evolved to have both. Liberals are for finding worthy new things to adopt, and conservatives are for deciding what about our society is worth keeping, and defending. We need each other—we *all* need each other. Humans need Quatro. Quatro need Kaithe. Kaithe need Wingers, and Wingers need Tumbra. If we allow ourselves to fragment and fight each other, then we're lost. To lose sight of that is to play right into the enemy's hands, and the enemy will happily consume us for it."

His eyes fell on the officials sent by the president. "The IU doesn't get to slide into tyranny. You don't get to violate the principles of a democratic society just to impose your own misguided vision on the world. The people will rise up and tear you down for that. It's happened before and it'll happen again. But we don't have time for it." Husher shook his head. "You can have the alliance with the Assembly of Elders, because we need it. But that doesn't mean imitating them, and it doesn't mean letting them influence how we govern ourselves. We live in a free society, where everyone has the opportunity to make something of themselves—and yes, where we help each other out. But we don't tear one group down to help another.

"I hope that's all very well understood," he said. "Because like I said, there are certain things I'll stand for, and certain things I won't. And if I have to come after anyone for destabilizing our society again, I'm not going to do it with any mercy. Because anyone doing that is helping the Progenitors destroy us. And I don't take kindly to that." He raised his eyebrows. "Any questions?"

Lisa Sato stood from among her Oneiri teammates, and Husher turned toward her. "Yes, Sato?"

But she didn't speak. Instead, she drew her sidearm and placed it against Price's head.

Everything seemed to happen at once. Cries of alarm rose, and Husher reached for his own sidearm, knowing he was too late.

Near Sato and Price, Maeve leapt from her seat and tackled Sato. The gun fired, and Price fell.

Husher sprinted across the chamber and stomped on Sato's gun hand, which caused her to drop the firearm. He picked it up, safetied it, and tucked it inside his belt.

As Ash Sweeney and Beth Arkanian restrained Sato, Husher knelt beside Price, hands probing the seaman's head.

The bullet had left a furrow in the side of Jake's skull, and through the blood it was difficult to tell how deep it went.

Husher wrenched his com from its holster to summon paramedics from the Cybele General Hospital.

CHAPTER 64

Sleeper Agent

"So Husher is back in the IU's good books?" Bronson said, staring across the table at Eve Quinn. They were having lunch in Tartarus Station's cafeteria, as they did regularly, so that they could touch base about progress on the Project.

"He was never in our good books," Quinn said. "But he does remain annoyingly relevant to the war effort. The Progenitors pose an existential threat. There's no getting around that. So certain elements inside the government—such as the agency I work for, for example—are thinking that maybe it's best to wait till after the war to make our move. In the meantime, we can quietly prepare. Which is what you and I are doing, Bronson."

"You really think there's an 'after the war,' huh? You say it with such confidence."

"I'm a confident gal. You know that." Quinn's lips spread into her usual smile, which made him feel like she was making fun of him even when she wasn't speaking. "Husher will be dealt with in time. For now, we've decided we'll be following the Darkstream model when it comes to implementation. Sell the military on the idea of using implants to more efficiently pilot craft of all sorts—just like the mech pilots do. What if a Python pilot could *become* the Python? What if a Nav officer could *be* the warship? And once everyone starts to appreciate the military applications, we'll start selling the public on them. Lucid tech will be adopted kind of like Oculenses were, except in reverse: military first, then public."

"I find this all deeply ironic," Bronson said.

They compared notes a while longer, until Quinn had to go. Bronson watched her leave the cafeteria, then he got up too, leaving their trays for the cleaning staff to take care of.

Since arriving on Tartarus, he'd learned that the agency Quinn worked for was called the Galactic Intelligence Bureau, or GIB. As far as he could tell, they had an incredibly long reach, which made him impressed that they'd managed to conceal their existence from the public for so long. *The Darkstream board could have learned a thing or two from them.*

He entered his modest quarters fifteen minutes later, climbing onto his bed to lie on his back, without bothering to take off his boots. Before Imbros, he'd always been used to more comfort than this, though not too much more. He *had* spent most of his life on warships.

After Imbros, this felt like the lap of luxury. It was a lot better than sleeping in damp alleyways.

"Bronson," a voice said, and he cried out.

Sitting up, he saw one of the Progenitors' telepresence robots standing in the middle of the room. "Are you really here?"

"No."

"Okay." Swinging his legs over the side of the bed, he fought to steady his breathing. "What is it? Why have you contacted me?"

"Our sleeper agent was activated, and she succeeded in creating a conflict within the IU by informing them about a Quatro fugitive being given refuge aboard the *Vesta*. But she failed to neutralize one of our primary targets, and she has now been apprehended."

"What does that have to do with me?"

"It has everything to do with you. It's your turn, now, Bronson. Your time has come.".

EPILOGUE

Identify Yourself

As they drew closer to the Progenitors' home dimension, the silence inside the *Spire*'s CIC grew uneasier.

Sitting at the Tactical Station felt odd to Fesky—wrong, almost. She'd quickly grown accustomed to the command seat's centrality. From it, she could easily see every officer's console. Here, she had to twist uncomfortably to look at Nav or Helm, and when she did, the empty command seat always caught her eye.

"We're here," Nav said.

Fesky turned to her sensor operator, hating that she still had to deal with him after his screwups back in Larkspur. If they'd been able to rejoin the *Vesta* before coming here, she could have replaced him, and found a new Tactical officer. Now they were inside enemy territory with a crew she was far from happy with.

"What do you see?" she asked Yvan, who was staring hard at his console.

"Nothing that makes sense," he muttered.

"Yvan! Describe to me what you see!"

The sensor operator jerked in his seat. "Sorry, Captain. It's just—well, we're in a star system filled with Progenitor ships. Thousands and thousands of them, all in heliocentric orbit, just sitting there. There are shuttles going back and forth between them and various stations and colonies, but none of the ships have reacted to our presence yet. We're at the edge of the system, near a large asteroid belt, and it's possible they've yet to distinguish us from the asteroids."

"That doesn't sound so far off what we expected," Fesky said. "What about this doesn't make sense?"

"A couple of things, ma'am. For one, just past the asteroid belt, space seems to just...stop. There aren't any other stars shining in the universe. There's nothing. Just pitch-black nothing."

Fesky sat in silence for a moment, puzzling over what Yvan had told her.

"I just picked up on an asteroid whose course is taking it toward the edge," Yvan said. "Should I put it on visual?"

"Yes."

The main display changed to a zoomed-in visual of the asteroid, and they all watched as it neared the strange border.

When the asteroid hit, it disintegrated, and ripples of electric-blue energy spread out from the point of impact.

"It's like the forcefield Teth generated around Klaxon's moon," Fesky murmured. *But is it meant to keep things in or something else out?* "You said there were two things, Yvan."

The sensor operator nodded. "Yes, ma'am. This system—the configuration of planets, the star's profile—if I'm not mistaken, this is the Sol System."

That left Fesky just as baffled, but she didn't have time to think about it. On her console's tactical display, one of the Progenitor ships had broken off from the immense fleet and was heading directly for them.

"Should we transition out, ma'am?" her Nav officer asked.

"Standby to do that, but don't do it yet," Fesky said. "They'll enter real-time coms range before they can threaten us with Ravagers or their particle beam. Let's see if they have anything to say."

The *Spire* sat there for hours, next to what had to be the Kuiper Belt, if they were truly in this universe's equivalent of the Sol System. Meanwhile, they continued to observe the system, collecting as much data as they could in the time they had. *Anything the IGF can use.*

Sure enough, as the Progenitor ship—a destroyer—drew near, Fesky's Coms officer turned to her. "We're getting a transmission request, ma'am."

Fesky nodded. "Put it on the display."

When she saw the man who appeared on her CIC's main display, it felt like a fist of ice had punched her in the stomach. He bore a scar that ran diagonally across his face, from his temple to his chin, and it had healed poorly, leaving his mouth misshapen. But otherwise, Fesky would have recognized that face anywhere.

"Unknown vessel, identify yourself at once or prepare to be attacked," he said.

Fesky tried to speak, but couldn't at first. Then, finally, she managed it: "*Husher?*"

He narrowed his eyes, though otherwise he didn't react. For the first time, Fesky sensed the coldness that exuded from him—as though he was ready to kill her without a glimmer of remorse. For her, that was the most jarring thing of all.

"How do you know my name?" he said.

Acknowledgments

Thank you to Rex Bain, Sheila Beitler, Bruce A. Brandt, Michael Friend, Maikel Hölzel, Jason Pennock, and Jeff Rudolph for offering insightful editorial input and helping to make this book as strong as it could be.

Thank you to Tom Edwards for creating such stunning cover art.

Thank you to my family - your support means everything.

Thank you to Cecily, my heart.

Thank you to the people who read my stories, write reviews, and help spread the word. I couldn't do this without you.

About the Author

Scott Bartlett was born in St. John's, Newfoundland – the easternmost province of Canada. During his decade-long journey to become a full-time author, he supported himself by working a number of different jobs: salmon hatchery technician, grocery clerk, youth care worker, ghostwriter, research assistant, pita maker, and freelance editor.

In 2014, he succeeded in becoming a full-time novelist, and he's been writing science fiction at light speed ever since.

Visit scottplots.com to learn about Scott's other books.